Lord of the Flies
Educational Edition

Books by
Sir William Golding
1911–1993
Nobel Prize in Literature

Fiction
Lord of the Flies
The Inheritors
Pincher Martin
Free Fall
The Spire
The Pyramid
The Scorpion God
Darkness Visible
Rites of Passage
The Paper Men
Close Quarters
Fire Down Below
To the Ends of the Earth
(comprising *Rites of Passage*, *Close Quarters* and *Fire Down Below*
in a revised text; foreword by the author)
The Double Tongue

Essays
The Hot Gates
A Moving Target

Travel
An Egyptian Journal

Plays
The Brass Butterfly
Lord of the Flies
adapted for the stage by Nigel Williams

LORD OF THE FLIES

William Golding

Educational Edition

With notes prepared by the English Department
of Loxford School of Science and Technology

faber and faber

First published in 1954
by Faber and Faber Limited
Bloomsbury House
74–77 Great Russell Street
London WC1B 3DA
This educational edition first published in 2012

Typeset by Donald Sommerville
Printed and bound by CPI Group (UK) Ltd, Croydon, CR0 4YY

All rights reserved
© William Golding, 1954
'Fable' © William Golding, 1965
Introduction and study notes © Faber and Faber Ltd, 2012

The right of William Golding to be identified as author of this work
has been asserted in accordance with Section 77 of the Copyright,
Designs and Patents Act 1988

*This book is sold subject to the condition that it shall not, by way of trade
or otherwise, be lent, resold, hired out or otherwise circulated without the
publisher's prior consent in any form of binding or cover other than that in which
it is published and without a similar condition including this condition being
imposed on the subsequent purchaser*

A CIP record for this book
is available from the British Library

ISBN 978–0–571–29571–5

CONTENTS

PREFACE

First published in 1954, *Lord of the Flies* is a novel that has captivated schoolchildren for decades. A teacher himself, Golding clearly understood what excites and interests children. It is not only a gripping story, with strong, sympathetic characters, but it also raises timeless and profound questions.

Part of its lasting appeal, particularly in schools, surely arises from the way it tackles universal issues. The novel is a catalyst for thought-provoking discussion and analysis, particularly concerning the capabilities of humans for good and evil and the fragility of moral inhibition. The boys' struggle to find a way of existing in a community with no fixed boundaries invites readers to evaluate the concepts involved in social and political constructs and moral frameworks we take for granted. Ideas of community, leadership, and the rule of law are called into question as the reader has to consider who has a right to power, why, and what the consequences of the acquisition of power may be. Effective teaching and learning can ensure that discussions about such concerns – as vital today as ever – are made relevant to today's students.

This educational edition encourages original and independent thought from students, as well as guiding them through the text. The introductory material includes a biographical section on William Golding and provides information about the novel's historical context, which will be ideal for students completing GCSE and A-Level courses. At the end of the text there are chapter summaries, comprehension questions,

Preface

discussion points and activities which inform the teaching and learning of the text. There is a glossary of less familiar words and phrases. This edition includes William Golding's essay 'Fable', which gives an insight into the author's view of the novel. For advanced students, it also includes essays introducing readers to some theoretical interpretations of the text. All of these are intended to inspire and generate creative teaching, learning and love of the novel.

English Department of Loxford School
of Science and Technology, 2012

INTRODUCTORY MATERIALS

PROFILE OF WILLIAM GOLDING

Life and Family

> He was born in 1911, in his grandmother's house in Cornwall.
> He grew up in Marlborough, Wiltshire.
> His father, Alec, was a teacher with socialist views.
> His mother, Mildred, campaigned for women's suffrage.
> He had an older brother, Joseph, also a teacher.
> He married Ann Brookfield, an analytical chemist, in 1939.
> He had two children, named David and Judith Diana.
> He died in 1993.

Education

> He attended Marlborough Grammar School, 1921–30.
> In 1930, he went to Oxford University. He read Natural Sciences for two years but then changed to English Literature.

Career

> He served in the Royal Navy during the Second World War.
> Between 1945 and 1961, he taught at Bishop Wordsworth School in Salisbury.
> He had four books published while he was teaching – many publishers had earlier turned his books down.

> Charles Monteith at Faber and Faber saw the quality of *Lord of the Flies* and published it in 1954.

Role during the Second World War

> He joined the Royal Navy in 1940.
> He took part in the pursuit of the German battleship *Bismarck*.
> He took part in the invasion of Normandy on D-Day.
> By the end of the war in 1945 he was a lieutenant in command of a rocket landing craft.

Writing

> *Lord of the Flies*, his first novel, was published in 1954.
> Other key texts include:
> > *The Inheritors* (novel) 1955
> > *The Brass Butterfly* (play) 1958
> > *The Spire* (novel) 1964
> > *The Scorpion God* (three short novels) 1971
> > *Darkness Visible* (novel) 1979
> > *Rites of Passage* (novel) 1980
> > *Close Quarters* (novel) 1987
> > *Fire Down Below* (novel) 1989

Recognition

> In 1980, he won the Booker Prize for *Rites of Passage* (the first novel in the trilogy titled *To the Ends of the Earth*).
> In 1983, he was awarded the Nobel Prize in Literature.
> In 1988, he was knighted.

TIMELINE

1500s   British exploration of the New World;
         British colonization begins.
1600s   British settlements in Virginia, Newfoundland,
         Bermuda, and elsewhere;
         East India Company formed.
1776   American independence from Britain.
1807   British abolition of slave trading.
1833   Abolition of slavery in the British Empire.
1837   Victoria becomes Queen of Great Britain and Ireland.
1877   Queen Victoria proclaimed Empress of India.
1901   Death of Queen Victoria; Edward VII becomes king.
1914   Assassination of Archduke Franz Ferdinand, amongst
         other factors, sparks World War I.
1918   11 November: World War I ends.
1924   The British Empire Exhibition held at Wembley.
1939   3 September: Britain and France declare war on
         Germany.
1940   'The Blitz' begins, lasting until May 1941.
1941   Sinking of the *Bismarck* – a key ship in the German
         Navy.
1944   6 June: D-Day landings in Normandy.
1945   7 May: Germany concedes defeat;
         8 May: 'VE Day', the end of war in Europe.
         6 and 8 August: use of atomic weapons on
         Hiroshima and Nagasaki.
1947   India granted independence.

Introductory Materials

HISTORICAL CONTEXT

Britain and Imperialism

The British Empire was arguably the most extensive empire ever to have existed, at its peak covering almost a quarter of the world's land and governing a fifth of the world's population. The phrase 'the sun never sets on the British Empire' derived from the idea that the Empire was so widespread that it was always daytime in at least one part of it.

Discovery and Exploration turn to Settlement

English exploration of the 'New World' began at the end of the fifteenth century, first becoming significant with the essentially rapacious activities of adventurers like Walter Raleigh in the Americas. The first half of the seventeenth century saw the emergence of colonial ambitions result in the establishment of the first permanent English settlements in Virginia, Bermuda and the Caribbean island of Barbados, amongst others. The failure of the Kingdom of Scotland's own endeavours to form an empire in the Americas was one of the primary causes for the integration of Scotland into Great Britain in 1707.

Trade

New settlements outside Europe brought territorial expansion and sometimes great mineral wealth. They always offered prospects of access to new resources and opportunities. 'New World' crop discoveries included potatoes, tomatoes and tobacco. The creation of new trade routes magnified Britain's own export opportunities, further stimulating the economy. Another type of trade supported British colonial expansion from the seventeenth century: the burgeoning slave trade. Hundreds of thousands of Africans were transported to British colonies in the West Indies and North America until Britain's abolition of slave trading in 1807. From the late eighteenth century (particularly after American independence from Britain was declared in 1776) the focus of Empire moved from west to east – especially to India (but also to locations as distant as the region of Australasia). The privately owned East India Company amassed incredible power, maintaining its own army and governing an ever-increasing proportion of the Indian subcontinent; it was the dominant power among India's rulers until the mid-nineteenth century, when the British government formally took charge of its domains.

The Dominance of the Royal Navy

The key to Britain's imperial expansion was its power at sea. The Royal Navy emerged in the reign of Henry VIII but was not professionalized until the eighteenth century. The defeat of the French Navy at the Battle of Trafalgar in 1805, followed by the defeat of the French Army at the Battle of Waterloo in 1815, left Britain as the dominant extra-European power and marked the beginning of what can be seen as Britain's imperial century, roughly covering the life of Queen Victoria (1819–1901). In the eighteenth and nineteenth centuries, Britain's overseas trade and its industries expanded massively, each fuelling the other, and Britain maintained its mastery of the seas with developments in navigational technology, cartography, and the manufacture of ships and armaments. From the time of the suppression of the slave trade in the early nineteenth century until well into the twentieth century the Royal Navy was regarded by many Britons as a romantic symbol of exploration, civility, order and Christianity in the exotic world of the savage 'other'. Nevertheless, its role was to support an empire essentially beneficial to Britain.

Peak and Decline

The post-World War I settlement saw the British Empire further extend its boundaries, as it took control of many of the former German and Ottoman empires' territories, yet the twentieth century is, in fact, notable for the demise of the British Empire. By the end of World War I it was clear that the self-governing 'white dominions', notably Australia and Canada, would no longer automatically follow the lead of the 'mother country' in wars or foreign affairs. The creation of the Irish Free State in 1922 was another blow to the union of the empire. Furthermore, after the Second World War, it became increasingly difficult for Britain to maintain imperial claims over its colonies in the face of increasing calls for self-governance; this principle was supported in the charter of the new United Nations and, after all, Britain had gone to war supposedly to support Poland's desire to resist Nazi quasi-colonial expansion. With considerable opposition from those traditional Britons who idolized the British Empire, independence was granted to India in 1947 and to other colonies in Asia and Africa through the 1950s and 1960s. In the same period British forces also left Palestine, Egypt and other regions of the Middle East which had been British-controlled but were not formally part of the Empire.

Legacy

The British Empire was a great source of pride to Britons. For many years, it was regarded as the pillar which supported the world's most powerful economy and Britain's armed services acted in part as a global police force. Rule of the empire allowed the export not only of British products but also industrial capitalism and parliamentary democracy. However, as well as its former (though not unique) role in the slave trade, Britain was also the perpetrator of extensive colonial brutalities, which have become increasingly well documented in recent decades. In the second half of the twentieth century and in the twenty-first, faith in the 'civilizing' effect of the British Empire has also been much undermined by the years of political and social turmoil in post-colonial nations around the world from Afghanistan to Sierra Leone and from Bangladesh to Iraq.

Post-War British Society

William Golding began writing *Lord of the Flies* in 1951, six years after the Second World War ended (although it was not published until 1954). Fear and change were dominant themes for British people. By 1951 the Americans and the

Soviets were menacing human existence with the threat of atomic weapons and many in Britain saw world communism as being as dangerous a threat as Hitler's Germany had been. The post-war governments had implemented an austerity programme to rebuild the shattered British economy. How that might be achieved and society be remodelled in the process remained uncertain.

The Impact of War

The Second World War shook the foundations of British society, not only because around 260,000 Britons died on active service. Civilians were targeted to an unprecedented degree: some 60,000 died in the Blitz of Britain's great cities and industrial centres and in other attacks. Many historical accounts describe how British society responded with a unity of determination, perhaps most memorably represented even before the Blitz by the 'spirit of Dunkirk', where flotillas of civilian ships helped rescue defeated British troops from extermination or capture on the beaches of France.

Virtually everyone participated in the war effort in some way. The young men in the armed services came from every part of the United Kingdom and many of those too old or too young to fight, or exempt from military service because they worked in war industries, joined the Home Guard. Many women contributed to the war effort, producing munitions, working on farms or serving in non-combat military roles.

The war caused trauma and destruction but also, to a limited degree, eroded some of the persistent social inequality in Britain. Conscription into the armed forces applied to all able-bodied men, no matter how privileged their background, and the evacuation of children from cities threatened by bombing brought the urban and rural communities into closer contact. Rationing affected rich and poor while, for the second time in a quarter of a century, women proved their worth as workers not just as wives and mothers.

Political Consensus: The Welfare State

With victory in 1945, many Britons began asking why, if a collective effort had won the war, peacetime collectivism should not regenerate Britain into a beacon of social harmony. By 1950, the so-called welfare state had been created: secondary education and pension provision had been reformed and expanded; social security supported those unable to work; virtually full employment for all those capable of working had been achieved and the National Health Service had been established. None of this was based on the socialist principle of redistributing wealth but rather on the idea of national insurance: every working individual paid a contribution to be guaranteed a 'national minimum' in the event of unemployment, sickness or old age. Post-war Britons had rejected both fascist and Stalinist totalitarianism and the widespread poverty and unemployment of the 1930s. A consensus developed and successive governments expanded rather than dismantled the welfare state.

Education in Post-War Britain

An important element in post-war welfare development was the extension of the school-leaving age to fifteen for all British children. Universal education was a reality but there remained a disparity in the quality of educational provision and the future prospects it provided. Fee-paying schools gave unparalleled opportunities to those from richer families, and grammar schools taught academic subjects to students from largely middle-class families. A small number of technical schools taught vocational skills, mainly to children from working-class backgrounds, but the majority of children went to secondary modern schools and were expected to end their full-time education with few qualifications and enter the workforce at the age of fifteen. Social mobility had increased dramatically since the inter-war period but the school system remained a significant obstacle to equality of opportunity in Britain.

The Horrors of War

There was a universal reaction of shock and disgust as the full extent of the Holocaust was realized at the end of the war. The Nazi genocide of approximately six million Jews and the extermination of millions of other minorities appalled the British public. At this point, the even more extensive atrocities committed by Stalin in the Soviet Union remained largely unknown. Public support for military intervention in opposition to the 1950 invasion of South Korea by North Korea might appear surprising given the legacy of the Second World War, but many people feared appeasing aggression after such an approach had failed so dramatically in response to Nazi Germany. Such concerns were amplified by the fear that the development of the Soviet atom bomb would encourage the spread of international communism. The potential for mass destruction demonstrated by the atomic attacks on Hiroshima and Nagasaki in 1945 played on many Britons' imaginations and consciences. The 1950s saw the emergence of the Campaign for Nuclear Disarmament, with those opposing the nuclear deterrent arguing that a nuclear arms race would exacerbate tensions, heating up the Cold War rather than preventing conflict.

The Inevitability of British Moderation?

It is tempting to suppose that the people of Britain would always have rejected totalitarianism, that tolerance and fairness would inevitably characterize British sentiment. Yet such a view is simplistic. In the 1930s Britain had its own communist and fascist sympathizers and many Britons of all political persuasions had favoured appeasement of Nazi Germany, even though the brutality of Hitler's regime was already clear. Furthermore, whilst the Holocaust was the responsibility of Nazi Germany, British ideas had indirectly played their part. It was a British scientist, Sir Francis Galton, who advocated (and coined the term) eugenics, a powerful influence behind Hitler's plans for 'genetic cleansing'. Furthermore, during the Boer War, it was British generals who held South African civilians in concentration camps, where conditions and death rates were appalling. In this longer view of history, it would appear that the boundaries between collective good and evil have often been more blurred than one might like to think. To Britons of the 1950s, war and the horrors it brought might well result from an external attack but could also arise from hidden and subversive internal weaknesses.

TEXT

For my mother and father

CHAPTER ONE

The Sound of the Shell

———❦———

The boy with fair hair lowered himself down the last few feet of rock and began to pick his way towards the lagoon. Though he had taken off his school sweater and trailed it now from one hand, his grey shirt stuck to him and his hair was plastered to his forehead. All round him the long scar smashed into the jungle was a bath of heat. He was clambering heavily among the creepers and broken trunks when a bird, a vision of red and yellow, flashed upwards with a witch-like cry; and this cry was echoed by another.

"Hi!" it said, "wait a minute!"

The undergrowth at the side of the scar was shaken and a multitude of raindrops fell pattering.

"Wait a minute," the voice said, "I got caught up."

The fair boy stopped and jerked his stockings with an automatic gesture that made the jungle seem for a moment like the Home Counties.

The voice spoke again.

"I can't hardly move with all these creeper things."

The owner of the voice came backing out of the undergrowth so that twigs scratched on a greasy wind-breaker. The naked crooks of his knees were plump, caught and scratched by thorns. He bent down, removed the thorns carefully, and turned round. He was shorter than the fair boy and very fat. He came forward, searching out safe lodgements for his feet, and then looked up through thick spectacles.

"Where's the man with the megaphone?"

The fair boy shook his head.

"This is an island. At least I think it's an island. That's a reef out in the sea. Perhaps there aren't any grown-ups anywhere."

The fat boy looked startled.

"There was that pilot. But he wasn't in the passenger tube, he was up in the cabin in front."

The fair boy was peering at the reef through screwed-up eyes.

"All them other kids," the fat boy went on. "Some of them must have got out. They must have, mustn't they?"

The fair boy began to pick his way as casually as possible towards the water. He tried to be offhand and not too obviously uninterested, but the fat boy hurried after him.

"Aren't there any grown-ups at all?"

"I don't think so."

The fair boy said this solemnly; but then the delight of a realized ambition overcame him. In the middle of the scar he stood on his head and grinned at the reversed fat boy.

"No grown-ups!"

The fat boy thought for a moment.

"That pilot."

The fair boy allowed his feet to come down and sat on the steamy earth.

"He must have flown off after he dropped us. He couldn't land here. Not in a plane with wheels."

"We was attacked!"

"He'll be back all right."

The fat boy shook his head.

"When we was coming down I looked through one of them windows. I saw the other part of the plane. There were flames coming out of it."

He looked up and down the scar.

"And this is what the tube done."

The fair boy reached out and touched the jagged end of a trunk. For a moment he looked interested.

"What happened to it?" he asked. "Where's it got to now?"

"That storm dragged it out to sea. It wasn't half dangerous with all them tree trunks falling. There must have been some kids still in it."

He hesitated for a moment then spoke again.

"What's your name?"

"Ralph."

The fat boy waited to be asked his name in turn but this proffer of acquaintance was not made; the fair boy called Ralph smiled vaguely, stood up, and began to make his way once more towards the lagoon. The fat boy hung steadily at his shoulder.

"I expect there's a lot more of us scattered about. You haven't seen any others have you?"

Ralph shook his head and increased his speed. Then he tripped over a branch and came down with a crash.

The fat boy stood by him, breathing hard.

"My auntie told me not to run," he explained, "on account of my asthma."

"Ass-mar?"

"That's right. Can't catch me breath. I was the only boy

13

in our school what had asthma," said the fat boy with a touch of pride. "And I've been wearing specs since I was three."

He took off his glasses and held them out to Ralph, blinking and smiling, and then started to wipe them against his grubby wind-breaker. An expression of pain and inward concentration altered the pale contours of his face. He smeared the sweat from his cheeks and quickly adjusted the spectacles on his nose.

"Them fruit."

He glanced round the scar.

"Them fruit," he said, "I expect——"

He put on his glasses, waded away from Ralph, and crouched down among the tangled foliage.

"I'll be out again in just a minute——"

Ralph disentangled himself cautiously and stole away through the branches. In a few seconds the fat boy's grunts were behind him and he was hurrying towards the screen that still lay between him and the lagoon. He climbed over a broken trunk and was out of the jungle.

The shore was fledged with palm trees. These stood or leaned or reclined against the light and their green feathers were a hundred feet up in the air. The ground beneath them was a bank covered with coarse grass, torn everywhere by the upheavals of fallen trees, scattered with decaying coconuts and palm saplings. Behind this was the darkness of the forest proper and the open space of the scar. Ralph stood, one hand against a grey trunk, and screwed up his eyes against the shimmering water. Out there, perhaps a mile away, the white surf flinked on a coral reef, and beyond that the open sea was dark blue. Within the irregular arc of coral the lagoon was still as a mountain lake,—blue of all shades and shadowy green and purple. The beach between the palm terrace and the water was a thin bow-stave, endless apparently, for to Ralph's left the perspectives of palm and beach and water drew to a point at infinity; and always, almost visible, was the heat.

He jumped down from the terrace. The sand was thick over his black shoes and the heat hit him. He became conscious of the weight of clothes, kicked his shoes off fiercely and ripped off each stocking with its elastic garter in a single movement. Then he leapt back on the terrace, pulled off his shirt, and stood there among the skull-like coco-nuts with green shadows from the palms and the forest sliding over his skin. He undid the snake-clasp of his belt, lugged off his shorts and pants, and stood there naked, looking at the dazzling beach and the water.

He was old enough, twelve years and a few months, to have lost the prominent tummy of childhood; and not yet old enough for adolescence to have made him awkward. You could see now that he might make a boxer, as far as width and heaviness of shoulders went, but there was a mildness about his mouth and eyes that proclaimed no devil. He patted the palm trunk softly; and, forced at last to believe in the reality of the island, laughed delightedly again and stood on his head. He turned neatly on to his feet, jumped down to the beach, knelt and swept a double armful of sand into a pile against his chest. Then he sat back and looked at the water with bright, excited eyes.

"Ralph——"

The fat boy lowered himself over the terrace and sat down carefully, using the edge as a seat.

"I'm sorry I been such a time. Them fruit——"

He wiped his glasses and adjusted them on his button

nose. The frame had made a deep, pink "V" on the bridge. He looked critically at Ralph's golden body and then down at his own clothes. He laid a hand on the end of a zipper that extended down his chest.

"My auntie——"

Then he opened the zipper with decision and pulled the whole wind-breaker over his head.

"There!"

Ralph looked at him side-long and said nothing.

"I expect we'll want to know all their names," said the fat boy, "and make a list. We ought to have a meeting."

Ralph did not take the hint so the fat boy was forced to continue.

"I don't care what they call me," he said confidentially, "so long as they don't call me what they used to call me at school."

Ralph was faintly interested.

"What was that?"

The fat boy glanced over his shoulder, then leaned towards Ralph.

He whispered.

"They used to call me 'Piggy'."

Ralph shrieked with laughter. He jumped up.

"Piggy! Piggy!"

"Ralph—please!"

Piggy clasped his hands in apprehension.

"I said I didn't want——"

"Piggy! Piggy!"

Ralph danced out into the hot air of the beach and then returned as a fighter-plane, with wings swept back, and machine-gunned Piggy.

"Sche-aa-ow!"

He dived in the sand at Piggy's feet and lay there laughing.

"Piggy!"

Piggy grinned reluctantly, pleased despite himself at even this much recognition.

"So long as you don't tell the others——"

Ralph giggled into the sand. The expression of pain and concentration returned to Piggy's face.

"Half a sec'."

He hastened back into the forest. Ralph stood up and trotted along to the right.

Here the beach was interrupted abruptly by the square motif of the landscape; a great platform of pink granite thrust up uncompromisingly through forest and terrace and sand and lagoon to make a raised jetty four feet high. The top of this was covered with a thin layer of soil and coarse grass and shaded with young palm trees. There was not enough soil for them to grow to any height and when they reached perhaps twenty feet they fell and dried, forming a criss-cross pattern of trunks, very convenient to sit on. The palms that still stood made a green roof, covered on the underside with a quivering tangle of reflections from the lagoon. Ralph hauled himself on to this platform, noted the coolness and shade, shut one eye, and decided that the shadows on his body were really green. He picked his way to the seaward edge of the platform and stood looking down into the water. It was clear to the bottom and bright with the efflorescence of tropical weed and coral. A school of tiny, glittering fish flicked hither and thither. Ralph spoke to himself, sounding the bass strings of delight.

"Whizzoh!"

Beyond the platform there was more enchantment. Some

act of God—a typhoon perhaps, or the storm that had accompanied his own arrival—had banked sand inside the lagoon so that there was a long, deep pool in the beach with a high ledge of pink granite at the further end. Ralph had been deceived before now by the specious appearance of depth in a beach pool and he approached this one preparing to be disappointed. But the island ran true to form and the incredible pool, which clearly was only invaded by the sea at high tide, was so deep at one end as to be dark green. Ralph inspected the whole thirty yards carefully and then plunged in. The water was warmer than his blood and he might have been swimming in a huge bath.

Piggy appeared again, sat on the rocky ledge, and watched Ralph's green and white body enviously.

"You can't half swim."

"Piggy."

Piggy took off his shoes and socks, ranged them carefully on the ledge, and tested the water with one toe.

"It's hot!"

"What did you expect?"

"I didn't expect nothing. My auntie——"

"Sucks to your auntie!"

Ralph did a surface dive and swam under water with his eyes open; the sandy edge of the pool loomed up like a hillside. He turned over, holding his nose, and a golden light danced and shattered just over his face. Piggy was looking determined and began to take off his shorts. Presently he was palely and fatly naked. He tip-toed down the sandy side of the pool, and sat there up to his neck in water smiling proudly at Ralph.

"Aren't you going to swim?"

Piggy shook his head.

"I can't swim. I wasn't allowed. My asthma——"

"Sucks to your ass-mar!"

Piggy bore this with a sort of humble patience.

"You can't half swim well."

Ralph paddled backwards down the slope, immersed his mouth and blew a jet of water into the air. Then he lifted his chin and spoke.

"I could swim when I was five. Daddy taught me. He's a commander in the Navy. When he gets leave he'll come and rescue us. What's your father?"

Piggy flushed suddenly.

"My dad's dead," he said quickly, "and my mum——"

He took off his glasses and looked vainly for something with which to clean them.

"I used to live with my auntie. She kept a sweet-shop. I used to get ever so many sweets. As many as I liked. When'll your dad rescue us?"

"Soon as he can."

Piggy rose dripping from the water and stood naked, cleaning his glasses with a sock. The only sound that reached them now through the heat of the morning was the long, grinding roar of the breakers on the reef.

"How does he know we're here?"

Ralph lolled in the water. Sleep enveloped him like the swathing mirages that were wrestling with the brilliance of the lagoon.

"How does he know we're here?"

Because, thought Ralph, because, because. The roar from the reef became very distant.

"They'd tell him at the airport."

Piggy shook his head, put on his flashing glasses and looked down at Ralph.

"Not them. Didn't you hear what the pilot said? About the atom bomb? They're all dead."

Ralph pulled himself out of the water, stood racing Piggy, and considered this unusual problem.

Piggy persisted.

"This is an island, isn't it?"

"I climbed a rock," said Ralph slowly, "and I think this is an island."

"They're all dead," said Piggy, "an' this is an island. Nobody don't know we're here. Your dad don't know, nobody don't know——"

His lips quivered and the spectacles were dimmed with mist.

"We may stay here till we die."

With that word the heat seemed to increase till it became a threatening weight and the lagoon attacked them with a blinding effulgence.

"Get my clothes," muttered Ralph. "Along there."

He trotted through the sand, enduring the sun's enmity, crossed the platform and found his scattered clothes. To put on a grey shirt once more was strangely pleasing. Then he climbed the edge of the platform add sat in the green shade on a convenient trunk. Piggy hauled himself up, carrying most of his clothes under his arms. Then he sat carefully on a fallen trunk near the little cliff that fronted the lagoon; and the tangled reflections quivered over him.

Presently he spoke.

"We got to find the others. We got to do something."

Ralph said nothing. Here was a coral island. Protected from the sun, ignoring Piggy's ill-omened talk, he dreamed pleasantly.

Piggy insisted.

"How many of us are there?"

Ralph came forward and stood by Piggy.

"I don't know."

Here and there, little breezes crept over the polished waters beneath the haze of heat. When these breezes reached the platform the palm-fronds would whisper, so that spots of blurred sunlight slid over their bodies or moved like bright, winged things in the shade.

Piggy looked up at Ralph. All the shadows on Ralph's face were reversed; green above, bright below from the lagoon. A blur of sunlight was crawling across his hair.

"We got to do something."

Ralph looked through him. Here at last was the imagined but never fully realized place leaping into real life. Ralph's lips parted in a delighted smile and Piggy, taking this smile to himself as a mark of recognition, laughed with pleasure.

"If it really is an island——"

"What's that?"

Ralph had stopped smiling and was pointing into the lagoon. Something creamy lay among the ferny weeds.

"A stone."

"No. A shell."

Suddenly Piggy was a-bubble with decorous excitement.

"S'right. It's a shell! I seen one like that before. On someone's back wall. A conch he called it. He used to blow it and then his mum would come. It's ever so valuable——"

Near to Ralph's elbow, a palm sapling leaned out over the lagoon. Indeed, the weight was already pulling a lump from the poor soil and soon it would fall. He tore out the stem and began to poke about in the water, while the brilliant fish flicked away on this side and that. Piggy leaned dangerously.

"Careful! You'll break it——"

"Shut up."

Ralph spoke absently. The shell was interesting and pretty and a worthy plaything: but the vivid phantoms of his day-dream still interposed between him and Piggy, who in this context was an irrelevance. The palm sapling, bending, pushed the shell across the weeds. Ralph used one hand as a fulcrum and pressed down with the other till the shell rose, dripping, and Piggy could make a grab.

Now the shell was no longer a thing seen but not to be touched, Ralph too became excited. Piggy babbled:

"——a conch; ever so expensive. I bet if you wanted to buy one, you'd have to pay pounds and pounds and pounds —he had it on his garden wall, and my auntie——"

Ralph took the shell from Piggy and a little water ran down his arm. In colour the shell was deep cream, touched here and there with fading pink. Between the point, worn away into a little hole, and the pink lips of the mouth, lay eighteen inches of shell with a slight spiral twist and covered with a delicate, embossed pattern. Ralph shook sand out of the deep tube.

"——moo-ed like a cow," he said. "He had some white stones too, an' a bird cage with a green parrot. He didn't blow the white stones, of course, an' he said——"

Piggy paused for breath and stroked the glistening thing that lay in Ralph's hands.

"Ralph!"

Ralph looked up.

"We can use this to call the others. Have a meeting. They'll come when they hear us——"

He beamed at Ralph.

"That was what you meant, didn't you? That's why you got the conch out of the water?"

Ralph pushed back his fair hair.

"How did your friend blow the conch?"

"He kind of spat," said Piggy. "My auntie wouldn't let me blow on account of my asthma. He said you blew from down here." Piggy laid a hand on his jutting abdomen. "You try, Ralph. You'll call the others."

Doubtfully, Ralph laid the small end of the shell against his mouth and blew. There came a rushing sound from its mouth but nothing more. Ralph wiped the salt water off his lips and tried again, but the shell remained silent.

"He kind of spat."

Ralph pursed his lips and squirted air into the shell, which emitted a low, farting noise. This amused both boys so much that Ralph went on squirting for some minutes, between bouts of laughter.

"He blew from down here."

Ralph grasped the idea and hit the shell with air from his diaphragm. Immediately the thing sounded. A deep, harsh note boomed under the palms, spread through the intricacies of the forest and echoed back from the pink granite of the mountain. Clouds of birds rose from the tree-tops, and something squealed and ran in the undergrowth.

Ralph took the shell away from his lips.

"Gosh!"

His ordinary voice sounded like a whisper after the harsh note of the conch. He laid the conch against his lips, took a deep breath and blew once more. The note boomed again: and then at his firmer pressure, the note, fluking up an octave, became a strident blare more penetrating than before. Piggy was shouting something, his face pleased, his glasses flashing. The birds cried, small animals scuttered. Ralph's breath failed; the note dropped the octave, became a low wubber, was a rush of air.

The conch was silent, a gleaming tusk; Ralph's face was dark with breathlessness and the air over the island was full of bird-clamour and echoes ringing.

"I bet you can hear that for miles."

Ralph found his breath and blew a series of short blasts.

Piggy exclaimed: "There's one!"

A child had appeared among the palms, about a hundred yards along the beach. He was a boy of perhaps six years, sturdy and fair, his clothes torn, his face covered with a sticky mess of fruit. His trousers had been lowered for an obvious purpose and had only been pulled back half-way. He jumped off the palm terrace into the sand and his trousers fell about his ankles; he stepped out of them and trotted to the platform. Piggy helped him up. Meanwhile Ralph continued to blow till voices shouted in the forest. The small boy squatted in front of Ralph, looking up brightly and vertically. As he received the reassurance of something purposeful being done he began to look satisfied, and his only clean digit, a pink thumb, slid into his mouth.

Piggy leaned down to him.

"What's yer name?"

"Johnny."

Piggy muttered the name to himself and then shouted it to Ralph, who was not interested because he was still blowing. His face was dark with the violent pleasure of making this stupendous noise, and his heart was making the stretched shirt shake. The shouting in the forest was nearer.

Signs of life were visible now on the beach. The sand, trembling beneath the heat-haze, concealed many figures in its miles of length; boys were making their way towards the platform through the hot, dumb sand. Three small children, no older than Johnny, appeared from startlingly close at hand where they had been gorging fruit in the forest. A dark little boy, not much younger than Piggy, parted a tangle of undergrowth, walked on to the platform, and smiled cheerfully at everybody. More and more of them came. Taking their cue from the innocent Johnny, they sat down on the fallen palm trunks and waited. Ralph continued to blow short, penetrating blasts. Piggy moved among the crowd, asking names and frowning to remember them. The children gave him the same simple obedience that they had given to the men with megaphones. Some were naked and carrying their clothes: others half-naked, or more-or-less dressed, in school uniforms; grey, blue, fawn, jacketed or jerseyed. There were badges, mottoes even, stripes of colour in stockings and pullovers. Their heads clustered above the trunks in the green shade; heads brown, fair, black, chestnut, sandy, mouse-coloured; heads muttering, whispering, heads full of eyes that watched Ralph and speculated. Something was being done.

The children who came along the beach, singly or in twos, leapt into visibility when they crossed the line from heat-haze to nearer sand. Here, the eye was first attracted to a black, bat-like creature that danced on the sand, and only later perceived the body above it. The bat was the child's shadow, shrunk by the vertical sun to a patch between the hurrying feet. Even while he blew, Ralph noticed the last pair of bodies that reached the platform above a fluttering patch of black. The two boys, bullet-headed and with hair like tow, flung themselves down and lay grinning and panting at Ralph like dogs. They were twins, and the

eye was shocked and incredulous at such cheery duplica-
tion. They breathed together, they grinned together, they
were chunky and vital. They raised wet lips at Ralph, for
they seemed provided with not quite enough skin, so that
their profiles were blurred and their mouths pulled open.
Piggy bent his flashing glasses to them and could be heard
between the blasts, repeating their names.

"Sam, Eric, Sam, Eric."

Then he got muddled; the twins shook their heads and
pointed at each other and the crowd laughed.

At last Ralph ceased to blow and sat there, the conch
trailing from one hand, his head bowed on his knees. As
the echoes died away so did the laughter, and there was
silence.

Within the diamond haze of the beach something dark
was fumbling along. Ralph saw it first, and watched till the
intentness of his gaze drew all eyes that way. Then the
creature stepped from mirage on to clear sand, and they
saw that the darkness was not all shadow but mostly clothing. The creature was a party of boys, marching approximately in step in two parallel lines and dressed in strangely
eccentric clothing. Shorts, shirts, and different garments
they carried in their hands: but each boy wore a square
black cap with a silver badge in it. Their bodies, from
throat to ankle, were hidden by black cloaks which bore a
long silver cross on the left breast and each neck was finished
off with a hambone frill. The heat of the tropics, the descent,
the search for food, and now this sweaty march along the
blazing beach had given them the complexions of newly
washed plums. The boy who controlled them was dressed
in the same way though his cap badge was golden. When his
party was about ten yards from the platform he shouted an

order and they halted, gasping, sweating, swaying in the fierce light. The boy himself came forward, vaulted on to the platform with his cloak flying, and peered into what to him was almost complete darkness.

"Where's the man with the trumpet?"

Ralph, sensing his sun-blindness, answered him.

"There's no man with a trumpet. Only me."

The boy came close and peered down at Ralph, screwing up his face as he did so. What he saw of the fair-haired boy with the creamy shell on his knees did not seem to satisfy him. He turned quickly, his black cloak circling.

"Isn't there a ship, then?"

Inside the floating cloak he was tall, thin, and bony: and his hair was red beneath the black cap. His face was crumpled and freckled, and ugly without silliness. Out of this face stared two light blue eyes, frustrated now, and turning, or ready to turn, to anger.

"Isn't there a man here?"

Ralph spoke to his back.

"No. We're having a meeting. Come and join in."

The group of cloaked boys began to scatter from close line. The tall boy shouted at them.

"Choir! Stand still!"

Wearily obedient, the choir huddled into line and stood there swaying in the sun. None the less, some began to protest faintly.

"But, Merridew. Please, Merridew . . . can't we?"

Then one of the boys flopped on his face in the sand and the line broke up. They heaved the fallen boy to the platform and let him lie. Merridew, his eyes staring, made the best of a bad job.

"All right then. Sit down. Let him alone."

"But Merridew."

"He's always throwing a faint," said Merridew. "He did in Gib.; and Addis; and at matins over the precentor."

This last piece of shop brought sniggers from the choir, who perched like black birds on the criss-cross trunks and examined Ralph with interest. Piggy asked no names. He was intimidated by this uniformed superiority and the off-hand authority in Merridew 's voice. He shrank to the other side of Ralph and busied himself with his glasses.

Merridew turned to Ralph.

"Aren't there any grown-ups?"

"No."

Merridew sat down on a trunk and looked round the circle.

"Then we'll have to look after ourselves."

Secure on the other side of Ralph, Piggy spoke timidly.

"That's why Ralph made a meeting. So as we can decide what to do. We've heard names. That's Johnny. Those two —they're twins, Sam 'n Eric. Which is Eric—? You? No— you're Sam——"

"I'm Sam——"

" 'n I'm Eric."

"We'd better all have names," said Ralph, "so I'm Ralph."

"We got most names," said Piggy. "Got 'em just now."

"Kids' names," said Merridew. "Why should I be Jack? I'm Merridew."

Ralph turned to him quickly. This was the voice of one who knew his own mind.

"Then," went on Piggy, "that boy—I forget——"

"You're talking too much," said Jack Merridew. "Shut up, Fatty."

Laughter arose.

"He's not Fatty," cried Ralph, "his real name's Piggy!'

"Piggy!"

"Piggy!"

"Oh, Piggy!"

A storm of laughter arose and even the tiniest child joined in. For the moment the boys were a closed circuit of sympathy with Piggy outside: he went very pink, bowed his head and cleaned his glasses again.

Finally the laughter died away and the naming continued. There was Maurice, next in size among the choir boys to Jack, but broad and grinning all the time. There was a slight, furtive boy whom no one knew, who kept to himself with an inner intensity of avoidance and secrecy. He muttered that his name was Roger and was silent again. Bill, Robert, Harold, Henry; the choir boy who had fainted sat up against a palm trunk, smiled pallidly at Ralph and said that his name was Simon.

Jack spoke.

"We've got to decide about being rescued."

There was a buzz. One of the small boys, Henry, said that he wanted to go home.

"Shut up," said Ralph absently. He lifted the conch. "Seems to me we ought to have a chief to decide things."

"A chief! A chief!"

"I ought to be chief," said Jack with simple arrogance, "because I'm chapter chorister and head boy. I can sing C sharp."

Another buzz.

"Well then," said Jack, "I——"

He hesitated. The dark boy, Roger, stirred at last and spoke up.

"Let's have a vote."

"Yes!"

"Vote for chief!"

"Let's vote——"

This toy of voting was almost as pleasing as the conch. Jack started to protest but the clamour changed from the general wish for a chief to an election by acclaim of Ralph himself. None of the boys could have found good reason for this; what intelligence had been shown was traceable to Piggy while the most obvious leader was Jack. But there was a stillness about Ralph as he sat that marked him out: there was his size, and attractive appearance; and most obscurely, yet most powerfully, there was the conch. The being that had blown that, had sat waiting for them on the platform with the delicate thing balanced on his knees, was set apart.

"Him with the shell."

"Ralph! Ralph!"

"Let him be chief with the trumpet-thing."

Ralph raised a hand for silence.

"All right. Who wants Jack for chief?"

With dreary obedience the choir raised their hands.

"Who wants me?"

Every hand outside the choir except Piggy's was raised immediately. Then Piggy, too, raised his hand grudgingly into the air.

Ralph counted.

"I'm chief then."

The circle of boys broke into applause. Even the choir applauded; and the freckles on Jack's face disappeared under a blush of mortification. He started up, then changed his mind and sat down again while the air rang. Ralph looked at him, eager to offer something.

"The choir belongs to you, of course."

"They could be the army——"

"Or hunters——"

"They could be——"

The suffusion drained away from Jack's face. Ralph waved again for silence.

"Jack's in charge of the choir. They can be—what do you want them to be?"

"Hunters."

Jack and Ralph smiled at each other with shy liking. The rest began to talk eagerly.

Jack stood up.

"All right, choir. Take off your togs."

As if released from class, the choir boys stood up, chattered, piled their black cloaks on the grass. Jack laid his on the trunk by Ralph. His grey shorts were sticking to him with sweat. Ralph glanced at them admiringly, and when Jack saw his glance he explained.

"I tried to get over that hill to see if there was water all round. But your shell called us."

Ralph smiled and held up the conch for silence.

"Listen, everybody. I've got to have time to think things out. I can't decide what to do straight off. If this isn't an island we might be rescued straight away. So we've got to decide if this is an island. Everybody must stay round here and wait and not go away. Three of us—if we take more we'd get all mixed, and lose each other—three of us will go on an expedition and find out. I'll go, and Jack, and, and. . . ."

He looked round the circle of eager faces. There was no lack of boys to choose from.

"And Simon."

The boys round Simon giggled, and he stood up, laugh-ing a little. Now that the pallor of his faint was over, he was a skinny, vivid little boy, with a glance coming up from under a hut of straight hair that hung down, black and coarse.

He nodded at Ralph.

"I'll come."

"And I——"

Jack snatched from behind him a sizable sheath-knife and clouted it into a trunk. The buzz rose and died away.

Piggy stirred.

"I'll come."

Ralph turned to him.

"You're no good on a job like this."

"All the same——"

"We don't want you," said Jack, flatly. "Three's enough."

Piggy's glasses flashed.

"I was with him when he found the conch. I was with him before anyone else was."

Jack and the others paid no attention. There was a gen-eral dispersal. Ralph, Jack and Simon jumped off the plat-form and walked along the sand past the bathing-pool. Piggy hung bumbling behind them.

"If Simon walks in the middle of us," said Ralph, "then we could talk over his head."

The three of them fell into step. This meant that every now and then Simon had to do a double shuffle to catch up with the others. Presently Ralph stopped and turned back to Piggy.

"Look."

Jack and Simon pretended to notice nothing. They walked on.

"You can't come."

Piggy's glasses were misted again—this time with humiliation.

"You told 'em. After what I said."

His face flushed, his mouth trembled.

"After I said I didn't want——"

"What on earth are you talking about?"

"About being called Piggy. I said I didn't care as long as they didn't call me Piggy; an' I said not to tell and then you went an' said straight out——"

Stillness descended on them. Ralph, looking with more understanding at Piggy, saw that he was hurt and crushed. He hovered between the two courses of apology or further insult.

"Better Piggy than Fatty," he said at last, with the directness of genuine leadership, "and anyway, I'm sorry if you feel like that. Now go back, Piggy, and take names. That's your job. So long."

He turned and raced after the other two. Piggy stood and the rose of indignation faded slowly from his cheeks. He went back to the platform.

The three boys walked briskly on the sand. The tide was low and there was a strip of weed-strewn beach that was almost as firm as a road. A kind of glamour was spread over them and the scene and they were conscious of the glamour and made happy by it. They turned to each other, laughing excitedly, talking, not listening. The air was bright. Ralph, faced by the task of translating all this into an explanation, stood on his head and fell over. When they had done laughing, Simon stroked Ralph's arm shyly; and they had to laugh again.

"Come on," said Jack presently, "we're explorers."

"We'll go to the end of the island", said Ralph, "and look round the corner."

"If it is an island——"

Now, towards the end of the afternoon, the mirages were settling a little. They found the end of the island, quite distinct and not magicked out of shape or sense. There was a jumble of the usual squareness, with one great block sitting out in the lagoon. Sea birds were nesting there.

"Like icing", said Ralph, "on a pink cake."

"We shan't see round this corner," said Jack, "because there isn't one. Only a slow curve—and you can see, the rocks get worse——"

Ralph shaded his eyes and followed the jagged outline of the crags up towards the mountain. This part of the beach was nearer the mountain than any other that they had seen.

"We'll try climbing the mountain from here," he said. "I should think this is the easiest way. There's less of that jungly stuff; and more pink rock. Come on."

The three boys began to scramble up. Some unknown force had wrenched and shattered these cubes so that they lay askew, often piled diminishingly on each other. The most usual feature of the rock was a pink cliff surmounted by a skewed block; and that again surmounted, and that again, till the pinkness became a stack of balanced rock projecting through the looped fantasy of the forest creepers. Where the pink cliffs rose out of the ground there were often narrow tracks winding upwards. They could edge along them, deep in the plant world, their faces to the rock.

"What made this track?"

Jack paused, wiping the sweat from his face. Ralph stood by him, breathless.

"Men?"

Jack shook his head.

"Animals."

Ralph peered into the darkness under the trees. The forest minutely vibrated.

"Come on."

The difficulty was not the steep ascent round the shoulders of rock, but the occasional plunges through the undergrowth to get to the next path. Here, the roots and stems of creepers were in such tangles that the boys had to thread through them like pliant needles. Their only guide, apart from the brown ground and occasional flashes of light through the foliage, was the tendency of slope: whether this hole, laced as it was with cables of creeper, stood higher than that.

Somehow, they moved up.

Immured in these tangles, at perhaps their most difficult moment, Ralph turned with shining eyes to the others.

"Wacco."

"Wizard."

"Smashing."

The cause of their pleasure was not obvious. All three were hot, dirty and exhausted. Ralph was badly scratched. The creepers were as thick as their thighs and left little but tunnels for further penetration. Ralph shouted experimentally and they listened to the muted echoes.

"This is real exploring," said Jack. "I bet nobody's been here before."

"We ought to draw a map," said Ralph, "only we haven't any paper."

"We could make scratches on bark", said Simon, "and rub black stuff in.'

Again came the solemn communion of shining eyes in the gloom.

"Wacco."

"Wizard."

There was no place for standing on one's head. This time Ralph expressed the intensity of his emotion by pretending to knock Simon down; and soon they were a happy, heaving pile in the under-dusk.

When they had fallen apart Ralph spoke first.

"Got to get on."

The pink granite of the next cliff was further back from the creepers and trees so that they could trot up the path. This again led into more open forest so that they had a glimpse of the spread sea. With openness came the sun; it dried the sweat that had soaked their clothes in the dark, damp heat. At last the way to the top looked like a scramble over pink rock, with no more plunging through darkness. The boys chose their way through defiles and over screes of sharp stone.

"Look! Look!"

High over this end of the island, the shattered rocks lifted up their stacks and chimneys. This one, against which Jack leaned, moved with a grating sound when they pushed.

"Come on——"

But not "Come on" to the top. The assault on the summit must wait while the three boys accepted this challenge. The rock was as large as a small motor car.

"Heave!"

Sway back and forth, catch the rhythm.

"Heave!"

Increase the swing of the pendulum, increase, increase,

come up and bear against that point of furthest balance—increase—increase——

"Heave!"

The great rock loitered, poised on one toe, decided not to return, moved through the air, fell, struck, turned over, leapt droning through the air and smashed a deep hole in the canopy of the forest. Echoes and birds flew, white and pink dust floated, the forest further down shook as with the passage of an enraged monster: and then the island was still.

"Wacco!"

"Like a bomb!"

"Whee-aa-oo!"

Not for five minutes could they drag themselves away from this triumph. But they left at last.

The way to the top was easy after that. As they reached the last stretch Ralph stopped.

"Golly!"

They were on the lip of a cirque, or a half-cirque, in the side of the mountain. This was filled with a blue flower, a rock plant of some sort; and the overflow hung down the vent and spilled lavishly among the canopy of the forest. The air was thick with butterflies, lifting, fluttering, settling.

Beyond the cirque was the square top of the mountain and soon they were standing on it.

They had guessed before that this was an island: clambering among the pink rocks, with the sea on either side, and the crystal heights of air, they had known by some instinct that the sea lay on every side. But there seemed something more fitting in leaving the last word till they stood on the top, and could see a circular horizon of water.

Ralph turned to the others.

"This belongs to us."

It was roughly boat-shaped: humped near this end with behind them the jumbled descent to the shore. On either side rocks, cliffs, tree-tops and a steep slope: forward there, the length of the boat, a tamer descent, tree-clad, with hints of pink: and then the jungly flat of the island, dense green, but drawn at the end to a pink tail. There, where the island petered out in water, was another island; a rock, almost detached, standing like a fort, facing them across the green with one bold, pink bastion.

The boys surveyed all this, then looked out to sea. They were high up and the afternoon had advanced; the view was not robbed of sharpness by mirage.

"That's a reef. A coral reef. I've seen pictures like that."

The reef enclosed more than one side of the island, lying perhaps a mile out and parallel to what they now thought of as their beach. The coral was scribbled in the sea as though a giant had bent down to reproduce the shape of the island in a flowing, chalk line but tired before he had finished. Inside was peacock water, rocks and weed showing as in an aquarium; outside was the dark blue of the sea. The tide was running so that long streaks of foam tailed away from the reef and for a moment they felt that the boat was moving steadily astern.

Jack pointed down.

"That's where we landed."

Beyond falls and cliffs there was a gash visible in the trees; there were the splintered trunks and then the drag, leaving only a fringe of palm between the scar and the sea. There, too, jutting into the lagoon, was the platform, with insect-like figures moving near it.

Ralph sketched a twining line from the bald spot on

which they stood down a slope, a gully, through flowers, round and down to the rock where the scar started.

"That's the quickest way back."

Eyes shining, mouths open, triumphant, they savoured the right of domination. They were lifted up: were friends.

"There's no village smoke, and no boats," said Ralph wisely. "We'll make sure later; but I think it's uninhabited."

"We'll get food," cried Jack. "Hunt. Catch things ... until they fetch us."

Simon looked at them both, saying nothing but nodding till his black hair flopped backwards and forwards: his face was glowing.

Ralph looked down the other way where there was no reef.

"Steeper," said Jack.

Ralph made a cupping gesture.

"That bit of forest down there ... the mountain holds it up."

Every coign of the mountain held up trees—flowers and trees. Now the forest stirred, roared, flailed. The nearer acres of rock flowers fluttered and for half a minute the breeze blew cool on their faces.

Ralph spread his arms.

"All ours."

They laughed and tumbled and shouted on the mountain.

"I'm hungry."

When Simon mentioned his hunger the others became aware of theirs.

"Come on," said Ralph. "We've found out what we wanted to know."

They scrambled down a rock slope, dropped among flowers and made their way under the trees. Here they

39

paused and examined the bushes round them curiously.

Simon spoke first.

"Like candles. Candle bushes. Candle buds."

The bushes were dark evergreen and aromatic and the many buds were waxen green and folded up against the light. Jack slashed at one with his knife and the scent spilled over them.

"Candle buds."

"You couldn't light them," said Ralph. "They just look like candles."

"Green candles," said Jack contemptuously, "we can't eat them. Come on."

They were in the beginnings of the thick forest, plonking with weary feet on a track, when they heard the noises—squeakings—and the hard strike of hoofs on a path. As they pushed forward the squeaking increased till it became a frenzy. They found a piglet caught in a curtain of creepers, throwing itself at the elastic traces in all the madness of extreme terror. Its voice was thin, needle-sharp and insistent. The three boys rushed forward and Jack drew his knife again with a flourish. He raised his arm in the air. There came a pause, a hiatus, the pig continued to scream and the creepers to jerk, and the blade continued to flash at the end of a bony arm. The pause was only long enough for them to understand what an enormity the downward stroke would be. Then the piglet tore loose from the creepers and scurried into the undergrowth. They were left looking at each other and the place of terror. Jack's face was white under the freckles. He noticed that he still held the knife aloft and brought his arm down replacing the blade in the sheath. Then they all three laughed ashamedly and began to climb back to the track.

"I was choosing a place," said Jack. "I was just waiting for a moment to decide where to stab him."

"You should stick a pig," said Ralph fiercely. "They always talk about sticking a pig."

"You cut a pig's throat to let the blood out," said Jack, "otherwise you can't eat the meat."

"Why didn't you——?"

They knew very well why he hadn't: because of the enormity of the knife descending and cutting into living flesh; because of the unbearable blood.

"I was going to," said Jack. He was ahead of them and they could not see his face. "I was choosing a place. Next time——!"

He snatched his knife out of the sheath and slammed it into a tree trunk. Next time there would be no mercy. He looked round fiercely, daring them to contradict. Then they broke out into the sunlight and for a while they were busy finding and devouring food as they moved down the scar towards the platform and the meeting.

CHAPTER TWO

Fire on the Mountain

———————◆———————

B y the time Ralph finished blowing the conch the platform was crowded. There were differences between
this meeting and the one held in the morning. The
afternoon sun slanted in from the other side of the platform
and most of the children, feeling too late the smart of sunburn, had put their clothes on. The choir, noticeably less of
a group, had discarded their cloaks.

Ralph sat on a fallen trunk, his left side to the sun. On
his right were most of the choir; on his left the larger boys
who had not known each other before the evacuation;
before him small children squatted in the grass.

Silence now. Ralph lifted the cream and pink shell to his
knees and a sudden breeze scattered light over the platform.
He was uncertain whether to stand up or remain sitting.
He looked sideways to his left, towards the bathing-pool.
Piggy was sitting near but giving no help.

Ralph cleared his throat.

"Well then."

All at once he found he could talk fluently and explain
what he had to say. He passed a hand through his fair hair
and spoke.

"We're on an island. We've been on the mountain-top

and seen water all round. We saw no houses, no smoke, no footprints, no boats, no people. We're on an uninhabited island with no other people on it."

Jack broke in.

"All the same you need an army—for hunting. Hunting pigs——"

"Yes. There are pigs on the island."

All three of them tried to convey the sense of the pink live thing struggling in the creepers.

"We saw——"

"Squealing——"

"It broke away——"

"Before I could kill it—but—next time!"

Jack slammed his knife into a trunk and looked round challengingly.

The meeting settled down again.

"So you see," said Ralph, "we need hunters to get us meat. And another thing."

He lifted the shell on his knees and looked round the sun-slashed faces.

"There aren't any grown-ups. We shall have to look after ourselves."

The meeting hummed and was silent.

"And another thing. We can't have everybody talking at once. We'll have to have 'Hands up' like at school."

He held the conch before his face and glanced round the mouth.

"Then I'll give him the conch."

"Conch?"

"That's what this shell's called. I'll give the conch to the next person to speak. He can hold it when he's speaking."

43

"But——"

"Look——"

"And he won't be interrupted. Except by me."

Jack was on his feet.

"We'll have rules!" he cried excitedly. "Lots of rules! Then when anyone breaks 'em——"

"Whee-oh!"

"Wacco!"

"Bong!"

"Doink!"

Ralph felt the conch lifted from his lap. Then Piggy was standing cradling the great cream shell and the shouting died down. Jack, left on his feet, looked uncertainly at Ralph who smiled and patted the log. Jack sat down. Piggy took off his glasses and blinked at the assembly while he wiped them on his shirt.

"You're hindering Ralph. You're not letting him get to the most important thing."

He paused effectively.

"Who knows we're here? Eh?"

"They knew at the airport."

"The man with a trumpet-thing——"

"My dad."

Piggy put on his glasses.

"Nobody knows where we are," said Piggy. He was paler than before and breathless. "Perhaps they knew where we was going to; and perhaps not. But they don't know where we are 'cos we never got there." He gaped at them for a moment, then swayed and sat down. Ralph took the conch from his hands.

"That's what I was going to say," he went on, "when you all, all. . . ." He gazed at their intent faces. "The plane was shot down in flames. Nobody knows where we are. We may be here a long time."

The silence was so complete that they could hear the fetch and miss of Piggy's breathing. The sun slanted in and lay golden over half the platform. The breezes that on the lagoon had chased their tails like kittens were finding their way across the platform and into the forest. Ralph pushed back the tangle of fair hair that hung on his forehead.

"So we may be here a long time."

Nobody said anything. He grinned suddenly.

"But this is a good island. We—Jack, Simon and me—we climbed the mountain. It's wizard. There's food and drink, and——"

"Rocks——"

"Blue flowers——"

Piggy, partly recovered, pointed to the conch in Ralph's hands, and Jack and Simon fell silent. Ralph went on.

"While we're waiting we can have a good time on this island."

He gesticulated widely.

"It's like in a book."

At once there was a clamour.

"Treasure Island——"

"Swallows and Amazons——"

"Coral Island——"

Ralph waved the conch.

"This is our island. It's a good island. Until the grownups come to fetch us we'll have fun."

Jack held out his hand for the conch.

"There's pigs," he said. "There's food; and bathing-water in that little stream along there—and everything. Didn't anyone find anything else?"

45

He handed the conch back to Ralph and sat down. Apparently no one had found anything.

The older boys first noticed the child when he resisted. There was a group of little boys urging him forward and he did not want to go. He was a shrimp of a boy, about six years old, and one side of his face was blotted out by a mulberry-coloured birthmark. He stood now, warped out of the perpendicular by the fierce light of publicity, and he bored into the coarse grass with one toe. He was muttering and about to cry.

The other little boys, whispering but serious, pushed him towards Ralph.

"All right," said Ralph, "come on then."

The small boy looked round in panic.

"Speak up!"

The small boy held out his hands for the conch and the assembly shouted with laughter; at once he snatched back his hands and started to cry.

"Let him have the conch!" shouted Piggy. "Let him have it!"

At last Ralph induced him to hold the shell but by then the blow of laughter had taken away the child's voice. Piggy knelt by him, one hand on the great shell, listening and interpreting to the assembly.

"He wants to know what you're going to do about the snake-thing."

Ralph laughed, and the other boys laughed with him. The small boy twisted further into himself.

"Tell us about the snake-thing."

"Now he says it was a beastie."

"Beastie?"

"A snake-thing. Ever so big. He saw it."

46

"Where?"

"In the woods."

Either the wandering breezes or perhaps the decline of the sun allowed a little coolness to lie under the trees. The boys felt it and stirred restlessly.

"You couldn't have a beastie, a snake-thing, on an island this size," Ralph explained kindly. "You only get them in big countries, like Africa, or India."

Murmur; and the grave nodding of heads.

"He says the beastie came in the dark."

"Then he couldn't see it!"

Laughter and cheers.

"Did you hear that? Says he saw the thing in the dark——"

"He still says he saw the beastie. It came and went away again an' came back and wanted to eat him——"

"He was dreaming."

Laughing, Ralph looked for confirmation round the ring of faces. The older boys agreed; but here and there among the little ones was the dubiety that required more than rational assurance.

"He must have had a nightmare. Stumbling about among all those creepers."

More grave nodding; they knew about nightmares.

"He says he saw the beastie, the snake-thing, and will it come back to-night?"

"But there isn't a beastie!"

"He says in the morning it turned into them things like ropes in the trees and hung in the branches. He says will it come back to-night?"

"But there isn't a beastie!"

There was no laughter at all now and more grave watching. Ralph pushed both hands through his hair and looked at the little boy in mixed amusement and exasperation.

Jack seized the conch.

"Ralph's right of course. There isn't a snake-thing. But if there was a snake we'd hunt it and kill it. We're going to hunt pigs to get meat for everybody. And we'll look for the snake too——"

"But there isn't a snake!"

"We'll make sure when we go hunting."

Ralph was annoyed and, for the moment, defeated. He felt himself facing something ungraspable. The eyes that looked so intently at him were without humour.

"But there isn't a beast!"

Something he had not known was there rose in him and compelled him to make the point, loudly and again.

"But I tell you there isn't a beast!"

The assembly was silent.

Ralph lifted the conch again and his good humour came back as he thought of what he had to say next.

"Now we come to the most important thing. I've been thinking. I was thinking while we were climbing the mountain." He flashed a conspiratorial grin at the other two. "And on the beach just now. This is what I thought. We want to have fun. And we want to be rescued."

The passionate noise of agreement from the assembly hit him like a wave and he lost his thread. He thought again.

"We want to be rescued; and of course we shall be rescued."

Voices babbled. The simple statement, unbacked by any proof but the weight of Ralph's new authority, brought light and happiness. He had to wave the conch before he could make them hear him.

"My father's in the navy. He said there aren't any unknown islands left. He says the Queen has a big room full of maps and all the islands in the world are drawn there. So the Queen's got a picture of this island."

Again came the sounds of cheerfulness and better heart.

"And sooner or later a ship will put in here. It might even be daddy's ship. So you see, sooner or later, we shall be rescued."

He paused, with the point made. The assembly was lifted towards safety by his words. They liked and now respected him. Spontaneously they began to clap and presently the platform was loud with applause. Ralph flushed, looking sideways at Piggy's open admiration, and then the other way at Jack who was smirking and showing that he too knew how to clap.

Ralph waved the conch.

"Shut up! Wait! Listen!"

He went on in the silence, borne on his triumph.

"There's another thing. We can help them to find us. If a ship comes near the island they may not notice us. So we must make smoke on top of the mountain. We must make a fire."

"A fire! Make a fire!"

At once half the boys were on their feet. Jack clamoured among them, the conch forgotten.

"Come on! Follow me!"

The space under the palm trees was full of noise and movement. Ralph was on his feet too, shouting for quiet, but no one heard him. All at once the crowd swayed towards the island and were gone—following Jack. Even the tiny children went and did their best among the leaves and broken branches. Ralph was left, holding the conch, with no one but Piggy.

Piggy's breathing was quite restored.

"Like kids!" he said scornfully. "Acting like a crowd of kids!"

Ralph looked at him doubtfully and laid the conch on the tree trunk,

"I bet it's gone tea-time," said Piggy. "What do they think they're going to do on that mountain?"

He caressed the shell respectfully, then stopped and looked up.

"Ralph! Hey! Where you going?"

Ralph was already clambering over the first smashed swathes of the scar. A long way ahead of him was crashing and laughter.

Piggy watched him in disgust.

"Like a crowd of kids——"

He sighed, bent, and laced up his shoes. The noise of the errant assembly faded up the mountain. Then, with the martyred expression of a parent who has to keep up with the senseless ebullience of the children, he picked up the conch, turned towards the forest, and began to pick his way over the tumbled scar.

Below the other side of the mountain-top was a platform of forest. Once more Ralph found himself making the cupping gesture.

"Down there we could get as much wood as we want."

Jack nodded and pulled at his underlip. Starting perhaps a hundred feet below them on the steeper side of the mountain, the patch might have been designed expressly for fuel. Trees, forced by the damp heat, found too little soil for full growth, fell early and decayed: creepers cradled them, and new saplings searched a way up.

Jack turned to the choir, who stood ready. Their black caps of maintenance were slid over one ear like berets.

"We'll build a pile. Come on."

They found the likeliest path down and began tugging at the dead wood. And the small boys who had reached the top came sliding too till everyone but Piggy was busy. Most of the wood was so rotten that when they pulled it broke up into a shower of fragments and woodlice and decay; but some trunks came out in one piece. The twins, Sam 'n Eric, were the first to get a likely log but they could do nothing till Ralph, Jack, Simon, Roger and Maurice found room for a hand-hold. Then they inched the grotesque dead thing up the rock and toppled it over on top. Each party of boys added a quota, less or more, and the pile grew. At the return Ralph found himself alone on a limb with Jack and they grinned at each other, sharing this burden. Once more, amid the breeze, the shouting, the slanting sunlight on the high mountain, was shed that glamour, that strange invisible light of friendship, adventure, and content.

"Almost too heavy."

Jack grinned back.

"Not for the two of us."

Together, joined in effort by the burden, they staggered up the last steep of the mountain. Together, they chanted One! Two! Three! and crashed the log on to the great pile. Then they stepped back, laughing with triumphant pleasure, so that immediately Ralph had to stand on his head. Below them, boys were still labouring, though some of the small ones had lost interest and were searching this new forest for fruit. Now the twins, with unsuspected intelligence, came up the mountain with armfuls of dried leaves and dumped them against the pile. One by one, as they sensed that the pile was complete, the boys stopped going back for more and stood, with the pink, shattered top of the mountain around them. Breath came even by now, and sweat dried.

Ralph and Jack looked at each other while society paused about them. The shameful knowledge grew in them and they did not know how to begin confession.

Ralph spoke first, crimson in the face.

"Will you?"

He cleared his throat and went on.

"Will you light the fire?"

Now the absurd situation was open, Jack blushed too. He began to mutter vaguely.

"You rub two sticks. You rub——"

He glanced at Ralph, who blurted out the last confession of incompetence.

"Has anyone got any matches?"

"You make a bow and spin the arrow," said Roger. He rubbed his hands in mime. "Psss. Psss."

A little air was moving over the mountain. Piggy came with it, in shorts and shirt, labouring cautiously out of the forest with the evening sunlight gleaming from his glasses. He held the conch under his arm.

Ralph shouted at him.

"Piggy! Have you got any matches?"

The other boys took up the cry till the mountain rang. Piggy shook his head and came to the pile.

"My! You've made a big heap, haven't you?"

Jack pointed suddenly.

"His specs—use them as burning glasses!"

Piggy was surrounded before he could back away.

"Here—Let me go!" His voice rose to a shriek of terror

as Jack snatched the glasses off his face. "Mind out! Give 'em back! I can hardly see! You'll break the conch!"

Ralph elbowed him to one side and knelt by the pile.

"Stand out of the light."

There was pushing and pulling and officious cries. Ralph moved the lenses back and forth, this way and that, till a glossy white image of the declining sun lay on a piece of rotten wood. Almost at once a thin trickle of smoke rose up and made him cough. Jack knelt too and blew gently, so that the smoke drifted away, thickening, and a tiny flame appeared. The flame, nearly invisible at first in that bright sunlight, enveloped a small twig, grew, was enriched with colour and reached up to a branch which exploded with a sharp crack. The flame flapped higher and the boys broke into a cheer.

"My specs!" howled Piggy. "Give me my specs!"

Ralph stood away from the pile and put the glasses into Piggy's groping hands. His voice subsided to a mutter.

"Jus' blurs, that's all. Hardly see my hand——"

The boys were dancing. The pile was so rotten, and now so tinder-dry, that whole limbs yielded passionately to the yellow flames that poured upwards and shook a great beard of flame twenty feet in the air. For yards round the fire the heat was like a blow, and the breeze was a river of sparks. Trunks crumbled to white dust.

Ralph shouted.

"More wood! All of you get more wood!"

Life became a race with the fire and the boys scattered through the upper forest. To keep a clean flag of flame flying on the mountain was the immediate end and no one looked further. Even the smallest boys, unless fruit claimed them, brought little pieces of wood and threw them in. The air

53

moved a little faster and became a light wind, so that lee-ward and windward side were clearly differentiated. On one side the air was cool, but on the other the fire thrust out a savage arm of heat that crinkled hair on the instant. Boys who felt the evening wind on their damp faces paused to enjoy the freshness of it and then found they were exhausted. They flung themselves down in the shadows that lay among the shattered rocks. The beard of flame diminished quickly; then the pile fell inwards with a soft, cindery sound, and sent a great tree of sparks upwards that leaned away and drifted downwind. The boys lay, panting like dogs.

Ralph raised his head off his forearms.

"That was no good."

Roger spat efficiently into the hot dust.

"What d'you mean?"

"There wasn't any smoke. Only flame."

Piggy had settled himself in a coign between two rocks, and sat with the conch on his knees.

"We haven't made a fire," he said, "what's any use. We couldn't keep a fire like that going, not if we tried."

"A fat lot you tried," said Jack contemptuously. "You just sat."

"We used his specs," said Simon, smearing a black cheek with his forearm. "He helped that way."

"I got the conch," said Piggy indignantly. "You let me speak!"

"The conch doesn't count on top of the mountain," said Jack, "so you shut up."

"I got the conch in my hand."

"Put on green branches," said Maurice. "That's the best way to make smoke."

"I got the conch——"

Jack turned fiercely.

"You shut up!"

Piggy wilted. Ralph took the conch from him and looked round the circle of boys.

"We've got to have special people for looking after the fire. Any day there may be a ship out there"—he waved his arm at the taut wire of the horizon—"and if we have a signal going they'll come and take us off. And another thing. We ought to have more rules. Where the conch is, that's a meeting. The same up here as down there."

They assented. Piggy opened his mouth to speak, caught Jack's eye and shut it again. Jack held out his hands for the conch and stood up, holding the delicate thing carefully in his sooty hands.

"I agree with Ralph. We've got to have rules and obey them. After all, we're not savages. We're English; and the English are best at everything. So we've got to do the right things."

He turned to Ralph.

"Ralph—I'll split up the choir—my hunters, that is— into groups, and we'll be responsible for keeping the fire going——"

This generosity brought a spatter of applause from the boys, so that Jack grinned at them, then waved the conch for silence.

"We'll let the fire burn out now. Who would see smoke at night-time, anyway? And we can start the fire again whenever we like. Altos—you can keep the fire going this week; and trebles the next——"

The assembly assented gravely.

"And we'll be responsible for keeping a lookout too. If we see a ship out there"—they followed the direction of his

55

bony arm with their eyes—"we'll put green branches on. Then there'll be more smoke."

They gazed intently at the dense blue of the horizon, as if a little silhouette might appear there at any moment.

The sun in the west was a drop of burning gold that slid nearer and nearer the sill of the world. All at once they were aware of the evening as the end of light and warmth.

Roger took the conch and looked round at them gloomily.

"I've been watching the sea. There hasn't been the trace of a ship. Perhaps we'll never be rescued."

A murmur rose and swept away. Ralph took back the conch.

"I said before we'll be rescued sometime. We've just got to wait; that's all."

Daring, indignant, Piggy took the conch.

"That's what I said! I said about our meetings and things and then you said shut up——"

His voice lifted into the whine of virtuous recrimination. They stirred and began to shout him down.

"You said you wanted a small fire and you been and built a pile like a hayrick. If I say anything," cried Piggy, with bitter realism, "you say shut up; but if Jack or Maurice or Simon——"

He paused in the tumult, standing, looking beyond them and down the unfriendly side of the mountain to the great patch where they had found dead wood. Then he laughed so strangely that they were hushed, looking at the flash of his spectacles in astonishment. They followed his gaze to find the sour joke.

"You got your small fire all right."

Smoke was rising here and there among the creepers that

56

festooned the dead or dying trees. As they watched, a flash of fire appeared at the root of one wisp, and then the smoke thickened. Small flames stirred at the bole of a tree and crawled away through leaves and brushwood, dividing and increasing. One patch touched a tree trunk and scrambled up like a bright squirrel. The smoke increased, sifted, rolled outwards. The squirrel leapt on the wings of the wind and clung to another standing tree, eating downwards. Beneath the dark canopy of leaves and smoke the fire laid hold on the forest and began to gnaw. Acres of black and yellow smoke rolled steadily towards the sea. At the sight of the flames and the irresistible course of the fire, the boys broke into shrill, excited cheering. The flames, as though they were a kind of wild life, crept as a jaguar creeps on its belly towards a line of birch-like saplings that fledged an outcrop of the pink rock. They flapped at the first of the trees, and the branches grew a brief foliage of fire. The heart of flame leapt nimbly across the gap between the trees and then went swinging and flaring along the whole row of them. Beneath the capering boys a quarter of a mile square of forest was savage with smoke and flame. The separate noises of the fire merged into a drum-roll that seemed to shake the mountain.

"You got your small fire all right."

Startled, Ralph realized that the boys were falling still and silent, feeling the beginnings of awe at the power set free below them. The knowledge and the awe made him savage.

"Oh, shut up!" *power*

"I got the conch," said Piggy, in a hurt voice. "I got a right to speak."

They looked at him with eyes that lacked interest in

what they saw, and cocked ears at the drum-roll of the fire.
Piggy glanced nervously into hell and cradled the conch.

"We got to let that burn out now. And that was our fire-
wood."

He licked his lips.

"There ain't nothing we can do. We ought to be more
careful. I'm scared——"

Jack dragged his eyes away from the fire.

"You're always scared. Yah—Fatty!"

"I got the conch," said Piggy bleakly. He turned to
Ralph. "I got the conch, ain't I Ralph?"

Unwillingly Ralph turned away from the splendid, awful
sight.

"What's that?"

"The conch. I got a right to speak."

The twins giggled together.

"We wanted smoke——"

"Now look——"

A pall stretched for miles away from the island. All the
boys except Piggy started to giggle; presently they were
shrieking with laughter.

Piggy lost his temper.

"I got the conch! Just you listen! The first thing we
ought to have made was shelters down there by the beach.
It wasn't half cold down there in the night. But the first
time Ralph says 'fire' you goes howling and screaming up
this here mountain. Like a pack of kids!"

By now they were listening to the tirade.

"How can you expect to be rescued if you don't put first
things first and act proper?"

He took off his glasses and made as if to put down the
conch; but the sudden motion towards it of most of the

older boys changed his mind. He tucked the shell under his arm, and crouched back on a rock.

"Then when you get here you build a bonfire that isn't no use. Now you been and set the whole island on fire. Won't we look funny if the whole island burns up? Cooked fruit, that's what we'll have to eat, and roast pork. And that's nothing to laugh at! You said Ralph was chief and you don't give him time to think. Then when he says something you rush off, like, like——"

He paused for breath, and the fire growled at them.

"And that's not all. Them kids. The little 'uns. Who took any notice of 'em? Who knows how many we got?"

Ralph took a sudden step forward.

"I told you to. I told you to get a list of names!"

"How could I," cried Piggy indignantly, "all by myself? They waited for two minutes, then they fell in the sea; they went into the forest; they just scattered everywhere. How was I to know which was which?"

Ralph licked pale lips.

"Then you don't know how many of us there ought to be?"

"How could I with them little 'uns running round like insects? Then when you three came back, as soon as you said make a fire, they all ran away, and I never had a chance——"

"That's enough!" said Ralph sharply, and snatched back the conch. "If you didn't you didn't."

"—then you come up here an' pinch my specs——"

Jack turned on him.

"You shut up!"

"—and them little 'uns was wandering about down there where the fire is. How d'you know they aren't still there?"

59

Piggy stood up and pointed to the smoke and flames. A murmur rose among the boys and died away. Something strange was happening to Piggy, for he was gaping for breath.

"That little 'un—" gasped Piggy—"him with the mark on his face, I don't see him. Where is he now?"

The crowd was as silent as death.

"Him that talked about the snakes. He was down there——"

A tree exploded in the fire like a bomb. Tall swathes of creepers rose for a moment into view, agonized, and went down again. The little boys screamed at them.

"Snakes! Snakes! Look at the snakes!"

In the west, and unheeded, the sun lay only an inch or two above the sea. Their faces were lit redly from beneath. Piggy fell against a rock and clutched it with both hands.

"That little 'un that had a mark on his—face—where is —he now? I tell you I don't see him."

The boys looked at each other fearfully, unbelieving.

"—where is he now?"

Ralph muttered the reply as if in shame.

"Perhaps he went back to the, the——"

Beneath them, on the unfriendly side of the mountain, the drum-roll continued.

CHAPTER THREE

Huts on the Beach

—————◆◆◆◆◆◆◆◆◆◆◆◆◆◆◆◆◆◆◆—————

Jack was bent double. He was down like a sprinter, his nose only a few inches from the humid earth. The tree trunks and the creepers that festooned them lost themselves in a green dusk thirty feet above him; and all about was the undergrowth. There was only the faintest indication of a trail here; a cracked twig and what might be the impression of one side of a hoof. He lowered his chin and stared at the traces as though he would force them to speak to him. Then dog-like, uncomfortably on all fours yet unheeding his discomfort, he stole forward five yards and stopped. Here was loop of creeper with a tendril pendant from a node. The tendril was polished on the underside; pigs, passing through the loop, brushed it with their bristly hide.

Jack crouched with his face a few inches away from this clue, then stared forward into the semi-darkness of the undergrowth. His sandy hair, considerably longer than it had been when they dropped in, was lighter now; and his bare back was a mass of dark freckles and peeling sunburn. A sharpened stick about five feet long trailed from his right hand; and except for a pair of tattered shorts held up by his knife-belt he was naked. He closed his eyes, raised his head and breathed in gently with flared nostrils, assessing the current of warm air for information. The forest and he were very still.

At length he let out his breath in a long sigh and opened his eyes. They were bright blue, eyes that in this frustration seemed bolting and nearly mad. He passed his tongue across dry lips and scanned the uncommunicative forest. Then again he stole forward and cast this way and that over the ground.

The silence of the forest was more oppressive than the heat, and at this hour of the day there was not even the whine of insects. Only when Jack himself roused a gaudy bird from a primitive nest of sticks was the silence shattered and echoes set ringing by a harsh cry that seemed to come out of the abyss of ages. Jack himself shrank at this cry with a hiss of indrawn breath; and for a minute became less a hunter than a furtive thing, ape-like among the tangle of trees. Then the trail, the frustration, claimed him again and he searched the ground avidly. By the bole of a vast tree that grew pale flowers on a grey trunk he checked, closed his eyes, and once more drew in the warm air; and this time his breath came short, there was even a passing pallor in his face, and then the surge of blood again. He passed like a shadow under the darkness of the tree and crouched, looking down at the trodden ground at his feet.

The droppings were warm. They lay piled among turned earth. They were olive green, smooth, and they steamed a little. Jack lifted his head and stared at the inscrutable masses of creeper that lay across the trail. Then he raised his spear and sneaked forward. Beyond the creeper, the trail joined a pig-run that was wide enough and trodden enough to be a path. The ground was hardened by an accustomed tread and as Jack rose to his full height he heard something moving on it. He swung back his right arm and hurled the spear with all his strength. From the pig-run came the quick, hard patter of hoofs, a castanet sound, seductive, maddening—the promise of meat. He rushed out of the undergrowth and snatched up his spear. The pattering of pig's trotters died away in the distance.

Jack stood there, streaming with sweat, streaked with brown earth, stained by all the vicissitudes of a day's hunting. Swearing, he turned off the trail and pushed his way through until the forest opened a little and instead of bald trunks supporting a dark roof there were light grey trunks and crowns of feathery palm. Beyond these was the glitter of the sea and he could hear voices. Ralph was standing by a contraption of palm trunks and leaves, a rude shelter that faced the lagoon, and seemed very near to falling down. He did not notice when Jack spoke.

"Got any water?"

Ralph looked up, frowning, from the complication of leaves. He did not notice Jack even when he saw him.

"I said have you got any water? I'm thirsty."

Ralph withdrew his attention from the shelter and realized Jack with a start.

"Oh, hullo. Water? There by the tree. Ought to be some left."

Jack took up a coco-nut shell that brimmed with fresh water from among a group that were arranged in the shade, and drank. The water splashed over his chin and neck and chest. He breathed noisily when he had finished.

"Needed that."

Simon spoke from inside the shelter.

"Up a bit."

63

Ralph turned to the shelter and lifted a branch with a whole tiling of leaves.

The leaves came apart and fluttered down. Simon's contrite face appeared in the hole.

"Sorry."

Ralph surveyed the wreck with distaste.

"Never get it done."

He flung himself down at Jack's feet. Simon remained, looking out of the hole in the shelter. Once down, Ralph explained.

"Been working for days now. And look!"

Two shelters were in position, but shaky. This one was a ruin.

"And they keep running off. You remember the meeting? How everyone was going to work hard until the shelters were finished?"

"Except me and my hunters——"

"Except the hunters. Well, the littluns are——"

He gesticulated, sought for a word.

"They're hopeless. The older ones aren't much better. D'you see? All day I've been working with Simon. No one else. They're off bathing, or eating, or playing."

Simon poked his head out carefully.

"You're chief. You tell 'em off."

Ralph lay flat and looked up at the palm trees and the sky.

"Meetings. Don't we love meetings? Every day. Twice a day. We talk." He got on one elbow. "I bet if I blew the conch this minute, they'd come running. Then we'd be, you know, very solemn, and someone would say we ought to build a jet, or a submarine, or a TV set. When the meeting was over they'd work for five minutes then wander off or go hunting."

Jack flushed.

"We want meat."

"Well, we haven't got any yet. And we want shelters. Besides, the rest of your hunters came back hours ago. They've been swimming."

"I went on," said Jack. "I let them go. I had to go on. I——"

He tried to convey the compulsion to track down and kill that was swallowing him up.

"I went on. I thought, by myself——"

The madness came into his eyes again.

"I thought I might kill."

"But you didn't."

"I thought I might."

Some hidden passion vibrated in Ralph's voice.

"But you haven't yet."

His invitation might have passed as casual, were it not for the undertone.

"You wouldn't care to help with the shelters, I suppose?"

"We want meat——"

"And we don't get it"

Now the antagonism was audible.

"But I shall! Next time! I've got to get a barb on this spear! We wounded a pig and the spear fell out. If we could only make barbs——"

"We need shelters."

Suddenly Jack shouted in rage.

"Are you accusing——"

"All I'm saying is we've worked dashed hard. That's all." They were both red in the face and found looking at each other difficult. Ralph rolled on his stomach and began to play with the grass.

"If it rains like when we dropped in we'll need shelters all right. And then another thing. We need shelters because of the——"

He paused for a moment and they both pushed their anger away. Then he went on with the safe, changed subject.

"You've noticed, haven't you?"

Jack put down his spear and squatted.

"Noticed what?"

"Well. They're frightened."

He rolled over and peered into Jack's fierce, dirty face.

"I mean the way things are. They dream. You can hear 'em. Have you been awake at night?"

Jack shook his head.

"They talk and scream. The littluns. Even some of the others. As if——"

"As if it wasn't a good island."

Astonished at the interruption, they looked up at Simon's serious face.

"As if", said Simon, "the beastie, the beastie or the snake-thing, was real. Remember?"

The two older boys flinched when they heard the shameful syllable. Snakes were not mentioned now, were not mentionable.

"As if this wasn't a good island," said Ralph slowly. "Yes, that's right."

Jack sat up and stretched out his legs.

"They're batty."

"Crackers. Remember when we went exploring?"

They grinned at each other, remembering the glamour of the first day. Ralph went on.

"So we need shelters as a sort of——"

"Home."

"That's right."

Jack drew up his legs, clasped his knees, and frowned in an effort to attain clarity.

"All the same—in the forest. I mean when you're hunting—not when you're getting fruit, of course, but when you're on your own——"

He paused for a moment, not sure if Ralph would take him seriously.

"Go on."

"If you're hunting sometimes you catch yourself feeling as if——" He flushed suddenly.

"There's nothing in it of course. Just a feeling. But you can feel as if you're not hunting, but—being hunted; as if something's behind you all the time in the jungle."

They were silent again: Simon intent, Ralph incredulous and faintly indignant. He sat up, rubbing one shoulder with a dirty hand.

"Well, I don't know."

Jack leapt to his feet and spoke very quickly.

"That's how you can feel in the forest. Of course there's nothing in it. Only—only——"

He took a few rapid steps towards the beach, then came back.

"Only I know how they feel. See? That's all."

"The best thing we can do is get ourselves rescued."

Jack had to think for a moment before he could remember what rescue was.

"Rescue? Yes, of course! All the same, I'd like to catch a pig first——" He snatched up his spear and dashed it into the ground. The opaque, mad look came into his eyes again. Ralph looked at him critically through his tangle of fair hair.

"So long as your hunters remember the fire——"

"You and your fire!"

The two boys trotted down the beach and, turning at the water's edge looked back at the pink mountain. The trickle of smoke sketched a chalky line up the solid blue of the sky, wavered high up and faded. Ralph frowned.

"I wonder how far off you could see that."

"Miles."

"We don't make enough smoke."

The bottom part of the trickle, as though conscious of their gaze, thickened to a creamy blur which crept up the feeble column.

"They've put on green branches," muttered Ralph. "I wonder!" He screwed up his eyes and swung round to search the horizon.

"Got it!"

Jack shouted so loudly that Ralph jumped.

"What? Where? Is it a ship?"

But Jack was pointing to the high declivities that led down from the mountain to the flatter part of the island.

"Of course! They'll lie up there—they must do, when the sun's too hot——"

Ralph gazed bewildered at his rapt face.

"—they get up high. High up and in the shade, resting during the heat, like cows at home——"

"I thought you saw a ship!"

"We could steal up on one—paint our faces so they wouldn't see—perhaps surround them and then——"

Indignation took away Ralph's control.

"I was talking about smoke! Don't you want to be rescued? All you can talk about is pig, pig, pig!"

"But we want meat!"

68

"And I work all day with nothing but Simon and you come back and don't even notice the huts!"

"I was working too——"

"But you like it!" shouted Ralph. "You want to hunt! While I——"

They faced each other on the bright beach, astonished at the rub of feeling. Ralph looked away first, pretending interest in a group of littluns on the sand. From beyond the platform came the shouting of the hunters in the swimming pool. On the end of the platform Piggy was lying flat, looking down into the brilliant water.

"People don't help much."

He wanted to explain how people were never quite what you thought they were.

"Simon. He helps." He pointed at the shelters.

"All the rest rushed off. He's done as much as I have. Only——"

"Simon's always about."

Ralph started back to the shelters with Jack by his side.

"Do a bit for you," muttered Jack, "before I have a bathe."

"Don't bother."

But when they reached the shelters Simon was not to be seen. Ralph put his head in the hole, withdrew it, and turned to Jack.

"He's buzzed off."

"Got fed up," said Jack, "and gone for a bathe."

Ralph frowned.

"He's queer. He's funny."

Jack nodded, as much for the sake of agreeing as anything, and by tacit consent they left the shelter and went towards the bathing-pool.

"And then," said Jack, "when I've had a bathe and something to eat, I'll just trek over to the other side of the mountain and see if I can see any traces. Coming?"

"But the sun's nearly set!"

"I might have time——"

They walked along, two continents of experience and feeling, unable to communicate.

"If I could only get a pig!"

"I'll come back and go on with the shelter."

They looked at each other, baffled, in love and hate. All the warm salt water of the bathing-pool and the shouting and splashing and laughing were only just sufficient to bring them together again.

Simon, whom they expected to find there, was not in the bathing-pool.

When the other two had trotted down the beach to look back at the mountain he had followed them for a few yards and then stopped. He had stood frowning down at a pile of sand on the beach where somebody had been trying to build a little house or hut. Then he turned his back on this and walked into the forest with an air of purpose. He was a small, skinny boy, his chin pointed, and his eyes so bright they had deceived Ralph into thinking him delightfully gay and wicked. The coarse mop of black hair was long and swung down, almost concealing a low, broad forehead. He wore the remains of shorts and his feet were bare like Jack's. Always darkish in colour, Simon was burned by the sun to a deep tan that glistened with sweat.

He picked his way up the scar, passed the great rock where Ralph had climbed on the first morning, then turned off to his right among the trees. He walked with an accustomed

tread through the acres of fruit trees, where the least ener-
getic could find an easy if unsatisfying meal. Flower and
fruit grew together on the same tree and everywhere was
the scent of ripeness and the booming of a million bees at
pasture. Here the littluns who had run after him caught up
with him. They talked, cried out unintelligibly, lugged him
towards the trees. Then, amid the roar of bees in the afternoon sunlight, Simon found for them the fruit they could
not reach, pulled off the choicest from up in the foliage,
passed them back down to the endless, outstretched hands.
When he had satisfied them he paused and looked round.
The littluns watched him inscrutably over double handfuls
of ripe fruit.

Simon turned away from them and went where the just
perceptible path led him. Soon high jungle closed in. Tall
trunks bore unexpected pale flowers all the way up to the
dark canopy where life went on clamorously. The air here
was dark too, and the creepers dropped their ropes like the
rigging of foundered ships. His feet left prints in the soft
soil and the creepers shivered throughout their lengths
when he bumped them.

He came at last to a place where more sunshine fell.
Since they had not so far to go for light the creepers had
woven a great mat that hung at the side of an open space in
the jungle; for here a patch of rock came close to the surface
and would not allow more than little plants and ferns to
grow. The whole space was walled with dark aromatic
bushes, and was a bowl of heat and light. A great tree, fallen
across one corner, leaned against the trees that still stood
and a rapid climber flaunted red and yellow sprays right to
the top.

Simon paused. He looked over his shoulder as Jack had

done at the close ways behind him and glanced swiftly round to confirm that he was utterly alone. For a moment his movements were almost furtive. Then he bent down and wormed his way into the centre of the mat. The creepers and the bushes were so close that he left his sweat on them and they pulled together behind him. When he was secure in the middle he was in a little cabin screened off from the open space by a few leaves. He squatted down, parted the leaves and looked out into the clearing. Nothing moved but a pair of gaudy butterflies that danced round each other in the hot air. Holding his breath he cocked a critical ear at the sounds of the island. Evening was advancing towards the island; the sounds of the bright fantastic birds, the bee-sounds, even the crying of the gulls that were returning to their roosts among the square rocks, were fainter. The deep sea breaking miles away on the reef made an undertone less perceptible than the susurration of the blood.

Simon dropped the screen of leaves back into place. The slope of the bars of honey-coloured sunlight decreased; they slid up the bushes, passed over the green candle-like buds, moved up towards the canopy, and darkness thickened under the trees. With the fading of the light the riotous colours died and the heat and urgency cooled away. The candle-buds stirred. Their green sepals drew back a little and the white tips of the flowers rose delicately to meet the open air.

Now the sunlight had lifted clear of the open space and withdrawn from the sky. Darkness poured out, submerging the ways between the trees till they were dim and strange as the bottom of the sea. The candle-buds opened their wide white flowers glimmering under the light that pricked down from the first stars. Their scent spilled out into the air and took possession of the island.

CHAPTER FOUR

Painted Faces and Long Hair

 ◆━━━━━━◆

The first rhythm that they became used to was the slow swing from dawn to quick dusk. They accepted the pleasures of morning, the bright sun, the whelming sea and sweet air, as a time when play was good and life so full that hope was not necessary and therefore forgotten. Towards noon, as the floods of light fell more nearly to the perpendicular, the stark colours of the morning were smoothed in pearl and opalescence; and the heat—as though the impending sun's height gave it momentum—became a blow that they ducked, running to the shade and lying there, perhaps even sleeping.

Strange things happened at midday. The glittering sea rose up, moved apart in planes of blatant impossibility; the coral reef and the few, stunted palms that clung to the more elevated parts would float up into the sky, would quiver, be plucked apart, run like rain-drops on a wire or be repeated as in an odd succession of mirrors. Sometimes land loomed where there was no land and flicked out like a bubble as the children watched. Piggy discounted all this learnedly as a "mirage"; and since no boy could reach even the reef over the stretch of water where the snapping sharks waited, they grew accustomed to these mysteries and

73

ignored them, just as they ignored the miraculous, throbbing stars. At midday the illusions merged into the sky and there the sun gazed down like an angry eye. Then, at the end of the afternoon, the mirage subsided and the horizon became level and blue and clipped as the sun declined. That was another time of comparative coolness but menaced by the coming of the dark. When the sun sank, darkness dropped on the island like an extinguisher and soon the shelters were full of restlessness, under the remote stars.

Nevertheless, the northern European tradition of work, play, and food right through the day, made it impossible for them to adjust themselves wholly to this new rhythm. The littlun Percival had early crawled into a shelter and stayed there for two days, talking, singing, and crying, till they thought him batty and were faintly amused. Ever since then he had been peaked, red-eyed, and miserable; a littlun who played little and cried often.

The smaller boys were known now by the generic title of "littluns". The decrease in size, from Ralph down, was gradual; and though there was a dubious region inhabited by Simon and Robert and Maurice, nevertheless no one had any difficulty in recognizing biguns at one end and littluns at the other. The undoubted littluns, those aged about six, led a quite distinct, and at the same time intense, life of their own. They ate most of the day, picking fruit where they could reach it and not particular about ripeness and quality. They were used now to stomach-aches and a sort of chronic diarrhoea. They suffered untold terrors in the dark and huddled together for comfort. Apart from food and sleep, they found time for play, aimless and trivial, among the white sand by the bright water. They cried for their mothers much less often than might have been expected; they were very brown, and filthily dirty. They obeyed the summons of the conch, partly because Ralph blew it, and he was big enough to be a link with the adult world of authority; and partly because they enjoyed the entertainment of the assemblies. But otherwise they seldom bothered with the biguns and their passionately emotional and corporate life was their own.

They had built castles in the sand at the bar of the little river. These castles were about one foot high and were decorated with shells, withered flowers, and interesting stones. Round the castles was a complex of marks, tracks, walls, railway lines, that were of significance only if inspected with the eye at beach-level. The littluns played here, if not happily at least with absorbed attention; and often as many as three of them would play the same game together.

Three were playing here now—Henry was the biggest of them. He was also a distant relative of that other boy whose mulberry-marked face had not been seen since the evening of the great fire; but he was not old enough to understand this, and if he had been told that the other boy had gone home in an aircraft, he would have accepted the statement without fuss or disbelief.

Henry was a bit of a leader this afternoon, because the other two were Percival and Johnny, the smallest boys on the island. Percival was mouse-coloured and had not been very attractive even to his mother; Johnny was well built, with fair hair and a natural belligerence. Just now he was being obedient because he was interested; and the three children, kneeling in the sand, were at peace.

Roger and Maurice came out of the forest. They were relieved from duty at the fire and had come down for a swim. Roger led the way straight through the castles, kicking them over, burying the flowers, scattering the chosen stones. Maurice followed, laughing, and added to the destruction. The three littluns paused in their game and looked up. As it happened, the particular marks in which they were interested had not been touched, so they made no protest. Only Percival began to whimper with an eyeful of sand and Maurice hurried away. In his other life Maurice had received chastisement for filling a younger eye with sand. Now, though there was no parent to let fall a heavy hand, Maurice still felt the unease of wrong-doing. At the back of his mind formed the uncertain outlines of an excuse. He muttered something about a swim and broke into a trot.

Roger remained, watching the littluns. He was not noticeably darker than when he had dropped in, but the shock of black hair, down his nape and low on his forehead, seemed to suit his gloomy face and made what had seemed at first an unsociable remoteness into something forbidding. Percival finished his whimper and went on playing, for the tears had washed the sand away. Johnny watched him with china-blue eyes; then began to fling up sand in a shower, and presently Percival was crying again.

When Henry tired of his play and wandered off along the beach, Roger followed him, keeping beneath the palms and drifting casually in the same direction. Henry walked at a distance from the palms and the shade because he was too young to keep himself out of the sun. He went down the beach and busied himself at the water's edge. The great Pacific tide was coming in and every few seconds the relatively still water of the lagoon heaved forwards an inch. There were creatures that lived in this last fling of the sea, tiny transparencies that came questing in with the water over the hot, dry sand. With impalpable organs of sense they examined this new field. Perhaps food had appeared where at the last incursion there had been none; bird droppings, insects perhaps, any of the strewn detritus of landward life. Like a myriad of tiny teeth in a saw, the transparencies came scavenging over the beach.

This was fascinating to Henry. He poked about with a bit of stick, that itself was wave-worn and whitened and a vagrant, and tried to control the motions of the scavengers. He made little runnels that the tide filled and tried to crowd them with creatures. He became absorbed beyond mere happiness as he felt himself exercising control over living things. He talked to them, urging them, ordering them. Driven back by the tide, his footprints became bays in which they were trapped and gave him the illusion of mastery. He squatted on his hams at the water's edge, bowed, with a shock of hair falling over his forehead and past his eyes, and the afternoon sun emptied down invisible arrows.

Roger waited too. At first he had hidden behind a great palm bole; but Henry's absorption with the transparencies was so obvious that at last he stood out in full view. He looked along the beach. Percival had gone off, crying, and Johnny was left in triumphant possession of the castles. He sat there, crooning to himself and throwing sand at an imaginary Percival. Beyond him, Roger could see the platform and the glints of spray where Ralph and Simon and Piggy and Maurice were diving in the pool. He listened carefully but could only just hear them.

A sudden breeze shook the fringe of palm trees, so that the fronds tossed and fluttered. Sixty feet above Roger, a cluster of nuts, fibrous lumps as big as rugby balls, were

loosed from their stems. They fell about him with a series
of hard thumps and he was not touched. Roger did not consider his escape, but looked from the nuts to Henry and
back again.

The subsoil beneath the palm trees was a raised beach;
and generations of palms had worked loose in this the
stones that had lain on the sands of another shore. Roger
stooped, picked up a stone, aimed, and threw it at Henry—
threw it to miss. The stone, that token of preposterous time,
bounced five yards to Henry's right and fell in the water.
Roger gathered a handful of stones and began to throw
them. Yet there was a space round Henry, perhaps six yards
in diameter, into which he dare not throw. Here, invisible
yet strong, was the taboo of the old life. Round the squatting
child was the protection of parents and school and police-
men and the law. Roger's arm was conditioned by a civilization that knew nothing of him and was in ruins.

Henry was surprised by the plopping sounds in the water.
He abandoned the noiseless transparencies and pointed at
the centre of the spreading rings like a setter. This side and
that the stones fell, and Henry turned obediently but always
too late to see the stones in the air. At last he saw one and
laughed, looking for the friend who was teasing him. But
Roger had whipped behind the palm bole again, was leaning
against it breathing quickly, his eyelids fluttering. Then
Henry lost interest in stones and wandered off.

"Roger."

Jack was standing under a tree about ten yards away.
When Roger opened his eyes and saw him, a darker shadow
crept beneath the swarthiness of his skin; but Jack noticed
nothing. He was eager, impatient, beckoning, so that Roger
went to him.

There was a pool at the end of the river, a tiny mere dammed back by sand and full of white water-lilies and needle-like reeds. Here Sam and Eric were waiting, and Bill. Jack, concealed from the sun, knelt by the pool and opened the two large leaves that he carried. One of them contained white clay, and the other red. By them lay a stick of charcoal brought down from the fire.

Jack explained to Roger as he worked.

"They don't smell me. They see me, I think. Something pink, under the trees."

He smeared on the clay.

"If only I'd some green!"

He turned a half-concealed face up to Roger and answered the incomprehension of his gaze.

"For hunting. Like in the war. You know—dazzle paint. Like things trying to look like something else——"

He twisted in the urgency of telling.

"—like moths on a tree trunk."

Roger understood and nodded gravely. The twins moved towards Jack and began to protest timidly about something. Jack waved them away.

"Shut up."

He rubbed the charcoal stick between the patches of red and white on his face.

"No. You two come with me."

He peered at his reflection and disliked it. He bent down, took up a double handful of lukewarm water and rubbed the mess from his face. Freckles and sandy eyebrows appeared.

Roger smiled, unwillingly.

"You don't half look a mess."

Jack planned his new face. He made one cheek and one eye-socket white, then he rubbed red over the other half of his face and slashed a black bar of charcoal across from right ear to left jaw. He looked in the mere for his reflection, but his breathing troubled the mirror.

"Samneric. Get me a coco-nut. An empty one."

He knelt, holding the shell of water. A rounded patch of sunlight fell on his face and a brightness appeared in the depths of the water. He looked in astonishment, no longer at himself but at an awesome stranger. He spilt the water and leapt to his feet, laughing excitedly. Beside the mere, his sinewy body held up a mask that drew their eyes and appalled them. He began to dance and his laughter became a bloodthirsty snarling. He capered towards Bill, and the mask was a thing on its own, behind which Jack hid, liberated from shame and self-consciousness. The face of red and white and black, swung through the air and jigged towards Bill. Bill started up laughing; then suddenly he fell silent and blundered away through the bushes.

Jack rushed towards the twins.

"The rest are making a line. Come on!"

"But——"

"—we——"

"Come on! I'll creep up and stab——"

The mask compelled them.

Ralph climbed out of the bathing-pool and trotted up the beach and sat in the shade beneath the palms. His fair hair was plastered over his eyebrows and he pushed it back. Simon was floating in the water and kicking with his feet, and Maurice was practising diving. Piggy was mooning about, aimlessly picking up things and discarding them. The rock-pools which so fascinated him were covered by the tide, so he was without an interest until the tide went back. Presently, seeing Ralph under the palms, he came and sat by him.

Piggy wore the remainders of a pair of shorts, his fat body was golden brown, and the glasses still flashed when he looked at anything. He was the only boy on the island whose hair never seemed to grow. The rest were shock-headed, but Piggy's hair still lay in wisps over his head as though baldness were his natural state, and this imperfect covering would soon go, like the velvet on a young stag's antlers.

"I've been thinking," he said, "about a clock. We could make a sundial. We could put a stick in the sand, and then——"

The effort to express the mathematical processes involved was too great. He made a few passes instead.

"And an airplane, and a TV set," said Ralph sourly, "and a steam engine."

Piggy shook his head.

"You have to have a lot of metal things for that," he said, "and we haven't got no metal. But we got a stick."

Ralph turned and smiled involuntarily. Piggy was a bore; his fat, his ass-mar and his matter-of-fact ideas were dull: but there was always a little pleasure to be got out of pulling his leg, even if one did it by accident.

Piggy saw the smile and misinterpreted it as friendliness. There had grown up tacitly among the biguns the opinion that Piggy was an outsider, not only by accent, which did not matter, but by fat, and ass-mar, and specs, and a certain disinclination for manual labour. Now, finding that something he had said made Ralph smile, he rejoiced and pressed his advantage.

"We got a lot of sticks. We could have a sundial each. Then we should know what the time was."

"A fat lot of good that would be."

"You said you wanted things done. So as we could be rescued."

"Oh, shut up."

He leapt to his feet and trotted back to the pool, just as Maurice did a rather poor dive. Ralph was glad of a chance to change the subject. He shouted as Maurice came to the surface.

"Belly flop! Belly flop!"

Maurice flashed a smile at Ralph who slid easily into the water. Of all the boys, he was the most at home there; but to-day, irked by the mention of rescue, the useless, footling mention of rescue, even the green depths of water and the shattered, golden sun held no balm. Instead of remaining and playing, he swam with steady strokes under Simon and crawled out of the other side of the pool to lie there, sleek and streaming like a seal. Piggy, always clumsy, stood up and came to stand by him, so that Ralph rolled on his stomach and pretended not to see. The mirages had died away and gloomily he ran his eye along the taut blue line of the horizon.

The next moment he was on his feet and shouting.

"Smoke! Smoke!"

Simon tried to sit up in the water and got a mouthful. Maurice, who had been standing ready to dive, swayed back on his heels, made a bolt for the platform, then swerved back to the grass under the palms. There he started to pull on his tattered shorts, to be ready for any-thing.

Ralph stood, one hand holding back his hair, the other clenched. Simon was climbing out of the water. Piggy was rubbing his glasses on his shorts and squinting at the sea.

Maurice had got both legs through one leg of his shorts—of all the boys, only Ralph was still.

"I can't see no smoke," said Piggy incredulously. "I can't see no smoke, Ralph—where is it?"

Ralph said nothing. Now both his hands were clenched over his forehead so that the fair hair was kept out of his eyes. He was leaning forward and already the salt was whitening his body.

"Ralph—where's the ship?"

Simon stood by, looking from Ralph to the horizon. Maurice's trousers gave way with a sigh and he abandoned them as a wreck, rushed towards the forest, and then came back again.

The smoke was a tight little knot on the horizon and was uncoiling slowly. Beneath the smoke was a dot that might be a funnel. Ralph's face was pale as he spoke to himself.

"They'll see our smoke."

Piggy was looking in the right direction now.

"It don't look much."

He turned round and peered up at the mountain. Ralph continued to watch the ship, ravenously. Colour was coming back into his face. Simon stood by him, silent.

"I know I can't see very much," said Piggy, "but have we got any smoke?"

Ralph moved impatiently, still watching the ship.

"The smoke on the moutain"

Maurice came running, and stared out to sea. Both Simon and Piggy were looking up at the mountain. Piggy screwed up his face but Simon cried out as though he had hurt himself.

"Ralph! Ralph!"

The quality of his speech slewed Ralph on the sand.

"You tell me," said Piggy anxiously. "Is there a signal?"

Ralph looked back at the dispersing smoke on the horizon, then up at the mountain.

"Ralph—please! Is there a signal?"

Simon put out his hand, timidly, to touch Ralph; but Ralph started to run, splashing through the shallow end of the bathing-pool, across the hot, white sand and under the palms. A moment later, he was battling with the complex undergrowth that was already engulfing the scar. Simon ran after him, then Maurice. Piggy shouted.

"Ralph! Please—Ralph!"

Then he too started to run, stumbling over Maurice's discarded shorts before he was across the terrace. Behind the four boys, the smoke moved gently along the horizon; and on the beach, Henry and Johnny were throwing sand at Percival who was crying quietly again; and all three were in complete ignorance of the excitement.

By the time Ralph had reached the landward end of the scar he was using precious breath to swear. He did desperate violence to his naked body among the rasping creepers so that blood was sliding over him. Just where the steep ascent of the mountain began, he stopped. Maurice was only a few yards behind him.

"Piggy's specs!" shouted Ralph, "if the fire's right out, we'll need them——"

He stopped shouting and swayed on his feet. Piggy was only just visible, bumbling up from the beach. Ralph looked at the horizon, then up to the mountain. Was it better to fetch Piggy's glasses, or would the ship have gone? Or if they climbed on, supposing the fire was right out, and they had to watch Piggy crawling nearer and the ship sinking under the horizon? Balanced on a high peak of need, agonized by indecision, Ralph cried out:

"Oh God, oh God!"

Simon, struggling with bushes, caught his breath. His face was twisted. Ralph blundered on, savaging himself, as the wisp of smoke moved on.

The fire was dead. They saw that straight away; saw what they had really known down on the beach when the smoke of home had beckoned. The fire was right out, smokeless and dead; the watchers were gone. A pile of unused fuel lay ready.

Ralph turned to the sea. The horizon stretched, impersonal once more, barren of all but the faintest trace of smoke. Ralph ran stumbling along the rocks, saved himself on the edge of the pink cliff, and screamed at the ship.

"Come back! Come back!"

He ran backwards and forwards along the cliff, his face always to the sea, and his voice rose insanely.

"Come back! Come back!"

Simon and Maurice arrived. Ralph looked at them with unwinking eyes. Simon turned away, smearing the water from his cheeks. Ralph reached inside himself for the worst word he knew.

"They let the bloody fire out."

He looked down the unfriendly side of the mountain. Piggy arrived, out of breath and whimpering like a littlun. Ralph clenched his fist and went very red. The intentness of his gaze, the bitterness of his voice pointed for him.

"There they are."

A procession had appeared, far down among the pink screes that lay near the water's edge. Some of the boys wore black caps but otherwise they were almost naked. They lifted sticks in the air together, whenever they came to an easy patch. They were chanting, something to do with the bundle that the errant twins carried so carefully. Ralph picked out Jack easily, even at that distance, tall, red-haired, and inevitably leading the procession.

Simon looked now, from Ralph to Jack, as he had looked from Ralph to the horizon, and what he saw seemed to make him afraid. Ralph said nothing more, but waited while the procession came nearer. The chant was audible but at that distance still wordless. Behind Jack walked the twins, carrying a great stake on their shoulders. The gutted carcass of a pig swung from the stake, swinging heavily as the twins toiled over the uneven ground. The pig's head hung down with gaping neck and seemed to search for something on the ground. At last the words of the chant floated up to them, across the bowl of blackened wood and ashes.

(*"Kill the pig. Cut her throat. Spill her blood."*)

Yet as the words became audible, the procession reached the steepest part of the mountain, and in a minute or two the chant had died away. Piggy snivelled and Simon shushed him quickly as though he had spoken too loudly in church.

Jack, his face smeared with clays, reached the top first and hailed Ralph excitedly, with lifted spear.

"Look! We've killed a pig—we stole up on them—we got in a circle——"

Voices broke in from the hunters.

"We got in a circle——"

"We crept up——"

"The pig squealed——"

The twins stood with the pig swinging between them, dropping black gouts on the rock. They seemed to share one wide, ecstatic grin. Jack had too many things to tell

86

Ralph at once. Instead, he danced a step or two, then remembered his dignity and stood still, grinning. He noticed blood on his hands and grimaced distastefully, looked for something on which to clean them, then wiped them on his shorts and laughed.

Ralph spoke.

"You let the fire out."

Jack checked, vaguely irritated by this irrelevance but too happy to let it worry him.

"We can light the fire again. You should have been with us, Ralph. We had a smashing time. The twins got knocked over——"

"We hit the pig——"

"—I fell on top——"

"I cut the pig's throat," said Jack, proudly, and yet twitched as he said it. "Can I borrow yours, Ralph, to make a nick in the hilt?"

The boys chattered and danced. The twins continued to grin.

"There was lashings of blood," said Jack, laughing and shuddering, "you should have seen it!"

"We'll go hunting every day——"

Ralph spoke again, hoarsely. He had not moved.

"You let the fire out."

This repetition made Jack uneasy. He looked at the twins and then back at Ralph.

"We had to have them in the hunt," he said, "or there wouldn't have been enough for a ring."

He flushed, conscious of a fault.

"The fire's only been out an hour or two. We can light up again——"

He noticed Ralph's scarred nakedness, and the sombre

87

silence of all four of them. He sought, charitable in his happiness, to include them in the thing that had happened. His mind was crowded with memories; memories of the knowledge that had come to them when they closed in on the struggling pig, knowledge that they had outwitted a living thing, imposed their will upon it, taken away its life like a long satisfying drink.

He spread his arms wide.

"You should have seen the blood!"

The hunters were more silent now, but at this they buzzed again. Ralph flung back his hair. One arm pointed at the empty horizon. His voice was loud and savage, and struck them into silence.

"There was a ship."

Jack, faced at once with too many awful implications, ducked away from them. He laid a hand on the pig and drew his knife. Ralph brought his arm down, fist clenched, and his voice shook.

"There was a ship. Out there. You said you'd keep the fire going and you let it out!" He took a step towards Jack who turned and faced him.

"They might have seen us. We might have gone home—"

This was too bitter for Piggy, who forgot his timidity in the agony of his loss. He began to cry out, shrilly:

"You and your blood, Jack Merridew! You and your hunting! We might have gone home——"

Ralph pushed Piggy on one side.

"I was chief; and you were going to do what I said. You talk. But you can't even build huts—then you go off hunting and let out the fire——"

He turned away, silent for a moment. Then his voice came again on a peak of feeling.

"There was a ship——"

One of the smaller hunters began to wail. The dismal truth was filtering through to everybody. Jack went very red as he hacked and pulled at the pig.

"The job was too much. We needed everyone."

Ralph turned.

"You could have had everyone when the shelters were finished. But you had to hunt——"

"We needed meat."

Jack stood up as he said this, the bloodied knife in his hand. The two boys faced each other. There was the brilliant world of hunting, tactics, fierce exhilaration, skill; and there was the world of longing and baffled common-sense. Jack transferred the knife to his left hand and smudged blood over his forehead as he pushed down the plastered hair.

Piggy began again.

"You didn't ought to have let that fire out. You said you'd keep the smoke going——"

This from Piggy, and the wails of agreement from some of the hunters drove Jack to violence. The bolting look came into his blue eyes. He took a step, and able at last to hit someone, stuck his fist into Piggy's stomach. Piggy sat down with a grunt. Jack stood over him. His voice was vicious with humiliation.

"You would, would you? Fatty!"

Ralph made a step forward and Jack smacked Piggy's head. Piggy's glasses flew off and tinkled on the rocks. Piggy cried out in terror:

"My specs!"

He went crouching and feeling over the rocks but Simon, who got there first, found them for him. Passions beat about Simon on the mountain-top with awful wings.

"One side's broken."

Piggy grabbed and put on the glasses. He looked male-volently at Jack.

"I got to have them specs. Now I only got one eye. Jus' you wait——"

Jack made a move towards Piggy who scrambled away till a great rock lay between them. He thrust his head over the top and glared at Jack through his one flashing glass.

"Now I only got one eye. Just you wait——"

Jack mimicked the whine and scramble.

"Jus' you wait—yah!"

Piggy and the parody were so funny that the hunters began to laugh. Jack felt encouraged. He went on scrambling and the laughter rose to a gale of hysteria. Unwillingly Ralph felt his lips twitch; he was angry with himself for giving way.

He muttered.

"That was a dirty trick."

Jack broke out of his gyration and stood facing Ralph. His words came in a shout.

"All right, all right!"

He looked at Piggy, at the hunters, at Ralph.

"I'm sorry. About the fire, I mean. There. I——"

He drew himself up.

"—I apologize."

The buzz from the hunters was one of admiration at this handsome behaviour. Clearly they were of the opinion that Jack had done the decent thing, had put himself in the right by his generous apology and Ralph, obscurely, in the wrong. They waited for an appropriately decent answer.

Yet Ralph's throat refused to pass one. He resented, as an addition to Jack's misbehaviour, this verbal trick. The fire was dead, the ship was gone. Could they not see? Anger instead of decency passed his throat.

"That was a dirty trick."

They were silent on the mountain-top while the opaque look appeared in Jack's eyes and passed away.

Ralph's final word was an ungracious mutter.

"All right. Light the fire."

With some positive action before them, a little of the tension died. Ralph said no more, did nothing, stood looking down at the ashes round his feet. Jack was loud and active. He gave orders, sang, whistled, threw remarks at the silent Ralph—remarks that did not need an answer, and therefore could not invite a snub; and still Ralph was silent. No one, not even Jack, would ask him to move and in the end they had to build the fire three yards away and in a place not really as convenient. So Ralph asserted his chieftainship and could not have chosen a better way if he had thought for days. Against this weapon, so indefinable and so effective, Jack was powerless and raged without knowing why. By the time the pile was built, they were on different sides of a high barrier.

When they had dealt with the fire another crisis arose. Jack had no means of lighting it. Then to his surprise, Ralph went to Piggy and took the glasses from him. Not even Ralph knew how a link between him and Jack had been snapped and fastened elsewhere.

"I'll bring 'em back."

"I'll come too."

Piggy stood behind him, islanded in a sea of meaningless colour, while Ralph knelt and focused the glossy spot. Instantly the fire was alight Piggy held out his hands and grabbed the glasses back.

Before these fantastically attractive flowers of violet and red and yellow, unkindness melted away. They became a circle of boys round a camp fire and even Piggy and Ralph were half-drawn in. Soon some of the boys were rushing down the slope for more wood while Jack hacked the pig. They tried holding the whole carcass on a stake over the fire, but the stake burnt more quickly than the pig roasted. In the end they skewered bits of meat on branches and held them in the flames: and even then almost as much boy was roasted as meat.

Ralph dribbled. He meant to refuse meat but his past diet of fruit and nuts, with an odd crab or fish, gave him too little resistance. He accepted a piece of half-raw meat and gnawed it like a wolf.

Piggy spoke, also dribbling.

"Aren't I having none?"

Jack had meant to leave him in doubt, as an assertion of power; but Piggy by advertising his omission made more cruelty necessary.

"You didn't hunt."

"No more did Ralph," said Piggy wetly, "nor Simon." He amplified. "There isn't more than a ha'porth of meat in a crab."

Ralph stirred uneasily. Simon, sitting between the twins and Piggy, wiped his mouth and shoved his piece of meat over the rocks to Piggy, who grabbed it. The twins giggled and Simon lowered his face in shame.

Then Jack leapt to his feet, slashed off a great hunk of meat, and flung it down at Simon's feet.

"Eat! Damn you!"

He glared at Simon.

"Take it!"

He spun on his heel, centre of a bewildered circle of boys.
"I got you meat!"

Numberless and inexpressible frustrations combined to make his rage elemental and awe-inspiring.

"I painted my face—I stole up. Now you eat—all of you —and I——"

Slowly the silence on the mountain-top deepened till the click of the fire and the soft hiss of roasting meat could be heard clearly. Jack looked round for understanding but found only respect. Ralph stood among the ashes of the signal fire, his hands full of meat, saying nothing.

Then at last Maurice broke the silence. He changed the subject to the only one that could bring the majority of them together.

"Where did you find the pig?"

Roger pointed down the unfriendly side.

"They were there—by the sea."

Jack, recovering, could not bear to have his story told. He broke in quickly.

"We spread round. I crept, on hands and knees. The spears fell out because they hadn't barbs on. The pig ran away and made an awful noise——"

"It turned back and ran into the circle, bleeding——"

All the boys were talking at once, relieved and excited.

"We closed in——"

The first blow had paralysed its hind quarters, so then the circle could close in and beat and beat—

"I cut the pig's throat——"

The twins, still sharing their identical grin, jumped up and ran round each other. Then the rest joined in, making pig-dying noises and shouting.

"One for his nob!"

"Give him a fourpenny one!"

Then Maurice pretended to be the pig and ran squealing into the centre, and the hunters, circling still, pretended to beat him. As they danced, they sang.

"*Kill the pig. Cut her throat. Bash her in.*"

Ralph watched them, envious and resentful. Not till they flagged and the chant died away, did he speak.

"I'm calling an assembly."

One by one, they halted, and stood watching him.

"With the conch. I'm calling a meeting even if we have to go on into the dark. Down on the platform. When I blow it. Now."

He turned away and walked off, down the mountain.

CHAPTER FIVE

Beast from Water

The tide was coming in and there was only a narrow strip of firm beach between the water and the white, stumbling stuff near the palm terrace. Ralph chose the firm strip as a path because he needed to think; and only here could he allow his feet to move without having to watch them. Suddenly, pacing by the water, he was overcome with astonishment. He found himself understanding the wearisomeness of this life, where every path was an improvisation and a considerable part of one's waking life was spent watching one's feet. He stopped, facing the strip; and remembering that first enthusiastic exploration as though it were part of a brighter childhood, he smiled jeeringly. He turned then and walked back towards the platform with the sun in his face. The time had come for the assembly and as he walked into the concealing splendours of the sunlight he went carefully over the points of his speech. There must be no mistake about this assembly, no chasing imaginary. . . .

He lost himself in a maze of thoughts that were rendered vague by his lack of words to express them. Frowning, he tried again.

This meeting must not be fun, but business.

At that he walked faster, aware all at once of urgency and

the declining sun and a little wind created by his speed that breathed about his face. This wind pressed his grey shirt against his chest so that he noticed—in this new mood of comprehension—how the folds were stiff like cardboard, and unpleasant; noticed too how the frayed edges of his shorts were making an uncomfortable, pink area on the front of his thighs. With a convulsion of the mind, Ralph discovered dirt and decay; understood how much he disliked perpetually flicking the tangled hair out of his eyes, and at last, when the sun was gone, rolling noisily to rest among dry leaves. At that, he began to trot.

The beach near the bathing-pool was dotted with groups of boys waiting for the assembly. They made way for him silently, conscious of his grim mood and the fault at the fire.

The place of assembly in which he stood was roughly a triangle; but irregular and sketchy, like everything they made. First there was the log on which he himself sat; a dead tree that must have been quite exceptionally big for the platform. Perhaps one of those legendary storms of the Pacific had shifted it here. This palm trunk lay parallel to the beach, so that when Ralph sat he faced the island but to the boys was a darkish figure against the shimmer of the lagoon. The two sides of the triangle of which the log was base were less evenly defined. On the right was a log polished by restless seats along the top, but not so large as the chief's and not so comfortable. On the left were four small logs, one of them—the furthest—lamentably springy. Assembly after assembly had broken up in laughter when someone had leaned too far back and the log had whipped and thrown half a dozen boys backwards into the grass. Yet now, he saw, no one had had the wit—not himself nor Jack, nor Piggy—to bring a stone and wedge the thing. So they would continue enduring the ill-balanced twister, because, because.... Again he lost himself in deep waters.

Grass was worn away in front of each trunk but grew tall and untrodden in the centre of the triangle. Then, at the apex, the grass was thick again because no one sat there. All round the place of assembly the grey trunks rose, straight or leaning, and supported the low roof of leaves. On two sides was the beach; behind, the lagoon; in front, the darkness of the island.

Ralph turned to the chief's seat. They had never had an assembly as late before. That was why the place looked so different. Normally the underside of the green roof was lit by a tangle of golden reflections, and their faces were lit upside down, like—thought Ralph, when you hold an electric torch in your hands. But now the sun was slanting in at one side, so that the shadows were where they ought to be.

Again he fell into that strange mood of speculation that was so foreign to him. If faces were different when lit from above or below—what was a face? What was anything?

Ralph moved impatiently. The trouble was, if you were a chief you had to think, you had to be wise. And then the occasion slipped by so that you had to grab at a decision. This made you think; because thought was a valuable thing, that got results....

Only, decided Ralph as he faced the chief's seat, I can't think. Not like Piggy.

Once more that evening Ralph had to adjust his values. Piggy could think. He could go step by step inside that fat head of his, only Piggy was no chief. But Piggy, for all his ludicrous body, had brains. Ralph was a specialist in thought now, and could recognize thought in another.

The sun in his eyes reminded him how time was passing,

so he took the conch down from the tree and examined the surface. Exposure to the air had bleached the yellow and pink to near-white, and transparency. Ralph felt a kind of affectionate reverence for the conch, even though he had fished the thing out of the lagoon himself. He faced the place of assembly and put the conch to his lips.

The others were waiting for this and came straight away. Those who were aware that a ship had passed the island while the fire was out were subdued by the thought of Ralph's anger; while those, including the littluns who did not know, were impressed by the general air of solemnity. The place of assembly filled quickly; Jack, Simon, Maurice, most of the hunters, on Ralph's right; the rest on the left, under the sun. Piggy came and stood outside the triangle. This indicated that he wished to listen, but would not speak; and Piggy intended it as a gesture of disapproval.

"The thing is: we need an assembly."

No one said anything but the faces turned to Ralph were intent. He flourished the conch. He had learnt as a practical business that fundamental statements like this had to be said at least twice, before everyone understood them. One had to sit, attracting all eyes to the conch, and drop words like heavy round stones among the little groups that crouched or squatted. He was searching his mind for simple words so that even the littluns would understand what the assembly was about. Later perhaps, practised debaters—Jack, Maurice, Piggy—would use their whole art to twist the meeting: but now at the beginning the subject of the debate must be laid out clearly.

"We need an assembly. Not for fun. Not for laughing and falling off the log"—the group of littluns on the twister giggled and looked at each other— "not for making jokes, or for"—he lifted the conch in an effort to find the compelling word—"for cleverness. Not for these things. But to put things straight."

He paused for a moment.

"I've been along. By myself I went, thinking what's what. I know what we need. An assembly to put things straight. And first of all, I'm speaking."

He paused for a moment and automatically pushed back his hair. Piggy tiptoed to the triangle, his ineffectual protest made, and joined the others.

Ralph went on.

"We have lots of assemblies. Everybody enjoys speaking and being together. We decide things. But they don't get done. We were going to have water brought from the stream and left in those coco-nut shells under fresh leaves. So it was, for a few days. Now there's no water. The shells are dry. People drink from the river."

There was a murmur of assent.

"Not that there's anything wrong with drinking from the river. I mean I'd sooner have water from that place—you know—the pool where the waterfall is—than out of an old coco-nut shell. Only we said we'd have the water brought. And now not. There were only two full shells there this afternoon."

He licked his lips.

"Then there's huts. Shelters."

The murmur swelled again and died away.

"You mostly sleep in shelters. To-night, except for Sam-neric up by the fire, you'll all sleep there. Who built the shelters?"

Clamour rose at once. Everyone had built the shelters. Ralph had to wave the conch once more.

"Wait a minute! I mean, who built all three? We all built the first one, four of us the second one, and me 'n Simon built the last one over there. That's why it's so tottery. No. Don't laugh. That shelter might fall down if the rain comes back. We'll need those shelters then."

He paused and cleared his throat.

"There's another thing. We chose those rocks right along beyond the bathing-pool as a lavatory. That was sensible too. The tide cleans the place up. You littluns know about that."

There were sniggers here and there and swift glances.

"Now people seem to use anywhere. Even near the shelters and the platform. You littluns, when you're getting fruit; if you're taken short——"

The assembly roared.

"I said if you're taken short you keep away from the fruit. That's dirty."

Laughter rose again.

"I said that's dirty!"

He plucked at his stiff, grey shirt.

"That's really dirty. If you're taken short you go right along the beach to the rocks. See?"

Piggy held out his hands for the conch but Ralph shook his head. This speech was planned, point by point.

"We've all got to use the rocks again. This place is getting dirty." He paused. The assembly, sensing a crisis, was tensely expectant. "And then: about the fire."

Ralph let out his spare breath with a little gasp that was echoed by his audience. Jack started to chip a piece of wood with his knife and whispered something to Robert, who looked away.

"The fire is the most important thing on the island. How

can we ever be rescued except by luck, if we don't keep a fire going? Is a fire too much for us to make?"

He flung out an arm.

"Look at us! How many are we? And yet we can't keep a fire going to make smoke. Don't you understand? Can't you see we ought to—ought to die before we let the fire out?"

There was a self-conscious giggling among the hunters. Ralph turned on them passionately.

"You hunters! You can laugh! But I tell you the smoke is more important than the pig, however often you kill one. Do all of you see?" He spread his arms wide and turned to the whole triangle.

"We've got to make smoke up there—or die."

He paused, feeling for his next point.

"And another thing."

Someone called out.

"Too many things."

There came mutters of agreement. Ralph overrode them.

"And another thing. We nearly set the whole island on fire. And we waste time, rolling rocks, and making little cooking fires. Now I say this and make it a rule, because I'm chief. We won't have a fire anywhere but on the mountain. Ever."

There was a row immediately. Boys stood up and shouted and Ralph shouted back.

"Because if you want a fire to cook fish or crab, you can jolly well go up the mountain. That way we'll be certain."

Hands were reaching for the conch in the light of the setting sun. He held on and leapt on the trunk.

"All this I meant to say. Now I've said it. You voted me for chief. Now you do what I say."

They quietened, slowly, and at last were seated again. Ralph dropped down and spoke in his ordinary voice.

"So remember. The rocks for a lavatory. Keep the fire going and smoke showing as a signal. Don't take fire from the mountain. Take your food up there."

Jack stood up, scowling in the gloom, and held out his hands.

"I haven't finished yet."

"But you've talked and talked!"

"I've got the conch."

Jack sat down, grumbling.

"Then the last thing. This is what people can talk about."

He waited till the platform was very still.

"Things are breaking up. I don't understand why. We began well; we were happy. And then——"

He moved the conch gently, looking beyond them at nothing, remembering the beastie, the snake, the fire, the talk of fear.

"Then people started getting frightened."

A murmur, almost a moan, rose and passed away. Jack had stopped whittling. Ralph went on, abruptly.

"But that's littluns' talk. We'll get that straight. So the last part, the bit we can all talk about, is kind of deciding on the fear."

The hair was creeping into his eyes again.

"We've got to talk about this fear and decide there's nothing in it. I'm frightened myself, sometimes; only that's nonsense! Like bogies. Then, when we've decided, we can start again and be careful about things like the fire." A picture of three boys walking along the bright beach flitted through his mind. "And be happy."

Ceremonially, Ralph laid the conch on the trunk beside

him as a sign that the speech was over. What sunlight reached them was level.

Jack stood up and took the conch.

"So this is a meeting to find out what's what. I'll tell you what's what. You littluns started all this, with the fear talk. Beasts! Where from? Of course we're frightened sometimes but we put up with being frightened. Only Ralph says you scream in the night. What does that mean but nightmares? Anyway, you don't hunt or build or help—you're a lot of cry-babies and sissies. That's what. And as for the fear—you'll have to put up with that like the rest of us."

Ralph looked at Jack open-mouthed, but Jack took no notice.

"The thing is—fear can't hurt you any more than a dream. There aren't any beasts to be afraid of on this island." He looked along the row of whispering littluns. "Serve you right if something did get you, you useless lot of cry-babies! But there *is* no animal——"

Ralph interrupted him testily.

"What is all this? Who said anything about an animal?"

"You did, the other day. You said they dream and cry out. Now they talk—not only the littluns, but my hunters sometimes—talk of a thing, a dark thing, a beast, some sort of animal. I've heard. You thought not, didn't you? Now listen. You don't get big animals on small islands. Only pigs. You only get lions and tigers in big countries like Africa and India——"

"And the Zoo——"

"I've got the conch. I'm not talking about the fear. I'm talking about the beast. Be frightened if you like. But as for the beast——"

Jack paused, cradling the conch, and turned to his hunters with their dirty black caps.

"Am I a hunter or am I not?"

They nodded, simply. He was a hunter all right. No one doubted that.

"Well then—I've been all over this island. By myself. If there were a beast I'd have seen it. Be frightened because you're like that—but there is no beast in the forest."

Jack handed back the conch and sat down. The whole assembly applauded him with relief. Then Piggy held out his hand.

"I don't agree with all Jack said, but with some. 'Course there isn't a beast in the forest. How could there be? What would a beast eat?"

"Pig."

"We eat pig."

"Piggy!"

"I got the conch!" said Piggy indignantly. "Ralph—they ought to shut up, oughtn't they? You shut up, you littluns! What I mean is that I don't agree about this here fear. Of course there isn't nothing to be afraid of in the forest. Why —I been there myself! You'll be talking about ghosts and such things next. We know what goes on and if there's something wrong, there's someone to put it right."

He took off his glasses and blinked at them. The sun had gone as if the light had been turned off.

He proceeded to explain.

"If you get a pain in your stomach, whether it's a little one or a big one——"

"Yours is a big one."

"When you done laughing perhaps we can get on with the meeting. And if them littluns climb back on the twister again they'll only fall off in a sec. So they might as well sit on the ground and listen. No. You have doctors for everything, even the inside of your mind. You don't really mean that we got to be frightened all the time of nothing? Life," said Piggy expansively, "is scientific, that's what it is. In a year or two when the war's over they'll be travelling to Mars and back. I know there isn't no beast—not with claws and all that, I mean—but I know there isn't no fear, either."

Piggy paused.

"Unless——"

Ralph moved restlessly.

"Unless what?"

"Unless we get frightened of people."

A sound, half-laugh, half-jeer, rose among the seated boys. Piggy ducked his head and went on hastily.

"So let's hear from that littlun who talked about a beast and perhaps we can show him how silly he is."

The littluns began to jabber among themselves, then one stood forward.

"What's your name?"

"Phil."

For a littlun he was self-confident, holding out his hands, cradling the conch as Ralph did, looking round at them to collect their attention before he spoke.

"Last night I had a dream, a horrid dream, fighting with things. I was outside the shelter by myself, fighting with things, those twisty things in the trees."

He paused, and the other littluns laughed in horrified sympathy.

"Then I was frightened and I woke up. And I was outside the shelter by myself in the dark and the twisty things had gone away."

The vivid horror of this, so possible and so nakedly terrifying, held them all silent. The child's voice went piping on from behind the white conch.

"And I was frightened and started to call out for Ralph and then I saw something moving among the trees, something big and horrid."

He paused, half-frightened by the recollection yet proud of the sensation he was creating.

"That was a nightmare," said Ralph, "he was walking in his sleep."

The assembly murmured in subdued agreement.

The littlun shook his head stubbornly.

"I was asleep when the twisty things were fighting and when they went away I was awake, and I saw something big and horrid moving in the trees."

Ralph held out his hands for the conch and the littlun sat down.

"You were asleep. There wasn't anyone there. How could anyone be wandering about in the forest at night? Was anyone? Did anyone go out?"

There was a long pause while the assembly grinned at the thought of anyone going out in the darkness. Then Simon stood up and Ralph looked at him in astonishment.

"You! What were you mucking about in the dark for?"

Simon grabbed the conch convulsively.

"I wanted—to go to a place—a place I know."

"What place?"

"Just a place I know. A place in the jungle."

He hesitated.

Jack settled the question for them with that contempt in his voice that could sound so funny and so final.

"He was taken short."

With a feeling of humiliation on Simon's behalf, Ralph took back the conch, looking Simon sternly in the face as he did so.

"Well, don't do it again. Understand? Not at night. There's enough silly talk about beasts, without the littluns seeing you gliding about like a——"

The derisive laughter that rose had fear in it and condemnation. Simon opened his mouth to speak but Ralph had the conch, so he backed to his seat.

When the assembly was silent Ralph turned to Piggy.

"Well, Piggy?"

"There was another one. Him."

The littluns pushed Percival forward then left him by himself. He stood knee-deep in the central grass, looking at his hidden feet, trying to pretend he was in a tent. Ralph remembered another small boy who had stood like this and he flinched away from the memory. He had pushed the thought down and out of sight, where only some positive reminder like this could bring it to the surface. There had been no further numberings of the littluns, partly because there was no means of ensuring that all of them were accounted for and partly because Ralph knew the answer to at least one question Piggy had asked on the mountain-top. There were little boys, fair, dark, freckled, and all dirty, but their faces were all dreadfully free of major blemishes. No one had seen the mulberry-coloured birthmark again. But that time Piggy had coaxed and bullied. Tacitly admitting that he remembered the unmentionable, Ralph nodded to Piggy.

"Go on. Ask him."

Piggy knelt, holding the conch.

"Now then. What's your name?"

The small boy twisted away into his tent. Piggy turned helplessly to Ralph, who spoke sharply.

"What's your name?"

Tormented by the silence and the refusal the assembly broke into a chant.

"What's your name? What's your name?"

"Quiet!"

Ralph peered at the child in the twilight.

"Now tell us. What's your name?"

"Percival Wemys Madison, The Vicarage, Harcourt St. Anthony, Hants, telephone, telephone, tele——"

As if this information was rooted far down in the springs of sorrow, the littlun wept. His face puckered, the tears leapt from his eyes, his mouth opened till they could see a square black hole. At first he was a silent effigy of sorrow; but then the lamentation rose out of him, loud and sustained as the conch.

"Shut up, you! Shut up!"

Percival Wemys Madison would not shut up. A spring had been tapped, far beyond the reach of authority or even physical intimidation. The crying went on, breath after breath, and seemed to sustain him upright as if he were nailed to it.

"Shut up! Shut up!"

For now the littluns were no longer silent. They were reminded of their personal sorrows; and perhaps felt themselves to share in a sorrow that was universal. They began to cry in sympathy, two of them almost as loud as Percival.

Maurice saved them. He cried out.

"Look at me!"

He pretended to fall over. He rubbed his rump and sat on the twister so that he fell in the grass. He clowned badly;

but Percival and the others noticed and sniffed and laughed. Presently they were all laughing so absurdly that the biguns joined in.

Jack was the first to make himself heard. He had not got the conch and thus spoke against the rules; but nobody minded.

"And what about the beast?"

Something strange was happening to Percival. He yawned and staggered, so that Jack seized and shook him.

"Where does the beast live?"

Percival sagged in Jack's grip.

"That's a clever beast," said Piggy, jeering, "if it can hide on this island."

"Jack's been everywhere——"

"Where could a beast live?"

"Beast my foot!"

Percival muttered something and the assembly laughed again. Ralph leaned forward.

"What does he say?"

Jack listened to Percival's answer and then let go of him. Percival, released, surrounded by the comfortable presence of humans, fell in the long grass and went to sleep.

Jack cleared his throat, then reported casually.

"He says the beast comes out of the sea."

The last laugh died away. Ralph turned involuntarily, a black, humped figure against the lagoon. The assembly looked with him; considered the vast stretches of water, the high sea beyond, unknown indigo of infinite possibility; heard silently the sough and whisper from the reef.

Maurice spoke—so loudly that they jumped.

"Daddy said they haven't found all the animals in the sea yet."

Argument started again. Ralph held out the glimmering conch and Maurice took it obediently. The meeting subsided.

"I mean when Jack says you can be frightened because people are frightened anyway that's all right. But when he says there's only pigs on this island I expect he's right but he doesn't know, not really, not certainly I mean"—Maurice took a breath—"My daddy says there's things, what d'you call'em that make ink—squids—that are hundreds of yards long and eat whales whole." He paused again and laughed gaily. "I don't believe in the beast of course. As Piggy says, life's scientific, but we don't know, do we? Not certainly, I mean——"

Someone shouted.

"A squid couldn't come up out of the water!"

"Could!"

"Couldn't!"

In a moment the platform was full of arguing, gesticulating shadows. To Ralph, seated, this seemed the breaking-up of sanity. Fear, beasts, no general agreement that the fire was all-important: and when one tried to get the thing straight the argument sheered off, bringing up fresh, unpleasant matter.

He could see a whiteness in the gloom near him so he grabbed it from Maurice and blew as loudly as he could. The assembly was shocked into silence. Simon was close to him, laying hands on the conch. Simon felt a perilous necessity to speak; but to speak in assembly was a terrible thing to him.

"Maybe," he said hesitantly, "maybe there is a beast."

The assembly cried out savagely and Ralph stood up in amazement.

"You, Simon? You believe in this?"

"I don't know," said Simon. His heartbeats were choking him. "But. . . ."

The storm broke.

"Sit down!"

"Shut up!"

"Take the conch!"

"Sod you!"

"Shut up!"

Ralph shouted.

"Hear him! He's got the conch!"

"What I mean is . . . maybe it's only us."

"Nuts!"

That was from Piggy, shocked out of decorum. Simon went on.

"We could be sort of. . . ."

Simon became inarticulate in his effort to express mankind's essential illness. Inspiration came to him.

"What's the dirtiest thing there is?"

As an answer Jack dropped into the uncomprehending silence that followed it the one crude expressive syllable. Release was like an orgasm. Those littluns who had climbed back on the twister fell off again and did not mind. The hunters were screaming with delight.

Simon's effort fell about him in ruins; the laughter beat him cruelly and he shrank away defenceless to his seat.

At last the assembly was silent again. Someone spoke out of turn.

"Maybe he means it's some sort of ghost."

Ralph lifted the conch and peered into the gloom. The lightest thing was the pale beach. Surely the littluns were nearer? Yes—there was no doubt about it, they were huddled into a tight knot of bodies in the central grass. A flurry of wind made the palms talk and the noise seemed very loud now that darkness and silence made it so noticeable. Two grey trunks rubbed each other with an evil squeaking that no one had noticed by day.

Piggy took the conch out of his hands. His voice was indignant.

"I don't believe in no ghosts—ever!"

Jack was up too, unaccountably angry.

"Who cares what you believe—Fatty!"

"I got the conch!"

There was the sound of a brief tussle and the conch moved to and fro.

"You gimme the conch back!"

Ralph pushed between them and got a thump on the chest. He wrested the conch from someone and sat down breathlessly.

"There's too much talk about ghosts. We ought to have left all this for daylight."

A hushed and anonymous voice broke in.

"Perhaps that's what the beast is—a ghost."

The assembly was shaken as by a wind.

"There's too much talking out of turn," Ralph said, "because we can't have proper assemblies if you don't stick to the rules."

He stopped again. The careful plan of this assembly had broken down.

"What d'you want me to say then? I was wrong to call this assembly so late. We'll have a vote on them; on ghosts I mean; and then go to the shelters because we're all tired. No—Jack is it?—wait a minute. I'll say here and now that I don't believe in ghosts. Or I don't think I do. But I don't like the thought of them. Not now that is, in the dark. But we were going to decide what's what."

He raised the conch for a moment.

"Very well then. I suppose what's what is whether there are ghosts or not——"

He thought for a moment, formulating the question.

"Who thinks there may be ghosts?"

For a long time there was silence and no apparent movement. Then Ralph peered into the gloom and made out the hands. He spoke flatly.

"I see."

The world, that understandable and lawful world, was slipping away. Once there was this and that; and now—and the ship had gone.

The conch was snatched from his hands and Piggy's voice shrilled.

"I didn't vote for no ghosts!"

He whirled round on the assembly.

"Remember that all of you!"

They heard him stamp.

"What are we? Humans? Or animals? Or savages? What's grown-ups going to think? Going off—hunting pigs—letting fires out—and now!"

A shadow fronted him tempestuously.

"You shut up, you fat slug!"

There was a moment's struggle and the glimmering conch jigged up and down. Ralph leapt to his feet.

"Jack! Jack! You haven't got the conch! Let him speak."

Jack's face swam near him.

"And you shut up! Who are you, anyway? Sitting there—telling people what to do. You can't hunt, you can't sing——"

"I'm chief. I was chosen."

"Why should choosing make any difference? Just giving orders that don't make any sense——"

"Piggy's got the conch."

"That's right—favour Piggy as you always do——"

"Jack!"

Jack's voice sounded in bitter mimicry.

"Jack! Jack!"

"The rules!" shouted Ralph, "you're breaking the rules!"

"Who cares?"

Ralph summoned his wits.

"Because the rules are the only thing we've got!"

But Jack was shouting against him.

"Bollocks to the rules! We're strong—we hunt! If there's a beast, we'll hunt it down! We'll close in and beat and beat and beat——"

He gave a wild whoop and leapt down to the pale sand. At once the platform was full of noise and excitement, scramblings, screams and laughter. The assembly shredded away and became a discursive and random scatter from the palms to the water and away along the beach, beyond nightsight. Ralph found his cheek touching the conch and took it from Piggy.

"What's grown-ups going to say?" cried Piggy again. "Look at 'em!"

The sound of mock hunting, hysterical laughter and real terror came from the beach.

"Blow the conch, Ralph."

Piggy was so close that Ralph could see the glint of his one glass.

"There's the fire. Can't they see?"

"You got to be tough now. Make 'em do what you want."

Ralph answered in the cautious voice of one who rehearses a theorem.

"If I blow the conch and they don't come back; then we've had it. We shan't keep the fire going. We'll be like animals. We'll never be rescued."

"If you don't blow, we'll soon be animals anyway. I can't see what they're doing but I can hear."

The dispersed figures had come together on the sand and were a dense black mass that revolved. They were chanting something and littluns that had had enough were staggering away, howling. Ralph raised the conch to his lips and then lowered it.

"The trouble is: Are there ghosts, Piggy? Or beasts?"

"Course there aren't."

"Why not?"

"'Cos things wouldn't make sense. Houses an' streets, an'—TV—they wouldn't work."

The dancing, chanting boys had worked themselves away till their sound was nothing but a wordless rhythm.

"But s'pose they don't make sense? Not here, on this island? Supposing things are watching us and waiting?"

Ralph shuddered violently and moved closer to Piggy, so that they bumped frighteningly.

"You stop talking like that! We got enough trouble, Ralph, an' I've had as much as I can stand. If there is ghosts——"

"I ought to give up being chief. Hear 'em."

"Oh lord! Oh no!"

Piggy gripped Ralph's arm.

"If Jack was chief he'd have all hunting and no fire. We'd be here till we died."

His voice ran up to a squeak.

"Who's that sitting there?"

"Me. Simon."

"Fat lot of good we are," said Ralph. "Three blind mice. I'll give up."

"If you give up," said Piggy, in an appalled whisper, "what'ud happen to me?"

"Nothing."

"He hates me. I dunno why. If he could do what he wanted—you're all right, he respects you. Besides—you'd hit him."

"You were having a nice fight with him just now."

"I had the conch," said Piggy simply. "I had a right to speak."

Simon stirred in the dark.

"Go on being chief."

"You shut up, young Simon! Why couldn't you say there wasn't a beast?"

"I'm scared of him," said Piggy, "and that's why I know him. If you're scared of someone you hate him but you can't stop thinking about him. You kid yourself he's all right really, an' then when you see him again; it's like asthma an' you can't breathe. I tell you what. He hates you too, Ralph——"

"Me? Why me?"

"I dunno. You got him over the fire; an' you're chief an' he isn't."

"But he's, he's, Jack Merridew!"

"I been in bed so much I done some thinking. I know about people. I know about me. And him. He can't hurt you: but if you stand out of the way he'd hurt the next thing. And that's me."

"Piggy's right, Ralph. There's you and Jack. Go on being chief."

"We're all drifting and things are going rotten. At home there was always a grown-up. Please, sir; please, miss; and then you got an answer. How I wish!"

"I wish my auntie was here."

"I wish my father . . O, what's the use?"

"Keep the fire going."

The dance was over and the hunters were going back to the shelters.

"Grown-ups know things," said Piggy. "They ain't afraid of the dark. They'd meet and have tea and discuss. Then things 'ud be all right——"

"They wouldn't set fire to the island. Or lose——"

"They'd build a ship——"

The three boys stood in the darkness, striving unsuccessfully to convey the majesty of adult life.

"They wouldn't quarrel——"

"Or break my specs——"

"Or talk about a beast——"

"If only they could get a message to us," cried Ralph desperately. "If only they could send us something grown-up . . . a sign or something."

A thin wail out of the darkness chilled them and set them grabbing for each other. Then the wail rose, remote and unearthly, and turned to an inarticulate gibbering. Percival Wemys Madison, of the Vicarage, Harcourt St. Anthony, lying in the long grass, was living through circumstances in which the incantation of his address was powerless to help him.

CHAPTER SIX

Beast from Air

<hr />

There was no light left save that of the stars. When they had understood what made this ghostly noise and Percival was quiet again, Ralph and Simon picked him up unhandily and carried him to a shelter. Piggy hung about near for all his brave words, and the three bigger boys went together to the next shelter. They lay restlessly and noisily among the dry leaves, watching the patch of stars that was the opening towards the lagoon. Sometimes a littlun cried out from the other shelters and once a bigun spoke in the dark. Then they too fell asleep.

A sliver of moon rose over the horizon, hardly large enough to make a path of light even when it sat right down on the water; but there were other lights in the sky, that moved fast, winked, or went out, though not even a faint popping came down from the battle fought at ten miles' height. But a sign came down from the world of grown-ups, though at the time there was no child awake to read it. There was a sudden bright explosion and a corkscrew trail across the sky; then darkness again and stars. There was a speck above the island, a figure dropping swiftly beneath a parachute, a figure that hung with dangling limbs. The changing winds of various altitudes took the figure where they would. Then, three miles up, the wind steadied and bore it in a descending curve round the sky and swept it in a great slant across the reef and the lagoon towards the mountain. The figure fell and crumpled among the blue flowers of the mountain-side, but now there was a gentle breeze at this height too and the parachute flopped and banged and pulled. So the figure, with feet that dragged behind it, slid up the mountain. Yard by yard, puff by puff, the breeze hauled the figure through the blue flowers, over the boulders and red stones, till it lay huddled among the shattered rocks of the mountain-top. Here the breeze was fitful and allowed the strings of the parachute to tangle and festoon; and the figure sat, its helmeted head between its knees, held by a complication of lines. When the breeze blew the lines would strain taut and some accident of this pull lifted the head and chest upright so that the figure seemed to peer across the brow of the mountain. Then, each time the wind dropped, the lines would slacken and the figure bow forward again, sinking its head between its knees. So as the stars moved across the sky, the figure sat on the mountain-top and bowed and sank and bowed again.

In the darkness of early morning there were noises by a rock a little way down the side of the mountain. Two boys rolled out of a pile of brushwood and dead leaves, two dim shadows talking sleepily to each other. They were the twins, on duty at the fire. In theory one should have been asleep and one on watch. But they could never manage to do things sensibly if that meant acting independently, and since staying awake all night was impossible, they had both gone to sleep. Now they approached the darker smudge that had been the signal fire, yawning, rubbing their eyes, treading with practised feet. When they reached it they stopped yawning, and one ran quickly back for brushwood and leaves.

The other knelt down.

"I believe it's out."

He fiddled with the sticks that were pushed into his hands.

"No."

He lay down and put his lips close to the smudge and blew softly. His face appeared, lit redly. He stopped blowing for a moment.

"Sam—give us——"

"—tinder wood."

Eric bent down and blew softly again till the patch was bright. Sam poked the piece of tinder wood into the hot spot, then a branch. The glow increased and the branch took fire. Sam piled on more branches.

"Don't burn the lot," said Eric, "you're putting on too much."

"Let's warm up."

"We'll only have to fetch more wood."

"I'm cold."

"So'm I."

"Besides, it's——"

"—dark. All right, then."

Eric squatted back and watched Sam make up the fire. He built a little tent of dead wood and the fire was safely alight.

"That was near."

"He'd have been——"

"Waxy"

"Huh."

For a few moments the twins watched the fire in silence. Then Eric sniggered.

"Wasn't he waxy?"

"About the——"

"Fire and the pig."

"Lucky he went for Jack, 'stead of us."

"Huh. Remember old Waxy at school?"

" 'Boy—you-are-driving-me-slowly-insane!' "

The twins shared their identical laughter, then remembered the darkness and other things and glanced round uneasily. The flames, busy about the tent, drew their eyes back again. Eric watched the scurrying wood-lice that were so frantically unable to avoid the flames, and thought of the first fire—just down there, on the steeper side of the mountains, where now was complete darkness. He did not like to remember it, and looked away at the mountain-top.

Warmth radiated now, and beat pleasantly on them. Sam amused himself by fitting branches into the fire as closely as possible. Eric spread out his hands, searching for the distance at which the heat was just bearable. Idly looking beyond the fire, he resettled the scattered rocks from their flat shadows into daylight contours. Just there was the big rock, and the three stones there, that split rock, and there beyond, was a gap—just there—

"Sam."

"Huh?"

"Nothing."

The flames were mastering the branches, the bark was curling and falling away, the wood exploding. The tent fell inwards and flung a wide circle of light over the mountaintop.

"Sam——"

"Huh?"

"Sam! Sam!"

Beast from Air

Sam looked at Eric irritably. The intensity of Eric's gaze made the direction in which he looked terrible, for Sam had his back to it. He scrambled round the fire, squatted by Eric, and looked to see. They became motionless, gripped in each other's arms, four unwinking eyes aimed and two mouths open.

Far beneath them, the trees of the forest sighed, then roared. The hair on their foreheads fluttered and flames blew out sideways from the fire. Fifteen yards away from them came the plopping noise of fabric blown open.

Neither of the boys screamed but the grip of their arms tightened and their mouths grew peaked. For perhaps ten seconds they crouched like that while the flailing fire sent smoke and sparks and waves of inconstant light over the top of the mountain.

Then as though they had but one terrified mind between them they scrambled away over the rocks and fled.

Ralph was dreaming. He had fallen asleep after what seemed hours of tossing and turning noisily among the dry leaves. Even the sounds of nightmare from the other shelters no longer reached him, for he was back from where he came from, feeding the ponies with sugar over the garden wall. Then someone was shaking his arm, telling him that it was time for tea.

"Ralph! Wake up!"

The leaves were roaring like the sea.

"Ralph, wake up!"

"What's the matter?"

"We saw—"

"—the beast——"

"—plain!"

"Who are you? The twins?"

"We jaw the beast——"

"Quiet. Piggy!"

The leaves were roaring still. Piggy bumped into him and a twin grabbed him as he made for the oblong of paling stars.

"You can't go out—it's horrible!"

"Piggy—where are the spears?"

"I can hear the——"

"Quiet then. Lie still."

They lay there listening, at first with doubt but then with terror to the description the twins breathed at them between bouts of extreme silence. Soon the darkness was full of claws, full of the awful unknown and menace. An interminable dawn faded the stars out, and at last light, sad and grey, filtered into the shelter. They began to stir though still the world outside the shelter was impossibly dangerous. The maze of the darkness sorted into near and far, and at the high point of the sky the cloudlets were warmed with colour. A single sea bird flapped upwards with a hoarse cry that was echoed presently, and something squawked in the forest. Now streaks of cloud near the horizon began to glow rosily, and the feathery tops of the palms were green.

Ralph knelt in the entrance to the shelter and peered cautiously round him.

"Sam'n Eric. Call them to an assembly. Quietly. Go on."

The twins, holding tremulously to each other, dared the few yards to the next shelter and spread the dreadful news. Ralph stood up and walked for the sake of dignity, though with his back pricking, to the platform. Piggy and Simon followed him and the other boys came sneaking after.

Ralph took the conch from where it lay on the polished

seat and held it to his lips; but then he hesitated and did not blow. He held the shell up instead and showed it to them and they understood.

The rays of the sun that were fanning upwards from below the horizon, swung downwards to eye-level. Ralph looked for a moment at the growing slice of gold that lit them from the right hand and seemed to make speech possible. The circle of boys before him bristled with hunting spears.

He handed the conch to Eric, the nearest of the twins.

"We've seen the beast with our own eyes. No—we weren't asleep——"

Sam took up the story. By custom now one conch did for both twins, for their substantial unity was recognized.

"It was furry. There was something moving behind its head—wings. The beast moved too——"

"That was awful. It kind of sat up——"

"The fire was bright——"

"We'd just made it up——"

"—more sticks on——"

"There were eyes——"

"Teeth——"

"Claws——"

"We ran as fast as we could——"

"Bashed into things——"

"The beast followed us——"

"I saw it slinking behind the trees——"

"Nearly touched me——"

Ralph pointed fearfully at Eric's face, which was striped with scars where the bushes had torn him.

"How did you do that?"

Eric felt his face.

"I'm all rough. Am I bleeding?"

The circle of boys shrank away in horror. Johnny, yawning still, burst into noisy tears and was slapped by Bill till he choked on them. The bright morning was full of threats and the circle began to change. It faced out, rather than in, and the spears of sharpened wood were like a fence. Jack called them back to the centre.

"This'll be a real hunt! Who'll come?"

Ralph moved impatiently.

"These spears are made of wood. Don't be silly."

Jack sneered at him.

"Frightened?"

"Course I'm frightened. Who wouldn't be?"

He turned to the twins, yearning but hopeless.

"I suppose you aren't pulling our legs?"

The reply was too emphatic for anyone to doubt them.

Piggy took the conch.

"Couldn't we—kind of—stay here? Maybe the beast won't come near us."

But for the sense of something watching them, Ralph would have shouted at him.

"Stay here? And be cramped into this bit of the island, always on the lookout? How should we get our food? And what about the fire?"

"Let's be moving," said Jack restlessly, "we're wasting time."

"No we're not. What about the littluns?"

"Sucks to the littluns!"

"Someone's got to look after them."

"Nobody has so far."

"There was no need! Now there is. Piggy'll look after them."

125

"That's right. Keep Piggy out of danger."

"Have some sense. What can Piggy do with only one eye?"

The rest of the boys were looking from Jack to Ralph, curiously.

"And another thing. You can't have an ordinary hunt because the beast doesn't leave tracks. If it did you'd have seen them. For all we know, the beast may swing through the trees like what's its name."

They nodded.

"So we've got to think."

Piggy took off his damaged glasses and cleaned the remaining lens.

"How about us, Ralph?"

"You haven't got the conch. Here."

"I mean—how about us? Suppose the beast comes when you're all away. I can't see proper, and if I get scared——"

Jack broke in, contemptuously.

"You're always scared."

"I got the conch——"

"Conch! Conch!" shouted Jack, "we don't need the conch any more. We know who ought to say things. What good did Simon do speaking, or Bill, or Walter? It's time some people knew they've got to keep quiet and leave deciding things to the rest of us——"

Ralph could no longer ignore his speech. The blood was hot in his cheeks.

"You haven't got the conch," he said. "Sit down."

Jack's face went so white that the freckles showed as clear, brown flecks. He licked his lips and remained standing.

"This is a hunter's job."

The rest of the boys watched intently. Piggy, finding himself uncomfortably embroiled, slid the conch to Ralph's

knees and sat down. The silence grew oppressive and Piggy
held his breath.

"This is more than a hunter's job," said Ralph at last,
"because you can't track the beast. And don't you want to
be rescued?"

He turned to the assembly.

"Don't you all want to be rescued?"

He looked back at Jack.

"I said before, the fire is the main thing. Now the fire
must be out——"

The old exasperation saved him and gave him the energy
to attack.

"Hasn't anyone got any sense? We've got to re-light that
fire. You never thought of that, Jack, did you? Or don't any
of you want to be rescued?"

Yes, they wanted to be rescued, there was no doubt about
that; and with a violent swing to Ralph's side, the crisis
passed. Piggy let out his breath with a gasp, reached for it
again and failed. He lay against a log, his mouth gaping,
blue shadows creeping round his lips. Nobody minded him.

"Now think, Jack. Is there anywhere on the island you
haven't been?"

Unwillingly Jack answered.

"There's only—but of course! You remember? The tail-
end part, where the rocks are all piled up. I've been near
there. The rock makes a sort of bridge. There's only one
way up."

"And the thing might live there."

All the assembly talked at once.

"Quiet! All right. That's where we'll look. If the beast
isn't there we'll go up the mountain and look; and light the
fire."

"Let's go."

"We'll eat first. Then go." Ralph paused. "We'd better take spears."

After they had eaten Ralph and the biguns set out along the beach. They left Piggy propped up on the platform. This day promised, like the others, to be a sunbath under a blue dome. The beach stretched away before them in a gentle curve till perspective drew it into one with the forest; for the day was not advanced enough to be obscured by the shifting veils of mirage. Under Ralph's direction, they picked a careful way along the palm terrace, rather than dare the hot sand down by the water. He let Jack lead the way; and Jack trod with theatrical caution though they could have seen an enemy twenty yards away. Ralph walked in the rear, thankful to have escaped responsibility for a time.

Simon, walking in front of Ralph, felt a flicker of in-credulity—a beast with claws that scratched, that sat on a mountain-top, that left no tracks and yet was not fast enough to catch Samneric. However Simon thought of the beast, there rose before his inward sight the picture of a human at once heroic and sick.

He sighed. Other people could stand up and speak to an assembly, apparently, without that dreadful feeling of the pressure of personality; could say what they would as though they were speaking to only one person. He stepped aside and looked back. Ralph was coming along, holding his spear over his shoulder. Diffidently, Simon allowed his pace to slacken until he was walking side by side with Ralph and looking up at him through the coarse black hair that fell now to his eyes. Ralph glanced sideways, smiled constrainedly as though he had forgotten that Simon had made a fool of himself, then looked away again at nothing. For a moment or two Simon was happy to be accepted and then he ceased to think about himself. When he bashed into a tree Ralph looked sideways impatiently and Robert sniggered. Simon reeled and a white spot on his forehead turned red and trickled. Ralph dismissed Simon and returned to his personal hell. They would reach the castle some time; and the chief would have to go forward.

Jack came trotting back.

"We're in sight now."

"All right. We'll get as close as we can."

He followed Jack towards the castle where the ground rose slightly. On their left was an impenetrable tangle of creepers and trees.

"Why couldn't there be something in that?"

"Because you can see. Nothing goes in or out."

"What about the castle then?"

"Look."

Ralph parted the screen of grass and looked out. There were only a few more yards of stony ground and then the two sides of the island came almost together so that one expected a peak of headland. But instead of this a narrow ledge of rock, a few yards wide and perhaps fifteen long, continued the island out into the sea. There lay another of those pieces of pink squareness that underlay the structure of the island. This side of the castle, perhaps a hundred feet high, was the pink bastion they had seen from the mountain-top. The rock of the cliff was split and the top littered with great lumps that seemed to totter.

Behind Ralph the tall grass had filled with silent hunters. Ralph looked at Jack.

"You're a hunter."

Jack went red.

'I know. All right."

Something deep in Ralph spoke for him.

"I'm chief. I'll go. Don't argue."

He turned to the others.

"You. Hide here. Wait for me."

He found his voice tended either to disappear or to come out too loud. He looked at Jack.

"Do you—think?"

Jack muttered.

"I've been all over. It must be here."

"I see."

Simon mumbled confusedly: "I don't believe in the beast."

Ralph answered him politely, as if agreeing about the weather.

"No. I suppose not."

His mouth was tight and pale. He put back his hair very slowly.

"Well. So long."

He forced his feet to move until they had carried him out on to the neck of land.

He was surrounded on all sides by chasms of empty air. There was nowhere to hide, even if one did not have to go on. He paused on the narrow neck and looked down. Soon, in a matter of centuries, the sea would make an island of the castle. On the right hand was the lagoon, troubled by the open sea; and on the left——

Ralph shuddered. The lagoon had protected them from the Pacific: and for some reason only Jack had gone right down to the water on the other side. Now he saw the landsman's view of the swell and it seemed like the breathing of some stupendous creature. Slowly the waters sank among the rocks, revealing pink tables of granite, strange growths of coral, polyp, and weed. Down, down, the waters went, whispering like the wind among the heads of the forest. There was one flat rock there, spread like a table, and the waters sucking down on the four weedy sides made them seem like cliffs. Then the sleeping leviathan breathed out —the waters rose, the weed streamed, and the water boiled over the table rock with a roar. There was no sense of the passage of waves; only this minute-long fall and rise and fall.

Ralph turned away to the red cliff. They were waiting behind him in the long grass, waiting to see what he would do. He noticed that the sweat in his palm was cool now; realized with surprise that he did not really expect to meet any beast and didn't know what he would do about it if he did.

He saw that he could climb the cliff but this was not necessary. The squareness of the rock allowed a sort of plinth round it, so that to the right, over the lagoon, one could inch along a ledge and turn the corner out of sight. It was easy going, and soon he was peering round the rock.

Nothing but what you might expect: pink, tumbled boulders with guano layered on them like icing; and a steep slope up to the shattered rocks that crowned the bastion.

A sound behind him made him turn. Jack was edging along the ledge.

"Couldn't let you do it on your own."

Ralph said nothing. He led the way over the rocks, inspected a sort of half-cave that held nothing more terrible than a clutch of rotten eggs and at last sat down, looking round him and tapping the rock with the butt of his spear.

Jack was excited.

"What a place for a fort!"

A column of spray wetted them.

"No fresh water."

"What's that then?"

There was indeed a long green smudge half-way up the rock. They climbed up and tasted the trickle of water.

"You could keep a coco-nut shell there, filling all the time."

"Not me. This is a rotten place."

Side by side they scaled the last height to where the diminishing pile was crowned by the last broken rock. Jack struck the near one with his fist and it grated slightly.

"Do you remember——?"

Consciousness of the bad times in between came to them both. Jack talked quickly.

"Shove a palm trunk under that and if an enemy came— look!"

A hundred feet below them was the narrow causeway, then the stony ground, then the grass dotted with heads, and behind that the forest.

"One heave," cried Jack, exulting, "and—wheee ——!"

He made a swooping movement with his hand. Ralph looked towards the mountain.

"What's the matter?"

Ralph turned.

"Why?"

"You were looking—I don't know how."

"There's no signal now. Nothing to show."

"You're nuts on the signal."

The taut blue horizon encircled them, broken only by the mountain-top.

"That's all we've got."

He leaned his spear against the rocking stone and pushed back two handfuls of hair.

"We'll have to go back and climb the mountain. That's where they saw the beast."

"The beast won't be there."

"What else can we do?"

The others, waiting in the grass, saw Jack and Ralph unharmed and broke cover into the sunlight. They forgot the beast in the excitement of exploration. They swarmed across the bridge and soon were climbing and shouting. Ralph stood now, one hand against an enormous red block, a block large as a millwheel that had been split off and hung, tottering. Sombrely he watched the mountain. He clenched his fist and beat hammer-wise on the red wall at his right. His lips were tightly compressed and his eyes yearned beneath the fringe of hair.

"Smoke."

He sucked his bruised fist.

"Jack! Come on."

But Jack was not there. A knot of boys, making a great noise that he had not noticed, were heaving and pushing at a rock. As he turned, the base cracked and the whole mass toppled into the sea so that a thunderous plume of spray leapt half-way up the cliff.

"Stop it! Stop it!"

His voice struck a silence among them.

"Smoke."

A strange thing happened in his head. Something flittered there in front of his mind like a bat's wing, obscuring his idea.

"Smoke."

At once the ideas were back, and the anger.

"We want smoke. And you go wasting your time. You roll rocks."

133

Roger shouted.

"We've got plenty of time!"

Ralph shook his head.

"We'll go to the mountain."

The clamour broke out. Some of the boys wanted to go back to the beach. Some wanted to roll more rocks. The sun was bright and danger had faded with the darkness.

"Jack. The beast might be on the other side. You can lead again. You've been."

"We could go by the shore. There's fruit."

Bill came up to Ralph.

"Why can't we stay here for a bit?"

"That's right."

"Let's have a fort——"

"There's no food here," said Ralph, "and no shelter. Not much fresh water."

"This would make a wizard fort."

"We can roll rocks——"

"Right on to the bridge——"

"I say we'll go on!" shouted Ralph furiously. "We've got to make certain. We'll go now."

"Let's stay here——"

"Back to the shelter——"

"I'm tired——"

"No!"

Ralph struck the skin off his knuckles. They did not seem to hurt.

"I'm chief. We've got to make certain. Can't you see the mountain? There's no signal showing. There may be a ship out there. Are you all off your rockers?"

Mutinously, the boys fell silent or muttering.

Jack led the way down the rock and across the bridge.

CHAPTER SEVEN

Shadows and Tall Trees

T he pig-run kept close to the jumble of rocks that lay
down by the water on the other side and Ralph was
content to follow Jack along it. If you could shut
your ears to the slow suck down of the sea and boil of the
return, if you could forget how dun and unvisited were the
ferny coverts on either side, then there was a chance that
you might put the beast out of mind and dream for a while.
The sun had swung over the vertical and the afternoon heat
was closing in on the island. Ralph passed a message forward to Jack and when they next came to fruit the whole
party stopped and ate.

Sitting, Ralph was aware of the heat for the first time
that day. He pulled distastefully at his grey shirt and wondered whether he might undertake the adventure of washing
it. Sitting under what seemed an unusual heat, even for this
island, Ralph planned his toilet. He would like to have a
pair of scissors and cut this hair—he flung the mass back—
cut this filthy hair right back to half an inch. He would like
to have a bath, a proper wallow with soap. He passed his
tongue experimentally over his teeth and decided that a
toothbrush would come in handy too. Then there were his
nails——

Ralph turned his hand over and examined them. They were bitten down to the quick though he could not remember when he had restarted this habit nor any time when he indulged it.

"Be sucking my thumb next——"

He looked round, furtively. Apparently no one had heard. The hunters sat, stuffing themselves with this easy meal, trying to convince themselves that they got sufficient kick out of bananas and that other olive-grey, jelly-like fruit. With the memory of his sometime clean self as a standard, Ralph looked them over. They were dirty, not with the spectacular dirt of boys who have fallen into mud or been brought down hard on a rainy day. Not one of them was an obvious subject for a shower, and yet—hair, much too long, tangled here and there, knotted round a dead leaf or a twig; faces cleaned fairly well by the process of eating and sweating but marked in the less accessible angles with a kind of shadow; clothes, worn away, stiff like his own with sweat, put on, not for decorum or comfort but out of custom; the skin of the body, scurfy with brine——

He discovered with a little fall of the heart that these were the conditions he took as normal now and that he did not mind. He sighed and pushed away the stalk from which he had stripped the fruit. Already the hunters were stealing away to do their business in the woods or down by the rocks. He turned and looked out to sea.

Here, on the other side of the island, the view was utterly different. The filmy enchantments of mirage could not endure the cold ocean water and the horizon was hard, clipped blue. Ralph wandered down to the rocks. Down here, almost on a level with the sea, you could follow with your eye the ceaseless, bulging passage of the deep sea waves.

They were miles wide, apparently not breakers or the banked ridges of shallow water. They travelled the length of the island with an air of disregarding it and being set on other business; they were less a progress than a momentous rise and fall of the whole ocean. Now the sea would suck down, making cascades and waterfalls of retreating water, would sink past the rocks and plaster down the seaweed like shining hair: then, pausing, gather and rise with a roar, irresistibly swelling over point and outcrop, climbing the little cliff, sending at last an arm of surf up a gully to end a yard or so from him in fingers of spray.

Wave after wave, Ralph followed the rise and fall until something of the remoteness of the sea numbed his brain. Then gradually the almost infinite size of this water forced itself on his attention. This was the divider, the barrier. On the other side of the island, swathed at midday with mirage, defended by the shield of the quiet lagoon, one might dream of rescue; but here, faced by the brute obtuseness of the ocean, the miles of division, one was clamped down, one was helpless, one was condemned, one was——

Simon was speaking almost in his ear. Ralph found that he had rock painfully gripped in both hands, found his body arched, the muscles of his neck stiff, his mouth strained open.

"You'll get back to where you came from."

Simon nodded as he spoke. He was kneeling on one knee, looking down from a higher rock which he held with both hands; his other leg stretched down to Ralph's level.

Ralph was puzzled and searched Simon's face for a clue.

"It's so big, I mean——"

Simon nodded.

"All the same. You'll get back all right. I think so, anyway."

137

Some of the strain had gone from Ralph's body. He glanced at the sea and then smiled bitterly at Simon.

"Got a ship in your pocket?"

Simon grinned and shook his head.

"How do you know, then?"

When Simon was still silent Ralph said curtly, "You're batty."

Simon shook his head violently till the coarse black hair flew backwards and forwards across his face.

"No, I'm not. I just *think you'll get back all right*."

For a moment nothing more was said. And then they suddenly smiled at each other.

Roger called from the coverts.

"Come and see!"

The ground was turned over near the pig-run and there were droppings that steamed. Jack bent down to them as though he loved them.

"Ralph—we need meat even if we are hunting the other thing."

"If you mean going the right way, we'll hunt."

They set off again, the hunters bunched a little by fear of the mentioned beast, while Jack quested ahead. They went more slowly than Ralph had bargained for; yet in a way he was glad to loiter, cradling his spear. Jack came up against some emergency of his craft and soon the procession stopped. Ralph leaned against a tree and at once the day-dreams came swarming up. Jack was in charge of the hunt and there would be time to get to the mountain——

Once, following his father from Chatham to Devonport, they had lived in a cottage on the edge of the moors. In the succession of houses that Ralph had known, this one stood out with particular clarity because after that house he had been sent away to school. Mummy had still been with them and Daddy had come home every day. Wild ponies came to the stone wall at the bottom of the garden, and it had snowed. Just behind the cottage there was a sort of shed and you could lie up there, watching the flakes swirl past. You could see the damp spot where each flake died; then you could mark the first flake that lay down without melting and watch the whole ground turn white. You could go in-doors when you were cold and look out of the window, past that bright copper kettle and the plate with the little blue men——

When you went to bed there was a bowl of cornflakes with sugar and cream. And the books—they stood on the shelf by the bed, leaning together with always two or three laid flat on top because he had not bothered to put them back properly. They were dog-eared and scratched. There was the bright, shining one about Topsy and Mopsy that he never read because it was about two girls; there was the one about the Magician which you read with a kind of tied-down terror, skipping page twenty-seven with the awful picture of the spider; there was a book about people who had dug things up, Egyptian things; there was the *Boy's Book of Trains*, *The Boy's Book of Ships*. Vividly they came before him; he could have reached up and touched them, could feel the weight and slow slide with which the *Mammoth Book for Boys* would come out and slither down. . . . Everything was all right; everything was good-humoured and friendly.

The bushes crashed ahead of them. Boys flung them-

139

selves wildly from the pig track and scrabbled in the creepers, screaming. Ralph saw Jack nudged aside and fall. Then there was a creature bounding along the pig track towards him, with tusks gleaming and an intimidating grunt. Ralph found he was able to measure the distance coldly and take aim. With the boar only five yards away, he flung the foolish wooden stick that he carried, saw it hit the great snout and hang there for a moment. The boar's note changed to a squeal and it swerved aside into the covert. The pig-run filled with shouting boys again, Jack came running back, and poked about in the undergrowth.

"Through here——"

"But he'd do us!"

"Through here, I said——"

The boar was floundering away from them. They found another pig-run parallel to the first and Jack raced away. Ralph was full of fright and apprehension and pride.

"I hit him! The spear stuck in——"

Now they came, unexpectedly, to an open space by the sea. Jack cast about on the bare rock and looked anxious.

"He's gone."

"I hit him," said Ralph again, "and the spear stuck in a bit."

He felt the need of witnesses.

"Didn't you see me?"

Maurice nodded.

"I saw you. Right bang on his snout—Wheee!"

Ralph talked on, excitedly.

"I hit him all right. The spear stuck in. I wounded him!"

He sunned himself in their new respect and felt that hunting was good after all.

"I walloped him properly. That was the beast, I think!" Jack came back.

"That wasn't the beast. That was a boar."

"I hit him."

"Why didn't you grab him? I tried——"

Ralph's voice ran up.

"But a boar!"

Jack flushed suddenly.

"You said he'd do us. What did you want to throw for? Why didn't you wait?"

He held out his arm.

"Look."

He turned his left forearm for them all to see. On the outside was a rip; not much, but bloody.

"He did that with his tusks. I couldn't get my spear down in time."

Attention focused on Jack.

"That's a wound," said Simon, "and you ought to suck it. Like Berengaria."

Jack sucked.

"I hit him," said Ralph indignantly. "I hit him with my spear, I wounded him."

He tried for their attention.

"He was coming along the path. I threw, like this——"

Robert snarled at him. Ralph entered into the play and everybody laughed. Presently they were all jabbing at Robert who made mock rushes.

Jack shouted.

"Make a ring!"

The circle moved in and round. Robert squealed in mock terror, then in real pain.

"Ow! Stop it! You're hurting!"

butt end of a spear fell on his back as he blundered
g them.

Hold him!"

They got his arms and legs. Ralph, carried away by a
sudden thick excitement, grabbed Eric's spear and jabbed
at Robert with it.

"Kill him! Kill him!"

All at once, Robert was screaming and struggling with
the strength of frenzy. Jack had him by the hair and was
brandishing his knife. Behind him was Roger, fighting to
get close. The chant rose ritually, as at the last moment of
a dance or a hunt.

"*Kill the pig! Cut his throat! Kill the pig! Bash him in!*"

Ralph too was fighting to get near, to get a handful of
that brown, vulnerable flesh. The desire to squeeze and
hurt was over-mastering.

Jack's arm came down; the heaving circle cheered and
made pig-dying noises. Then they lay quiet, panting, listening to Robert's frightened snivels. He wiped his face with
a dirty arm, and made an effort to retrieve his status.

"Oh, my bum!"

He rubbed his rump ruefully. Jack rolled over.

"That was a good game."

"Just a game," said Ralph uneasily. "I got jolly badly
hurt at rugger once."

"We ought to have a drum," said Maurice, "then we
could do it properly."

Ralph looked at him.

"How properly?"

"I dunno. You want a fire, I think, and a drum, and you
keep time to the drum."

"You want a pig," said Roger, "like in a real hunt."

"Or someone to pretend," said Jack. "You could get someone to dress up as a pig and then he could act—you know, pretend to knock me over and all that——"

"You want a real pig," said Robert, still caressing his rump, "because you've got to kill him."

"Use a littlun," said Jack, and everybody laughed.

Ralph sat up.

"Well. We shan't find what we're looking for at this rate."

One by one they stood up, twitching rags into place.

Ralph looked at Jack.

"Now for the mountain."

"Shouldn't we go back to Piggy," said Maurice, "before dark?"

The twins nodded like one boy.

"Yes, that's right. Let's go up there in the morning."

Ralph looked out and saw the sea.

"We've got to start the fire again."

"You haven't got Piggy's specs," said Jack, "so you can't."

"Then we'll find out if the mountain's clear."

Maurice spoke, hesitating, not wanting to seem a funk.

"Supposing the beast's up there?"

Jack brandished his spear.

"We'll kill it."

The sun seemed a little cooler. He slashed with the spear.

"What are we waiting for?"

"I suppose," said Ralph, "if we keep on by the sea this way, we'll come out below the burnt bit and then we can climb the mountain."

Once more Jack led them along by the suck and heave of the blinding sea.

Once more Ralph dreamed, letting his skilful feet deal with the difficulties of the path. Yet here his feet seemed less skilful than before. For most of the way they were forced right down to the bare rock by the water and had to edge along between that and the dark luxuriance of the forest. There were little cliffs to be scaled, some to be used as paths, lengthy traverses where one used hands as well as feet. Here and there they could clamber over wave-wet rock, leaping across clear pools that the tide had left. They came to a gully that split the narrow foreshore like a defence. This seemed to have no bottom and they peered awe-stricken into the gloomy crack where water gurgled. Then the wave came back, the gully boiled before them and spray dashed up to the very creeper so that the boys were wet and shrieking. They tried the forest but it was thick and woven like a bird's nest. In the end they had to jump one by one, waiting till the water sank; and even so, some of them got a second drenching. After that the rocks seemed to be growing impassable so they sat for a time, letting their rags dry and watching the clipped outlines of the rollers that moved so slowly past the island. They found fruit in a haunt of bright little birds that hovered like insects. Then Ralph said they were going too slowly. He himself climbed a tree and parted the canopy, and saw the square head of the mountain seeming still a great way off. Then they tried to hurry along the rocks and Robert cut his knee quite badly and they had to recognize that this path must be taken slowly if they were to be safe. So they proceeded after that as if they were climbing a dangerous mountain, until the rocks became an uncompromising cliff, overhung with impossible jungle and falling sheer into the sea.

Ralph looked at the sun critically.

"Early evening. After tea-time, at any rate."

"I don't remember this cliff," said Jack, crest-fallen, "so this must be the bit of the coast I missed."

Ralph nodded.

"Let me think."

By now, Ralph had no self-consciousness in public thinking but would treat the day's decisions as though he were playing chess. The only trouble was that he would never be a very good chess player. He thought of the littluns and Piggy. Vividly he imagined Piggy by himself, huddled in a shelter that was silent except for the sounds of nightmare.

"We can't leave the littluns alone with Piggy. Not all night."

The other boys said nothing but stood round, watching him.

"If we went back we should take hours."

Jack cleared his throat and spoke in a queer, tight voice.

"We musn't let anything happen to Piggy, must we?"

Ralph tapped his teeth with the dirty point of Eric's spear.

"If we go across——"

He glanced round him.

"Someone's got to go across the island and tell Piggy we'll be back after dark."

Bill spoke, unbelieving.

"Through the forest by himself? Now?"

"We can't spare more than one."

Simon pushed his way to Ralph's elbow.

"I'll go if you like. I don't mind, honestly."

Before Ralph had time to reply, he smiled quickly, turned and climbed into the forest.

Ralph looked back at Jack, seeing him, infuriatingly, for the first time.

"Jack—that time you went the whole way to the castle rock."

Jack glowered.

"Yes?"

"You came along part of this shore—below the mountain, beyond there."

"Yes."

"And then?"

"I found a pig-run. It went for miles."

Ralph nodded. He pointed at the forest.

"So the pig-run must be somewhere in there."

Everybody agreed, sagely.

"All right then. We'll smash a way through till we find the pig-run."

He took a step and halted.

"Wait a minute though! Where does the pig-run go to?"

"The mountain," said Jack, "I told you." He sneered. "Don't you want to go to the mountain?"

Ralph sighed, sensing the rising antagonism, understanding that this was how Jack felt as soon as he ceased to lead.

"I was thinking of the light. We'll be stumbling about."

"We were going to look for the beast——"

"There won't be enough light."

"I don't mind going," said Jack hotly. "I'll go when we get there. Won't you? Would you rather go back to the shelters and tell Piggy?"

Now it was Ralph's turn to flush but he spoke despairingly, out of the new understanding that Piggy had given him.

"Why do you hate me?"

The boys stirred uneasily, as though something indecent had been said. The silence lengthened.

Ralph, still hot and hurt, turned away first.

"Come on."

He led the way and set himself as by right to hack at the tangles. Jack brought up the rear, displaced and brooding.

The pig-track was a dark tunnel, for the sun was sliding quickly towards the edge of the world and in the forest shadows were never far to seek. The track was broad and beaten and they ran along at a swift trot. Then the roof of leaves broke up and they halted, breathing quickly, looking at the few stars that pricked round the head of the mountain.

"There you are."

The boys peered at each other doubtfully. Ralph made a decision.

"We'll go straight across to the platform and climb to-morrow."

They murmured agreement; but Jack was standing by his shoulder.

"If you're frightened of course——"

Ralph turned on him.

"Who went first on the castle rock?"

"I went too. And that was daylight."

"All right. Who wants to climb the mountain now?"

Silence was the only answer.

"Samneric? What about you?"

"We ought to go an' tell Piggy——"

"—yes, tell Piggy that——"

"But Simon went!"

"We ought to tell Piggy—in case——"

"Robert? Bill?"

They were going straight back to the platform now. Not, of course, that they were afraid—but tired.

Ralph turned back to Jack.

"You see?"

"I'm going up the mountain."

The words came from Jack viciously, as though they were a curse. He looked at Ralph, his thin body tensed, his spear held as if he threatened him.

"I'm going up the mountain to look for the beast—now."

Then the supreme sting, the casual, bitter word.

"Coming?"

At that word the other boys forgot their urge to be gone and turned back to sample this fresh rub of two spirits in the dark. The word was too good, too bitter, too successfully daunting to be repeated. It took Ralph at low water when his nerve was relaxed for the return to the shelter and the still, friendly waters of the lagoon.

"I don't mind."

Astonished, he heard his voice come out, cool and casual, so that the bitterness of Jack's taunt fell powerless.

"If you don't mind, of course."

"Oh, not at all."

Jack took a step.

"Well then——"

Side by side, watched by silent boys, the two started up the mountain.

Ralph stopped.

"We're silly. Why should only two go? If we find anything, two won't be enough——"

There came the sound of boys scuttling away. Astonishingly, a dark figure moved against the tide.

"Roger?"

"Yes."

"That's three, then."

Once more they set out to climb the slope of the mountain. The darkness seemed to flow round them like a tide. Jack, who had said nothing, began to choke and cough; and a gust of wind set all three spluttering. Ralph's eyes were blinded with tears.

"Ashes. We're on the edge of the burnt patch."

Their footsteps and the occasional breeze were stirring up small devils of dust. Now that they stopped again, Ralph had time while he coughed to remember how silly they were. If there was no beast—and almost certainly there was no beast—in that case, well and good; but if there was something waiting on top of the mountain—what was the use of three of them, handicapped by the darkness and carrying only sticks?

"We're being fools."

Out of the darkness came the answer.

"Windy?"

Irritably Ralph shook himself. This was all Jack's fault.

"'Course I am. But we're still being fools."

"If you don't want to go on," said the voice sarcastically, "I'll go up by myself."

Ralph heard the mockery and hated Jack. The sting of ashes in his eyes, tiredness, fear, enraged him.

"Go on then! We'll wait here."

There was silence.

"Why don't you go? Are you frightened?"

A stain in the darkness, a stain that was Jack, detached itself and began to draw away.

"All right. So long."

The stain vanished. Another took its place.

Ralph felt his knee against something hard and rocked a

charred trunk that was edgy to the touch. He felt the sharp cinders that had been bark push against the back of his knee and knew that Roger had sat down. He felt with his hands and lowered himself beside Roger, while the trunk rocked among invisible ashes. Roger, uncommunicative by nature, said nothing. He offered no opinion on the beast nor told Ralph why he had chosen to come on this mad expedition. He simply sat and rocked the trunk gently. Ralph noticed a rapid and infuriating tapping noise and realized that Roger was banging his silly wooden stick against something.

So they sat, the rocking, tapping, impervious Roger and Ralph, fuming; round them the close sky was loaded with stars, save where the mountain punched up a hole of blackness.

There was a slithering noise high above them, the sound of someone taking giant and dangerous strides on rock or ash. Then Jack found them, and was shivering and croaking in a voice they could just recognize as his.

"I saw a thing on top."

They heard him blunder against the trunk which rocked violently. He lay silent for a moment, then muttered.

"Keep a good lookout. It may be following."

A shower of ash pattered round them. Jack sat up.

"I saw a thing bulge on the mountain."

"You only imagined it," said Ralph shakily, "because nothing would bulge. Not any sort of creature."

Roger spoke; they jumped for they had forgotten him.

"A frog."

Jack giggled and shuddered.

"Some frog. There was a noise too. A kind of 'plop' noise. Then the thing bulged."

Ralph surprised himself, not so much by the quality of his voice, which was even, but by the bravado of its intention.

"We'll go and look."

For the first time since he had first known Jack, Ralph could feel him hesitate.

"Now——?"

His voice spoke for him.

"Of course."

He got off the trunk and led the way across the clinking cinders up into the dark, and the others followed.

Now that his physical voice was silent the inner voice of reason, and other voices too, made themselves heard. Piggy was calling him a kid. Another voice told him not to be a fool; and the darkness and desperate enterprise gave the night a kind of dentist's chair unreality.

As they came to the last slope, Jack and Roger drew near, changed from ink-stains to distinguishable figures. By common consent they stopped and crouched together. Behind them, on the horizon, was a patch of lighter sky where in a moment the moon would rise. The wind roared once in the forest and pushed their rags against them.

Ralph stirred.

"Come on."

They crept forward, Roger lagging a little. Jack and Ralph turned the shoulder of the mountain together. The glittering lengths of the lagoon lay below them and beyond that a long white smudge that was the reef. Roger joined them.

Jack whispered.

"Let's creep forward on hands and knees. Maybe it's asleep."

Roger and Ralph moved on, this time leaving Jack in the rear, for all his brave words. They came to the flat top where the rock was hard to hands and knees.

A creature that bulged.

Ralph put his hand in the cold, soft ashes of the fire and smothered a cry. His hand and shoulder were twitching from the unlooked-for contact. Green lights of nausea appeared for a moment and ate into the darkness. Roger lay behind him and Jack's mouth was at his ear.

"Over there, where there used to be a gap in the rock. A sort of hump—see?"

Ashes blew into Ralph's face from the dead fire. He could not see the gap or anything else, because the green lights were opening again and growing, and the top of the mountain was sliding sideways.

Once more, from a distance, he heard Jack's whisper.

"Scared?"

Not scared so much as paralysed; hung up here immovable on the top of a diminishing, moving mountain. Jack slid away from him, Roger bumped, fumbled with a hiss of breath, and passed onwards. He heard them whispering.

"Can you see anything?"

"There——"

In front of them, only three or four yards away, was a rock-like hump where no rock should be. Ralph could hear a tiny chattering noise coming from somewhere—perhaps from his own mouth. He bound himself together with his will, fused his fear and loathing into a hatred, and stood up. He took two leaden steps forward.

Behind them the sliver of moon had drawn clear of the horizon. Before them, something like a great ape was sitting asleep with its head between its knees. Then the wind roared in the forest, there was confusion in the darkness and the creature lifted its head, holding towards them the ruin of a face.

Ralph found himself taking giant strides among the ashes, heard other creatures crying out and leaping and dared the impossible on the dark slope; presently the mountain was deserted, save for the three abandoned sticks and the thing that bowed.

CHAPTER EIGHT

Gift for the Darkness

Piggy looked up miserably from the dawn-pale beach to the dark mountain.

"Are you sure? Really sure, I mean?"

"I told you a dozen times now," said Ralph, "we saw it."

"D'you think we're safe down here?"

"How the hell should I know?"

Ralph jerked away from him and walked a few paces along the beach. Jack was kneeling and drawing a circular pattern in the sand with his forefinger. Piggy's voice came to them, hushed.

"Are you sure? Really?"

"Go up and see," said Jack contemptuously, "and good riddance."

"No fear."

"The beast had teeth," said Ralph, "and big black eyes."

He shuddered violently. Piggy took off his one round of glass and polished the surface.

"What we going to do?"

Ralph turned towards the platform. The conch glimmered among the trees, a white blob against the place where the sun would rise. He pushed back his mop.

"I don't know."

He remembered the panic flight down the mountain-side.

"I don't think we'd ever fight a thing that size, honestly, you know. We'd talk but we wouldn't fight a tiger. We'd hide. Even Jack'ud hide."

Jack still looked at the sand.

"What about my hunters?"

Simon came stealing out of the shadows by the shelters. Ralph ignored Jack's question. He pointed to the touch of yellow above the sea.

"As long as there's light we're brave enough. But then? And now that thing squats by the fire as though it didn't want us to be rescued——"

He was twisting his hands now, unconsciously. His voice rose.

"So we can't have a signal fire. . . . We're beaten."

A point of gold appeared above the sea and at once all the sky lightened.

"What about my hunters?"

"Boys armed with sticks."

Jack got to his feet. His face was red as he marched away. Piggy put on his one glass and looked at Ralph.

"Now you done it. You been rude about his hunters."

"Oh shut up!"

The sound of the inexpertly blown conch interrupted them. As though he were serenading the rising sun, Jack went on blowing till the shelters were astir and the hunters crept to the platform and the littluns whimpered as now they so frequently did. Ralph rose obediently, and Piggy and they went to the platform.

"Talk," said Ralph bitterly, "talk, talk, talk."

He took the conch from Jack.

"This meeting——"

Jack interrupted him.

"I called it."

"If you hadn't called it I should have. You just blew the conch."

"Well isn't that?"

"Oh, take it! Go on—talk!"

Ralph thrust the conch into Jack's arms and sat down on the trunk.

"I've called an assembly," said Jack, "because of a lot of things. First—you know now, we've seen the beast. We crawled up. We were only a few feet away. The beast sat up and looked at us. I don't know what it does. We don't even know what it is——"

"The beast comes out of the sea——"

"Out of the dark——"

"Trees——"

"Quiet!" shouted Jack. "You, listen. The beast is sitting up there, whatever it is——"

"Perhaps it's waiting——"

"Hunting——"

"Yes, hunting."

"Hunting," said Jack. He remembered his age-old tremors in the forest. "Yes. The beast is a hunter. Only—shut up! The next thing is that we couldn't kill it. And the next thing is that Ralph said my hunters are no good."

"I never said that!"

"I've got the conch. Ralph thinks you're cowards, running away from the boar and the beast. And that's not all."

There was a kind of sigh on the platform as if everyone knew what was coming. Jack's voice went on, tremulous yet determined, pushing against the unco-operative silence.

"He's like Piggy. He says things like Piggy. He isn't a proper chief."

Jack clutched the conch to him.

"He's a coward himself."

For a moment he paused and then went on.

"On top, when Roger and me went on—he stayed back."

"I went too!"

"After."

The two boys glared at each other through screens of hair.

"I went on too," said Ralph, "then I ran away. So did you."

"Call me a coward then."

Jack turned to the hunters.

"He's not a hunter. He'd never have got us meat. He isn't a prefect and we don't know anything about him. He just gives orders and expects people to obey for nothing. All this talk——"

"All this talk!" shouted Ralph. "Talk, talk! Who wanted it? who called the meeting?"

Jack turned, red in the face, his chin sunk back. He glowered up under his eyebrows.

"All right then," he said in tones of deep meaning, and menace, "all right."

He held the conch against his chest with one hand and stabbed the air with his index finger.

"Who thinks Ralph oughtn't to be chief?"

He looked expectantly at the boys ranged round, who had frozen. Under the palms there was deadly silence.

"Hands up," said Jack strongly, "whoever wants Ralph not to be chief?"

The silence continued, breathless and heavy and full of shame. Slowly the red drained from Jack's cheeks, then came back with a painful rush. He licked his lips and turned his head at an angle, so that his gaze avoided the embarrassment of linking with another's eye.

"How many think——"

His voice tailed off. The hands that held the conch shook. He cleared his throat, and spoke loudly.

"All right then."

He laid the conch with great care in the grass at his feet. The humiliating tears were running from the corner of each eye.

"I'm not going to play any longer. Not with you."

Most of the boys were looking down now, at the grass or their feet. Jack cleared his throat again.

"I'm not going to be part of Ralph's lot——"

He looked along the right-hand logs, numbering the hunters that had been a choir.

"I'm going off by myself. He can catch his own pigs. Anyone who wants to hunt when I do can come too."

He blundered out of the triangle towards the drop to the white sand.

"Jack!"

Jack turned and looked back at Ralph. For a moment he paused and then cried out, high-pitched, enraged.

"—No!"

He leapt down from the platform and ran along the beach, paying no heed to the steady fall of his tears; and until he dived into the forest Ralph watched him.

Piggy was indignant.

"I been talking Ralph, and you just stood there like——"

Softly, looking at Piggy and not seeing him, Ralph spoke to himself.

"He'll come back. When the sun goes down he'll come."
He looked at the conch in Piggy's hand.

"What?"

"Well there!"

Piggy gave up the attempt to rebuke Ralph. He polished his glass again and went back to his subject.

"We can do without Jack Merridew. There's others besides him on this island. But now we really got a beast, though I can't hardly believe it, we'll need to stay close to the platform; there'll be less need of him and his hunting. So now we can really decide on what's what."

"There's no help. Piggy. Nothing to be done."

For a while they sat in depressed silence. Then Simon stood up and took the conch from Piggy, who was so astonished that he remained on his feet. Ralph looked up at Simon.

"Simon? What is it this time?"

A half-sound of jeering ran round the circle and Simon shrank from it.

"I thought there might be something to do. Something we——"

Again the pressure of the assembly took his voice away. He sought for help and sympathy and chose Piggy. He turned half towards him, clutching the conch to his brown chest.

"I think we ought to climb the mountain."

The circle shivered with dread. Simon broke off and turned to Piggy who was looking at him with an expression of derisive incomprehension.

"What's the good of climbing up to this here beast when Ralph and the other two couldn't do nothing?"

Simon whispered his answer.

"What else is there to do?"

His speech made, he allowed Piggy to lift the conch out of his hands. Then he retired and sat as far away from the others as possible.

Piggy was speaking now with more assurance and with what, if the circumstances had not been so serious, the others would have recognized as pleasure.

"I said we could all do without a certain person. Now I say we got to decide on what can be done. And I think I could tell you what Ralph's going to say next. The most important thing on the island is the smoke and you can't have no smoke without a fire."

Ralph made a restless movement.

"No go, Piggy. We've got no fire. That thing sits up there—we'll have to stay here."

Piggy lifted the conch as though to add power to his next words.

"We got no fire on the mountain. But what's wrong with a fire down here? A fire could be built on them rocks. On the sand, even. We'd make smoke just the same."

"That's right!"

"Smoke!"

"By the bathing-pool!"

The boys began to babble. Only Piggy could have the intellectual daring to suggest moving the fire from the mountain.

"So we'll have the fire down here," said Ralph. He looked about him. "We can build it just here between the bathing-pool and the platform. Of course——"

He broke off, frowning, thinking the thing out, unconsciously tugging at the stub of a nail with his teeth.

"Of course the smoke won't show so much, not be seen so far away. But we needn't go near; near the——"

The others nodded in perfect comprehension. There would be no need to go near.

"We'll build the fire now."

The greatest ideas are the simplest. Now there was something to be done they worked with passion. Piggy was so full of delight and expanding liberty in Jack's departure, so full of pride in his contribution to the good of society, that he helped to fetch wood. The wood he fetched was close at hand, a fallen tree on the platform that they did not need for the assembly; yet to the others the sanctity of the platform had protected even what was useless there. Then the twins realized they would have a fire near them as a comfort in the night and this set a few littluns dancing and clapping hands.

The wood was not so dry as the fuel they had used on the mountain. Much of it was damply rotten and full of insects that scurried; logs had to be lifted from the soil with care or they crumbled into sodden powder. More than this, in order to avoid going deep into the forest the boys worked near at hand on any fallen wood no matter how tangled with new growth. The skirts of the forest and the scar were familiar, near the conch and the shelters and sufficiently friendly in daylight. What they might become in darkness nobody cared to think. They worked therefore with great energy and cheerfulness, though as time crept by there was a suggestion of panic in the energy and hysteria in the cheerfulness. They built a pyramid of leaves and twigs, branches and logs, on the bare sand by the platform. For the first time on the island, Piggy himself removed his one glass, knelt down and focused the sun on tinder. Soon there was a ceiling of smoke and a bush of yellow flame.

The littluns who had seen few fires since the first catastrophe became wildly excited. They danced and sang and there was a partyish air about the gathering.

At last Ralph stopped work and stood up, smudging the sweat from his face with a dirty forearm.

"We'll have to have a small fire. This one's too big to keep up."

Piggy sat down carefully on the sand and began to polish his glass.

"We could experiment. We could find out how to make a small hot fire and then put green branches on to make smoke. Some of them leaves must be better for that than the others."

As the fire died down so did the excitement. The littluns stopped singing and dancing and drifted away towards the sea or the fruit trees or the shelters.

Ralph flopped down in the sand.

"We'll have to make a new list of who's to look after the fire."

"If you can find 'em."

He looked round. Then for the first time he saw how few biguns there were and understood why the work had been so hard.

"Where's Maurice?"

Piggy wiped his glass again.

"I expect . . . no, he wouldn't go into the forest by himself, would he?"

Ralph jumped up, ran swiftly round the fire and stood by Piggy, holding up his hair.

"But we've got to have a list! There's you and me and Samneric and——"

He would not look at Piggy but spoke casually.

"Where's Bill and Roger?"

Piggy leaned forward and put a fragment of wood on the fire.

"I expect they've gone. I expect they won't play either."

Ralph sat down and began to poke little holes in the sand. He was surprised to see that one had a drop of blood by it. He examined his bitten nail closely and watched the little globe of blood that gathered where the quick was gnawed away.

Piggy went on speaking.

"I seen them stealing off when we was gathering wood. They went that way. The same way as he went himself."

Ralph finished his inspection and looked up into the air. The sky, as if in sympathy with the great changes among them, was different to-day and so misty that in some places the hot air seemed white. The disc of the sun was dull silver as though it were nearer and not so hot, yet the air stifled.

"They always been making trouble, haven't they?"

The voice came near his shoulder and sounded anxious.

"We can do without 'em. We'll be happier now, won't we?"

Ralph sat. The twins came, dragging a great log and grinning in their triumph. They dumped the log among the embers so that sparks flew.

"We can do all right on our own can't we?"

For a long time while the log dried, caught fire and turned red hot, Ralph sat in the sand and said nothing. He did not see Piggy go to the twins and whisper with them, nor how the three boys went together into the forest.

"Here you are."

He came to himself with a jolt. Piggy and the other two were by him. They were laden with fruit.

"I thought perhaps," said Piggy, "we ought to have a feast kind of."

The three boys sat down. They had a great mass of the fruit with them and all of it properly ripe. They grinned at Ralph as he took some and began to eat.

"Thanks," he said. Then with an accent of pleased surprise—"Thanks!"

"Do all right on our own," said Piggy. "It's them that haven't no common sense that make trouble on this island. We'll make a little hot fire——"

Ralph remembered what had been worrying him.

"Where's Simon?"

"I don't know."

"You don't think he's climbing the mountain?"

Piggy broke into noisy laughter and took more fruit.

"He might be." He gulped his mouthful. "He's cracked."

Simon had passed through the area of fruit trees but today the littluns had been too busy with the fire on the beach and they had not pursued him there. He went on among the creepers until he reached the great mat that was woven by the open space and crawled inside. Beyond the screen of leaves the sunlight pelted down and the butterflies danced in the middle their unending dance. He knelt down and the arrow of the sun fell on him. That other time the air had seemed to vibrate with heat; but now it threatened. Soon the sweat was running from his long coarse hair. He shifted restlessly but there was no avoiding the sun. Presently he was thirsty, and then very thirsty.

He continued to sit.

Far off along the beach, Jack was standing before a small group of boys. He was looking brilliantly happy.

"Hunting," he said. He sized them up. Each of them wore the remains of a black cap and ages ago they had stood in two demure rows and their voices had been the song of angels.

"We'll hunt. I'm going to be chief."

They nodded, and the crisis passed easily.

"And then—about the beast."

They moved, looked at the forest.

"I say this. We aren't going to bother about the beast."

He nodded at them.

"We're going to forget the beast."

"That's right!"

"Yes!"

"Forget the beast!"

If Jack was astonished by their fervour he did not show it.

"And another thing. We shan't dream so much down here. This is near the end of the island."

They agreed passionately out of the depths of their tormented private lives.

"Now listen. We might go later to the castle rock. But now I'm going to get more of the biguns away from the conch and all that. We'll kill a pig and give a feast." He paused and went on more slowly. "And about the beast. When we kill we'll leave some of the kill for it. Then it won't bother us, maybe."

He stood up abruptly.

"We'll go into the forest now and hunt."

He turned and trotted away and after a moment they followed him obediently.

They spread out, nervously, in the forest. Almost at once Jack found the dug and scattered roots that told of pig and soon the track was fresh. Jack signalled the rest of the hunt to be quiet and went forward by himself. He was happy and wore the damp darkness of the forest like his old clothes. He crept down a slope to rocks and scattered trees by the sea.

The pigs lay, bloated bags of fat, sensuously enjoying the shadows under the trees. There was no wind and they were unsuspicious; and practice had made Jack silent as the shadows. He stole away again and instructed his hidden hunters. Presently they all began to inch forward sweating in the silence and heat. Under the trees an ear flapped idly. A little apart from the rest, sunk in deep maternal bliss, lay the largest sow of the lot. She was black and pink; and the great bladder of her belly was fringed with a row of piglets that slept or burrowed and squeaked.

Fifteen yards from the drove Jack stopped; and his arm, straightening, pointed at the sow. He looked round in inquiry to make sure that everyone understood and the other boys nodded at him. The row of right arms slid back.

"Now!"

The drove of pigs started up; and at a range of only ten yards the wooden spears with fire-hardened points flew towards the chosen pig. One piglet, with a demented shriek, rushed into the sea trailing Roger's spear behind it. The sow gave a gasping squeal and staggered up, with two spears sticking in her fat flank. The boys shouted and rushed forward, the piglets scattered and the sow burst the advancing line and went crashing away through the forest.

"After her!"

They raced along the pig-track, but the forest was too dark and tangled so that Jack, cursing, stopped them and cast among the trees. Then he said nothing for a time but breathed fiercely so that they were awed by him and looked at each other in uneasy admiration. Presently he stabbed down at the ground with his finger.

"There——"

Before the others could examine the drop of blood, Jack had swerved off, judging a trace, touching a bough that gave. So he followed, mysteriously right and assured; and the hunters trod behind him.

He stopped before a covert.

"In there."

They surrounded the covert but the sow got away with the sting of another spear in her flank. The trailing butts hindered her and the sharp, cross-cut points were a torment. She blundered into a tree, forcing a spear still deeper; and after that any of the hunters could follow her easily by the drops of vivid blood. The afternoon wore on, hazy and dreadful with damp heat; the sow staggered her way ahead of them, bleeding and mad, and the hunters followed, wedded to her in lust, excited by the long chase and the dropped blood. They could see her now, nearly got up with her, but she spurted with her last strength and held ahead of them again. They were just behind her when she staggered into an open space where bright flowers grew and butterflies danced round each other and the air was hot and still.

Here, struck down by the heat, the sow fell and the hunters hurled themselves at her. This dreadful eruption from an unknown world made her frantic; she squealed and bucked and the air was full of sweat and noise and blood and terror. Roger ran round the heap, prodding with his spear whenever pigflesh appeared. Jack was on top of the sow, stabbing downward with his knife. Roger found a lodgment for his point and began to push till he was leaning with his whole weight. The spear moved forward inch by inch and the terrified squealing became a high-pitched scream. Then Jack found the throat and the hot blood spouted over his hands. The sow collapsed under them and they were heavy and fulfilled upon her. The butterflies still danced, preoccupied in the centre of the clearing.

At last the immediacy of the kill subsided. The boys drew back, and Jack stood up, holding out his hands.

"Look."

He giggled and flinked them while the boys laughed at his reeking palms. Then Jack grabbed Maurice and rubbed the stuff over his cheeks. Roger began to withdraw his spear and the boys noticed it for the first time. Robert stabilized the thing in a phrase which was received uproariously.

"Right up her ass!"

"Did you hear?"

"Did you hear what he said?"

"Right up her ass!"

This time Robert and Maurice acted the two parts; and Maurice's acting of the pig's efforts to avoid the advancing spear was so funny that the boys cried with laughter.

At length even this palled. Jack began to clean his bloody hands on the rock. Then he started work on the sow and paunched her, lugging out the hot bags of coloured guts, pushing them into a pile on the rock while the others watched him. He talked as he worked.

"We'll take the meat along the beach. I'll go back to the platform and invite them to a feast. That should give us time."

Roger spoke.

"Chief——"

"Uh——?"

"How can we make a fire?"

Jack squatted back and frowned at the pig.

"We'll raid them and take fire. There must be four of you; Henry and you, Bill and Maurice. We'll put on paint and sneak up; Roger can snatch a branch while I say what I want. The rest of you can get this back to where we were. We'll build the fire there. And after that——"

He paused and stood up, looking at the shadows under the trees. His voice was lower when he spoke again.

"But we'll leave part of the kill for . . ."

He knelt down again and was busy with his knife. The boys crowded round him. He spoke over his shoulder to Roger.

"Sharpen a stick at both ends."

Presently he stood up, holding the dripping sow's head in his hands.

"Where's that stick?"

"Here."

"Ram one end in the earth. Oh—it's rock. Jam it in that crack. There."

Jack held up the head and jammed the soft throat down on the pointed end of the stick which pierced through into the mouth. He stood back and the head hung there, a little blood dribbling down the stick.

Instinctively the boys drew back too; and the forest was very still. They listened, and the loudest noise was the buzzing of flies over the spilled guts.

Jack spoke in a whisper.

"Pick up the pig."

Maurice and Robert skewered the carcass, lifted the dead weight, and stood ready. In the silence, and standing over the dry blood, they looked suddenly furtive.

169

Jack spoke loudly.

"This head is for the beast. It's a gift."

The silence accepted the gift and awed them. The head remained there, dim-eyed, grinning faintly, blood blackening between the teeth. All at once they were running away, as fast as they could, through the forest towards the open beach.

Simon stayed where he was, a small brown image, concealed by the leaves. Even if he shut his eyes the sow's head still remained like an after-image. The half-shut eyes were dim with the infinite cynicism of adult life. They assured Simon that everything was a bad business.

"I know that."

Simon discovered that he had spoken aloud. He opened his eyes quickly and there was the head grinning amusedly in the strange daylight, ignoring the flies, the spilled guts, even ignoring the indignity of being spiked on a stick.

He looked away, licking his dry lips.

A gift for the beast. Might not the beast come for it? The head, he thought, appeared to agree with him. Run away, said the head silently, go back to the others. It was a joke really—why should you bother? You were just wrong, that's all. A little headache, something you ate, perhaps. Go back, child, said the head silently.

Simon looked up, feeling the weight of his wet hair, and gazed at the sky. Up there, for once, were clouds, great bulging towers that sprouted away over the island, grey and cream and copper-coloured. The clouds were sitting on the land; they squeezed, produced moment by moment, this close, tormenting heat. Even the butterflies deserted the open space where the obscene thing grinned and dripped.

Simon lowered his head, carefully keeping his e...
then sheltered them with his hand. There were no sha...
under the trees but everywhere a pearly stillness, so tha...
what was real seemed illusive and without definition. The
pile of guts was a black blob of flies that buzzed like a saw.
After a while these flies found Simon. Gorged, they alighted
by his runnels of sweat and drank. They tickled under his
nostrils and played leap-frog on his thighs. They were black
and iridescent green and without number; and in front of
Simon, the Lord of the Flies hung on his stick and grinned.
At last Simon gave up and looked back; saw the white teeth
and dim eyes, the blood—and his gaze was held by that
ancient, inescapable recognition. In Simon's right temple,
a pulse began to beat on the brain.

Ralph and Piggy lay in the sand, gazing at the fire and
idly flicking pebbles into its smokeless heart.

"That branch is gone."

"Where's Samneric?"

"We ought to get some more wood. We're out of green
branches."

Ralph sighed and stood up. There were no shadows
under the palms on the platform; only this strange light
that seemed to come from everywhere at once. High up
among the bulging clouds thunder went off like a gun.

"We're going to get buckets of rain."

"What about the fire?"

Ralph trotted into the forest and returned with a wide
spray of green which he dumped on the fire. The branch
crackled, the leaves curled and the yellow smoke expanded.

Piggy made an aimless little pattern in the sand with his
fingers.

"Trouble is, we haven't got enough people for a fire. You got to treat Samneric as one turn. They do everything together——"

"Of course."

"Well, that isn't fair. Don't you see? They ought to do two turns."

Ralph considered this and understood. He was vexed to find how little he thought like a grown-up and sighed again. The island was getting worse and worse.

Piggy looked at the fire.

"You'll want another green branch soon."

Ralph rolled over.

"Piggy. What are we going to do?"

"Just have to get on without 'em."

"But—the fire."

He frowned at the black and white mess in which lay the unburnt ends of branches. He tried to formulate.

"I'm scared."

He saw Piggy look up; and blundered on.

"Not of the beast. I mean I'm scared of that too. But nobody else understands about the fire. If someone threw you a rope when you were drowning. If a doctor said take this because if you don't take it you'll die—you would, wouldn't you? I mean?"

"'Course I would."

"Can't they see? Can't they understand? Without the smoke signal we'll die here? Look at that!"

A wave of heated air trembled above the ashes but without a trace of smoke.

"We can't keep one fire going. And they don't care. And what's more——"He looked intensely into Piggy's streaming face.

"What's more, *I* don't sometimes. Supposing I got like the others—not caring. What 'ud become of us?"

Piggy took off his glasses, deeply troubled.

"I dunno, Ralph. We just got to go on, that's all. That's what grown-ups would do."

Ralph, having begun the business of unburdening himself, continued.

"Piggy, what 's wrong?"

Piggy looked at him in astonishment.

"Do you mean the——?"

"No, not it . . . I mean . . . what makes things break up like they do?"

Piggy rubbed his glasses slowly and thought. When he understood how far Ralph had gone towards accepting him he flushed pinkly with pride.

"I dunno, Ralph. I expect it's him."

"Jack?"

"Jack." A taboo was evolving round that word too.

Ralph nodded solemnly.

"Yes," he said, "I suppose it must be."

The forest near them burst into uproar. Demoniac figures with faces of white and red and green rushed out howling, so that the littluns fled screaming. Out of the corner of his eye, Ralph saw Piggy running. Two figures rushed at the fire and he prepared to defend himself but they grabbed half-burnt branches and raced away along the beach. The three others stood still, watching Ralph; and he saw that the tallest of them, stark naked save for paint and a belt, was Jack.

Ralph had his breath back and spoke.

"Well?"

Jack ignored him, lifted his spear and began to shout.

173

"Listen all of you. Me and my hunters, we're living along the beach by a flat rock. We hunt and feast and have fun. If you want to join my tribe come and see us. Perhaps I'll let you join. Perhaps not."

He paused and looked round. He was safe from shame or self-consciousness behind the mask of his paint and could look at each of them in turn. Ralph was kneeling by the remains of the fire like a sprinter at his mark and his face was half-hidden by hair and smut. Samneric peered together round a palm tree at the edge of the forest. A littlun howled, creased and crimson, by the bathing-pool and Piggy stood on the platform, the white conch gripped in his hands.

"To-night we're having a feast. We've killed a pig and we've got meat. You can come and eat with us if you like."

Up in the cloud canyons the thunder boomed again. Jack and the two anonymous savages with him swayed, looked up, and then recovered. The littlun went on howling. Jack was waiting for something. He whispered urgently to the others.

"Go on—now!"

The two savages murmured. Jack spoke sharply.

"Go on!"

The two savages looked at each other, raised their spears together and spoke in time.

"The Chief has spoken."

Then the three of them turned and trotted away.

Presently Ralph rose to his feet, looking at the place where the savages had vanished. Samneric came, talking in an awed whisper.

"I thought it was——"

"—and I was——"

"—scared."

Piggy stood above them on the platform, still holding the conch.

"That was Jack and Maurice and Robert," said Ralph. "Aren't they having fun?"

"I thought I was going to have asthma."

"Sucks to your ass-mar."

"When I saw Jack I was sure he'd go for the conch. Can't think why."

The group of boys looked at the white shell with affectionate respect. Piggy placed it in Ralph's hands and the littluns, seeing the familiar symbol, started to come back.

"Not here."

He turned towards the platform, feeling the need for ritual. First went Ralph, the white conch cradled, then Piggy very grave, then the twins, then the littluns and the others.

"Sit down all of you. They raided us for fire. They're having fun. But the——"

Ralph was puzzled by the shutter that flickered in his brain. There was something he wanted to say; then the shutter had come down.

"But the——"

They were regarding him gravely, not yet troubled by any doubts about his sufficiency. Ralph pushed the idiot hair out of his eyes and looked at Piggy.

"But the . . . oh . . the fire! Of course, the fire!"

He started to laugh, then stopped and became fluent instead.

"The fire's the most important thing. Without the fire we can't be rescued. I'd like to put on war-paint and be a savage. But we must keep the fire burning. The fire's the most important thing on the island, because, because——"

He paused again and the silence became full of doubt and wonder.

Piggy whispered urgently.

"Rescue."

"Oh yes. Without the fire we can't be rescued. So we must stay by the fire and make smoke."

When he stopped no one said anything. After the many brilliant speeches that had been made on this very spot Ralph's remarks seemed lame, even to the littluns.

At last Bill held out his hands for the conch.

"Now we can't have the fire up there—because we can't have the fire up there—we need more people to keep it going. Let's go to this feast and tell them the fire's hard on the rest of us. And then hunting and all that—being savages I mean—it must be jolly good fun."

Samneric took the conch.

"That must be fun like Bill says—and as he's invited us——"

"—to a feast——"

"—meat——"

"—crackling——"

"—I could do with some meat——"

Ralph held up his hand.

"Why shouldn't we get our own meat?"

The twins looked at each other. Bill answered.

"We don't want to go in the jungle."

Ralph grimaced.

"He—you know—goes."

"He's a hunter. They're all hunters. That's different."

No one spoke for a moment, then Piggy muttered to the sand.

"Meat——"

The littluns sat, solemnly thinking of meat and dribbling. Overhead the cannon boomed again and the dry palm-fronds clattered in a sudden gust of hot wind.

"You are a silly little boy," said the Lord of the Flies, "just an ignorant, silly little boy."

Simon moved his swollen tongue but said nothing.

"Don't you agree?" said the Lord of the Flies. "Aren't you just a silly little boy?"

Simon answered him in the same silent voice.

"Well then," said the Lord of the Flies, "you'd better run off and play with the others. They think you're batty. You don't want Ralph to think you're batty, do you? You like Ralph a lot, don't you? And Piggy, and Jack?"

Simon's head was tilted slightly up. His eyes could not break away and the Lord of the Flies hung in space before him.

"What are you doing out here all alone? Aren't you afraid of me?"

Simon shook.

"There isn't anyone to help you. Only me. And I'm the Beast."

Simon's mouth laboured, brought forth audible words.

"Pig's head on a stick."

"Fancy thinking the Beast was something you could hunt and kill!" said the head. For a moment or two the forest and all the other dimly appreciated places echoed with the parody of laughter. "You knew, didn't you? I'm part of you? Close, close, close! I'm the reason why it's no go? Why things are what they are?"

The laughter shivered again.

"Come now," said the Lord of the Flies. "Get back to the others and we'll forget the whole thing."

Simon's head wobbled. His eyes were half-closed as though he were imitating the obscene thing on the stick. He knew that one of his times was coming on. The Lord of the Flies was expanding like a balloon.

"This is ridiculous. You know perfectly well you'll only meet me down there—so don't try to escape!"

Simon's body was arched and stiff. The Lord of the Flies spoke in the voice of a schoolmaster.

"This has gone quite far enough. My poor, misguided child, do you think you know better than I do?"

There was a pause.

"I'm warning you. I'm going to get waxy. D'you see? You're not wanted. Understand? We are going to have fun on this island. Understand? We are going to have fun on this island! So don't try it on, my poor misguided boy, or else——"

Simon found he was looking into a vast mouth. There was blackness within, a blackness that spread.

"—Or else," said the Lord of the Flies, "we shall do you. See? Jack and Roger and Maurice and Robert and Bill and Piggy and Ralph. Do you. See?"

Simon was inside the mouth. He fell down and lost consciousness.

CHAPTER NINE

A View to a Death

O ver the island the build-up of clouds continued.
A steady current of heated air rose all day from
the mountain and was thrust to ten thousand feet;
revolving masses of gas piled up the static until the air was
ready to explode. By early evening the sun had gone and a
brassy glare had taken the place of clear daylight. Even the
air that pushed in from the sea was hot and held no refresh-
ment. Colours drained from water and trees and pink sur-
faces of rock, and the white and brown clouds brooded.
Nothing prospered but the flies who blackened their lord
and made the spilt guts look like a heap of glistening coal.
Even when the vessel broke in Simon's nose and the blood
gushed out they left him alone, preferring the pig's high
flavour.

With the running of the blood Simon's fit passed into
the weariness of sleep. He lay in the mat of creepers while
the evening advanced and the cannon continued to play.
At last he woke and saw dimly the dark earth close by his
cheek. Still he did not move but lay there, his face sideways
on the earth, his eyes looking dully before him. Then he
turned over, drew his feet under him and laid hold of the
creepers to pull himself up. When the creepers shook the

flies exploded from the guts with a vicious note and clamped back on again. Simon got to his feet. The light was unearthly. The Lord of the Flies hung on his stick like a black ball.

Simon spoke aloud to the clearing.

"What else is there to do?"

Nothing replied. Simon turned away from the open space and crawled through the creepers till he was in the dusk of the forest. He walked drearily between the trunks, his face empty of expression, and the blood was dry round his mouth and chin. Only sometimes as he lifted the ropes of creeper aside and chose his direction from the trend of the land, he mouthed words that did not reach the air.

Presently the creepers festooned the trees less frequently and there was a scatter of pearly light from the sky down through the trees. This was the backbone of the island, the slightly higher land that lay beneath the mountain where the forest was no longer deep jungle. Here there were wide spaces interspersed with thickets and huge trees and the trend of the ground led him up as the forest opened. He pushed on, staggering sometimes with his weariness but never stopping. The usual brightness was gone from his eyes and he walked with a sort of glum determination like an old man.

A buffet of wind made him stagger and he saw that he was out in the open, on rock, under a brassy sky. He found his legs were weak and his tongue gave him pain all the time. When the wind reached the mountain-top he could see something happen, a flicker of blue stuff against brown clouds. He pushed himself forward and the wind came again, stronger now, cuffing the forest heads till they ducked and roared. Simon saw a humped thing suddenly sit up on the top and look down at him. He hid his face, and toiled on.

The flies had found the figure too. The life-like movement would scare them off for a moment so that they made a dark cloud round the head. Then as the blue material of the parachute collapsed the corpulent figure would bow forward, sighing, and the flies settle once more.

Simon felt his knees smack the rock. He crawled forward and soon he understood. The tangle of lines showed him the mechanics of this parody; he examined the white nasal bones, the teeth, the colours of corruption. He saw how pitilessly the layers of rubber and canvas held together the poor body that should be rotting away. Then the wind blew again and the figure lifted, bowed, and breathed foully at him. Simon knelt on all fours and was sick till his stomach was empty. Then he took the lines in his hands; he freed them from the rocks and the figure from the wind's indignity.

At last he turned away and looked down at the beaches. The fire by the platform appeared to be out, or at least making no smoke. Further along the beach, beyond the little river and near a great slab of rock, a thin trickle of smoke was climbing into the sky. Simon, forgetful of the flies, shaded his eyes with both hands and peered at the smoke. Even at that distance it was possible to see that most of the boys—perhaps all the boys—were there. So they had shifted camp then, away from the beast. As Simon thought this, he turned to the poor broken thing that sat stinking by his side. The beast was harmless and horrible; and the news must reach the others as soon as possible. He started down the mountain and his legs gave beneath him. Even with great care the best he could do was a stagger.

"Bathing," said Ralph, "that's the only thing to do."

Piggy was inspecting the looming sky through his glass.

"I don't like them clouds. Remember how it rained just after we landed?"

"Going to rain again."

Ralph dived into the pool. A couple of littluns were playing at the edge, trying to extract comfort from a wetness warmer than blood. Piggy took off his glasses, stepped primly into the water and then put them on again. Ralph came to the surface and squirted a jet of water at him.

"Mind my specs," said Piggy. "If I get water on the glass I got to get out and clean 'em."

Ralph squirted again and missed. He laughed at Piggy, expecting him to retire meekly as usual and in pained silence. Instead, Piggy beat the water with his hands.

"Stop it!" He shouted, "D'you hear?"

Furiously he drove the water into Ralph's face.

"All right, all right," said Ralph. "Keep your hair on."

Piggy stopped beating the water.

"I got a pain in my head. I wish the air was cooler."

"I wish the rain would come."

"I wish we could go home."

Piggy lay back against the sloping sand-side of the pool. His stomach protruded and the water dried on it. Ralph squirted up at the sky. One could guess at the movement of the sun by the progress of a light patch among the clouds. He knelt in the water and looked round.

"Where's everybody?"

Piggy sat up.

"P'raps they're lying in the shelter."

"Where's Samneric?"

"And Bill?"

Piggy pointed beyond the platform.

"That's where they've gone. Jack's party."

"Let them go," said Ralph, uneasily, "I don't care."

"Just for some meat——"

"And for hunting," said Ralph, wisely, "and for pretending to be a tribe, and putting on war-paint."

Piggy stirred the sand under water and did not look at Ralph.

"P'raps we ought to go too."

Ralph looked at him quickly and Piggy blushed.

"I mean—to make sure nothing happens."

Ralph squirted water again.

Long before Ralph and Piggy came up with Jack's lot, they could hear the party. There was a stretch of grass in a place where the palms left a wide band of turf between the forest and the shore. Just one step down from the edge of the turf was the white, blown sand of above high water, warm, dry, trodden. Below that again was a rock that stretched away towards the lagoon. Beyond was a short stretch of sand and then the edge of the water. A fire burned on the rock and fat dripped from the roasting pig-meat into the invisible flames. All the boys of the island, except Piggy, Ralph, Simon, and the two tending the pig, were grouped on the turf. They were laughing, singing, lying, squatting, or standing on the grass, holding food in their hands. But to judge by the greasy faces, the meat-eating was almost done; and some held coco-nut shells in their hands and were drinking from them. Before the party had started a great log had been dragged into the centre of the lawn and Jack, painted and garlanded, sat there like an idol. There were piles of meat on green leaves near him, and fruit, and coco-nut shells full of drink.

Piggy and Ralph came to the edge of the grassy platform;

and the boys, as they noticed them, fell silent one by one till only the boy next to Jack was talking. Then the silence intruded even there and Jack turned where he sat. For a time he looked at them and the crackle of the fire was the loudest noise over the bourdon of the reef. Ralph looked away; and Sam, thinking that Ralph had turned to him accusingly, put down his gnawed bone with a nervous giggle. Ralph took an uncertain step, pointed to a palm tree, and whispered something inaudible to Piggy; and they both giggled like Sam. Lifting his feet high out of the sand, Ralph started to stroll past. Piggy tried to whistle.

At this moment the boys who were cooking at the fire suddenly hauled off a great chunk of meat and ran with it towards the grass. They bumped Piggy who was burnt, and yelled and danced. Immediately, Ralph and the crowd of boys were united and relieved by a storm of laughter. Piggy once more was the centre of social derision so that everyone felt cheerful and normal.

Jack stood up and waved his spear.

"Take them some meat."

The boys with the spit gave Ralph and Piggy each a succulent chunk. They took the gift, dribbling. So they stood and ate beneath a sky of thunderous brass that rang with the storm-coming.

Jack waved his spear again.

"Has everybody eaten as much as they want?"

There was still food left, sizzling on the wooden spits, heaped on the green platters. Betrayed by his stomach, Piggy threw a picked bone down on the beach and stooped for more.

Jack spoke again, impatiently.

"Has everybody eaten as much as they want?"

His tone conveyed a warning, given out of the pride of ownership, and the boys ate faster while there was still time. Seeing there was no immediate likelihood of a pause, Jack rose from the log that was his throne and sauntered to the edge of the grass. He looked down from behind his paint at Ralph and Piggy. They moved a little further off over the sand and Ralph watched the fire as he ate. He noticed, without understanding, how the flames were visible now against the dull light. Evening was come, not with calm beauty but with the threat of violence.

Jack spoke.

"Give me a drink."

Henry brought him a shell and he drank, watching Piggy and Ralph over the jagged rim. Power lay in the brown swell of his forearms: authority sat on his shoulder and chattered in his ear like an ape.

"All sit down."

The boys ranged themselves in rows on the grass before him but Ralph and Piggy stayed a foot lower, standing on the soft sand. Jack ignored them for the moment, turned his mask down to the seated boys and pointed at them with the spear.

"Who is going to join my tribe?"

Ralph made a sudden movement that became a stumble. Some of the boys turned towards him.

"I gave you food," said Jack, "and my hunters will protect you from the beast. Who will join my tribe?"

"I'm chief," said Ralph, "because you chose me. And we were going to keep the fire going. Now you run after food——"

"You ran yourself!" shouted Jack. "Look at that bone in your hands!"

Ralph went crimson.

"I said you were hunters. That was your job."

Jack ignored him again.

"Who'll join my tribe and have fun?"

"I'm chief," said Ralph tremulously. "And what about the fire? And I've got the conch——"

"You haven't got it with you," said Jack, sneering. "You left it behind. See, clever? And the conch doesn't count at this end of the island——"

All at once the thunder struck. Instead of the dull boom there was a point of impact in the explosion.

"The conch counts here too," said Ralph, "and all over the island."

"What are you going to do about it then?"

Ralph examined the ranks of boys. There was no help in them and he looked away, confused and sweating. Piggy whispered.

"The fire—rescue."

"Who'll join my tribe?"

"I will."

"Me."

"I will."

"I'll blow the conch," said Ralph breathlessly, "and call an assembly."

"We shan't hear it."

Piggy touched Ralph's wrist.

"Come away. There's going to be trouble. And we've had our meat."

There was a blink of bright light beyond the forest and the thunder exploded again so that a littlun started to whine. Big drops of rain fell among them making individual sounds when they struck.

"Going to be a storm," said Ralph, "and you'll have rain like when we dropped here. Who's clever now? Where are your shelters? What are you going to do about that?"

The hunters were looking uneasily at the sky, flinching from the stroke of the drops. A wave of restlessness set the boys swaying and moving aimlessly. The flickering light became brighter and the blows of the thunder were only just bearable. The littluns began to run about, screaming.

Jack leapt on to the sand.

"Do our dance! Come on! Dance!"

He ran stumbling through the thick sand to the open space of rock beyond the fire. Between the flashes of lightning the air was dark and terrible; and the boys followed him, clamorously. Roger became the pig, grunting and charging at Jack, who side-stepped. The hunters took their spears, the cooks took spits, and the rest clubs of fire-wood. A circling movement developed and a chant. While Roger mimed the terror of the pig, the littluns ran and jumped on the outside of the circle. Piggy and Ralph, under the threat of the sky, found themselves eager to take a place in this demented but partly secure society. They were glad to touch the brown backs of the fence that hemmed in the terror and made it governable.

"*Kill the beast! Cut his throat! Spill his blood!*"

The movement became regular while the chant lost its first superficial excitement and began to beat like a steady pulse. Roger ceased to be a pig and became a hunter, so that the centre of the ring yawned emptily. Some of the littluns started a ring on their own; and the complementary circles went round and round as though repetition would achieve safety of itself. There was the throb and stamp of a single organism.

The dark sky was shattered by a blue-white scar. An instant later the noise was on them like the blow of a gigantic whip. The chant rose a tone in agony.

"*Kill the beast! Cut his throat! Spill his blood!*"

Now out of the terror rose another desire, thick, urgent, blind.

"*Kill the beast! Cut his throat! Spill his blood!*"

Again the blue-white scar jagged above them and the sulphurous explosion beat down. The littluns screamed and blundered about, fleeing from the edge of the forest, and one of them broke the ring of biguns in his terror.

"Him! Him!"

The circle became a horseshoe. A thing was crawling out of the forest. It came darkly, uncertainly. The shrill screaming that rose before the beast was like a pain. The beast stumbled into the horseshoe.

"*Kill the beast! Cut his throat! Spill his blood!*"

The blue-white scar was constant, the noise unendurable. Simon was crying out something about a dead man on a hill.

"*Kill the beast! Cut his throat! Spill his blood! Do him in!*"

The sticks fell and the mouth of the new circle crunched and screamed. The beast was on its knees in the centre, its arms folded over its face. It was crying out against the abominable noise something about a body on the hill. The beast struggled forward, broke the ring and fell over the steep edge of the rock to the sand by the water. At once the crowd surged after it, poured down the rock, leapt on to the beast, screamed, struck, bit, tore. There were no words, and no movements but the tearing of teeth and claws.

Then the clouds opened and let down the rain like a water-fall. The water bounded from the mountain-top, tore leaves and branches from the trees, poured like a cold shower over the struggling heap on the sand. Presently the heap broke up and figures staggered away. Only the beast lay still, a few yards from the sea. Even in the rain they could see how small a beast it was; and already its blood was staining the sand.

Now a great wind blew the rain sideways, cascading the water from the forest trees. On the mountain-top the parachute filled and moved; the figure slid, rose to its feet, spun, swayed down through a vastness of wet air and trod with ungainly feet the tops of the high trees; falling, still falling, it sank towards the beach and the boys rushed screaming into the darkness. The parachute took the figure forward, furrowing the lagoon, and bumped it over the reef and out to sea.

Towards midnight the rain ceased and the clouds drifted away, so that the sky was scattered once more with the incredible lamps of stars. Then the breeze died too and there was no noise save the drip and trickle of water that ran out of clefts and spilled down, leaf by leaf, to the brown earth of the island. The air was cool, moist, and clear; and presently even the sound of the water was still. The beast lay huddled on the pale beach and the stains spread, inch by inch.

The edge of the lagoon became a streak of phosphorescence which advanced minutely, as the great wave of the tide flowed. The clear water mirrored the clear sky and the angular bright constellations. The line of phosphorescence bulged about the sand grains and little pebbles; it held them each in a dimple of tension, then suddenly accepted them with an inaudible syllable and moved on.

A View to a Death

Along the shoreward edge of the shallows the advancing clearness was full of strange, moonbeam-bodied creatures with fiery eyes. Here and there a larger pebble clung to its own air and was covered with a coat of pearls. The tide swelled in over the rain-pitted sand and smoothed everything with a layer of silver. Now it touched the first of the stains that seeped from the broken body and the creatures made a moving patch of light as they gathered at the edge. The water rose further and dressed Simon's coarse hair with brightness. The line of his cheek silvered and the turn of his shoulder became sculptured marble. The strange, attendant creatures, with their fiery eyes and trailing vapours, busied themselves round his head. The body lifted a fraction of an inch from the sand and a bubble of air escaped from the mouth with a wet plop. Then it turned gently in the water.

Somewhere over the darkened curve of the world the sun and moon were pulling; and the film of water on the earth planet was held, bulging slightly on one side while the solid core turned. The great wave of the tide moved further along the island and the water lifted. Softly, surrounded by a fringe of inquisitive bright creatures, itself a silver shape beneath the steadfast constellations, Simon's dead body moved out towards the open sea.

CHAPTER TEN

The Shell and the Glasses

<hr style="border-top: 3px double #8c8b8b;" />

Piggy eyed the advancing figure carefully. Nowadays he sometimes found that he saw more clearly if he removed his glasses and shifted the one lens to the other eye; but even through the good eye, after what had happened, Ralph remained unmistakably Ralph. He came now out of the coco-nut trees, limping, dirty, with dead leaves hanging from his shock of yellow hair. One eye was a slit in his puffy cheek and a great scab had formed on his right knee. He paused for a moment and peered at the figure on the platform.

"Piggy? Are you the only one left?"

"There's some littluns."

"They don't count. No biguns?"

"Oh—Samneric. They're collecting wood."

"Nobody else?"

"Not that I know of."

Ralph climbed on to the platform carefully. The coarse grass was still worn away where the assembly used to sit; the fragile white conch still gleamed by the polished seat. Ralph sat down in the grass facing the Chief's seat and the conch. Piggy knelt at his left, and for a long minute there was silence.

At last Ralph cleared his throat and whispered something. Piggy whispered back.

"What you say?"

Ralph spoke up.

"Simon."

Piggy said nothing but nodded, solemnly. They continued to sit, gazing with impaired sight at the chief's seat and the glittering lagoon. The green light and the glossy patches of sunshine played over their befouled bodies.

At length Ralph got up and went to the conch. He took the shell caressingly with both hands and knelt, leaning against the trunk.

"Piggy."

"Uh?"

"What we going to do?"

Piggy nodded at the conch.

"You could——"

"Call an assembly?"

Ralph laughed sharply as he said the word and Piggy frowned.

"You're still Chief."

Ralph laughed again.

"You are. Over us."

"I got the conch."

"Ralph! Stop laughing like that. Look there ain't no need, Ralph! What's the others going to think?"

At last Ralph stopped. He was shivering.

"Piggy."

"Uh?"

"That was Simon."

"You said that before."

"Piggy."

"Uh?"

"That was murder."

"You stop it!" said Piggy, shrilly. "What good're you doing talking like that?"

He jumped to his feet and stood over Ralph.

"It was dark. There was that—that bloody dance. There was lightning and thunder and rain. We was scared!"

"I wasn't scared," said Ralph slowly, "I was—I don't know what I was."

"We was scared!" said Piggy excitedly. "Anything might have happened. It wasn't—what you said."

He was gesticulating, searching for a formula.

"Oh Piggy!"

Ralph's voice, low and stricken, stopped Piggy's gestures. He bent down and waited. Ralph, cradling the conch, rocked himself to and fro.

"Don't you understand, Piggy? The things we did——"

"He may still be——"

"No."

"P'raps he was only pretending——"

Piggy's voice tailed off at the sight of Ralph's face.

"You were outside. Outside the circle. You never really came in. Didn't you see what we—what they did?"

There was loathing, and at the same time a kind of feverish excitement in his voice.

"Didn't you see, Piggy?"

"Not all that well. I only got one eye now. You ought to know that, Ralph."

Ralph continued to rock to and fro.

"It was an accident," said Piggy suddenly, "that's what it was. An accident." His voice shrilled again. "Coming in the dark—he hadn't no business crawling like that out of the dark. He was batty. He asked for it." He gesticulated widely again. "It was an accident."

"You didn't see what they did——"

"Look, Ralph. We got to forget this. We can't do no good thinking about it, see?"

"I'm frightened. Of us. I want to go home. O God I want to go home."

"It was an accident," said Piggy stubbornly, "and that's that."

He touched Ralph's bare shoulder and Ralph shuddered at the human contact.

"And look, Ralph," Piggy glanced round quickly, then leaned close— "don't let on we was in that dance. Not to Samneric."

"But we were! All of us!"

Piggy shook his head.

"Not us till last. They never noticed in the dark. Anyway you said I was only on the outside——"

"So was I," muttered Ralph, "I was on the outside too."

Piggy nodded eagerly.

"That's right. We was on the outside. We never done nothing, we never seen nothing."

Piggy paused, then went on.

"We'll live on our own, the four of us——"

"Four of us. We aren't enough to keep the fire burning."

"We'll try. See? I lit it."

Samneric came dragging a great log out of the forest. They dumped it by the fire and turned to the pool. Ralph jumped to his feet.

"Hi! You two!"

The twins checked a moment, then walked on.

"They're going to bathe, Ralph."

"Better get it over."

The twins were very surprised to see Ralph. They flushed and looked past him into the air.

"Hullo. Fancy meeting you, Ralph."

"We just been in the forest——"

"—to get wood for the fire——"

"—we got lost last night."

Ralph examined his toes.

"You got lost after the . . ."

Piggy cleaned his lens.

"After the feast," said Sam in a stifled voice. Eric nodded. "Yes, after the feast."

"We left early," said Piggy quickly, "because we were tired."

"So did we——"

"—very early——"

"—we were very tired."

Sam touched a scratch on his forehead and then hurriedly took his hand away. Eric fingered his split lip.

"Yes. We were very tired," repeated Sam, "so we left early. Was it a good——"

The air was heavy with unspoken knowledge. Sam twisted and the obscene word shot out of him. "—dance?"

Memory of the dance that none of them had attended shook all four boys convulsively.

"We left early."

When Roger came to the neck of land that joined the Castle Rock to the mainland he was not surprised to be challenged. He had reckoned, during the terrible night, on finding at least some of the tribe holding out against the horrors of the island in the safest place.

195

The voice rang out sharply from on high, where the diminishing crags were balanced one on another.

"Halt! Who goes there?"

"Roger."

"Advance, friend."

Roger advanced.

"You could see who I was."

"The Chief said we got to challenge everyone."

Roger peered up.

"You couldn't stop me coming if I wanted."

"Couldn't I? Climb up and see."

Roger clambered up the ladder-like cliff.

"Look at this."

A log had been jammed under the topmost rock and another lever under that. Robert leaned lightly on the lever and the rock groaned. A full effort would send the rock thundering down to the neck of land. Roger admired.

"He's a proper Chief, isn't he?"

Robert nodded.

"He's going to take us hunting."

He jerked his head in the direction of the distant shelters where a thread of white smoke climbed up the sky. Roger, sitting on the very edge of the cliff, looked sombrely back at the island as he worked with his fingers at a loose tooth. His gaze settled on the top of the distant mountain and Robert changed the unspoken subject.

"He's going to beat Wilfred."

"What for?"

Robert shook his head doubtfully.

"I don't know. He didn't say. He got angry and made us tie Wilfred up. He's been"—he giggled excitedly—"he's been tied for hours, waiting——"

"But didn't the Chief say why?"

"I never heard him."

Sitting on the tremendous rocks in the torrid sun, Roger received this news as an illumination. He ceased to work at his tooth and sat still, assimilating the possibilities of irresponsible authority. Then, without another word, he climbed down the back of the rocks towards the cave and the rest of the tribe.

The chief was sitting there, naked to the waist, his face blocked out in white and red. The tribe lay in a semicircle before him. The newly beaten and untied Wilfred was sniffing noisily in the background. Roger squatted with the rest.

"To-morrow," went on the Chief, "we shall hunt again."

He pointed at this savage and that with his spear.

"Some of you will stay here to improve the cave and defend the gate. I shall take a few hunters with me and bring back meat. The defenders of the gate will see that the others don't sneak in——"

A savage raised his hand and the chief turned a bleak, painted face towards him.

"Why should they try to sneak in, Chief?"

The Chief was vague but earnest.

"They will. They'll try to spoil things we do. So the watchers at the gate must be careful. And then——"

The Chief paused. They saw a triangle of startling pink dart out, pass along his lips and vanish again.

"——and then; the beast might try to come in. You remember how he crawled——"

The semicircle shuddered and muttered in agreement.

"He came—disguised. He may come again even though

197

we gave him the head of our kill to eat. So watch; and be careful."

Stanley lifted his forearm off the rock and held up an interrogative finger.

"Well?"

"But didn't we, didn't we——?"

He squirmed and looked down.

"No!"

In the silence that followed each savage flinched away from his individual memory.

"No! How could we—kill—it?"

Half-relieved, half-daunted by the implication of further terrors, the savages murmured again.

"So leave the mountain alone," said the Chief, solemnly, "and give it the head if you go hunting."

Stanley flicked his finger again.

"I expect the beast disguised itself."

"Perhaps," said the Chief. A theological speculation presented itself. "We'd better keep on the right side of him, anyhow. You can't tell what he might do."

The tribe considered this; and then were shaken, as if by a flaw of wind. The Chief saw the effect of his words and stood abruptly.

"But to-morrow we'll hunt and when we've got meat we'll have a feast——"

Bill put up his hand.

"Chief."

"Yes?"

"What'll we use for lighting the fire?"

The Chief's blush was hidden by the white and red clay. Into his uncertain silence the tribe spilled their murmur once more. Then the Chief held up his hand.

"We shall take fire from the others. Listen. To-morrow we'll hunt and get meat. To-night I'll go along with two hunters—who'll come?"

Maurice and Roger put up their hands.

"Maurice——"

"Yes, Chief?"

"Where was their fire?"

"Back at the old place by the fire rock."

The Chief nodded.

"The rest of you can go to sleep as soon as the sun sets. But us three, Maurice, Roger and me, we've got work to do. We'll leave just before sunset——"

Maurice put up his hand.

"But what happens if we meet——"

The chief waved his objection aside.

"We'll keep along by the sands. Then if he comes we'll do our, our dance again."

"Only the three of us?"

Again the murmur swelled and died away.

Piggy handed Ralph his glasses and waited to receive back his sight. The wood was damp; and this was the third time they had lighted it. Ralph stood back, speaking to himself.

"We don't want another night without fire."

He looked round guiltily at the three boys standing by. This was the first time he had admitted the double function of the fire. Certainly one was to send up a beckoning column of smoke; but the other was to be a hearth now and a comfort until they slept. Eric breathed on the wood till it glowed and sent out a little flame. A billow of white and yellow smoke reeked up. Piggy took back his glasses and looked at the smoke with pleasure.

"If only we could make a radio!"

"Or a plane——"

"—or a boat."

Ralph dredged in his fading knowledge of the world.

"We might get taken prisoner by the reds."

Eric pushed back his hair.

"They'd be better than——"

He would not name people and Sam finished the sentence for him by nodding along the beach.

Ralph remembered the ungainly figure on a parachute.

"He said something about a dead man——" He flushed painfully at this admission that he had been present at the dance. He made urging motions at the smoke with his body. "Don't stop—go on up!"

"Smoke's getting thinner."

"We need more wood already, even when it's wet."

"My asthma——"

The response was mechanical.

"Sucks to your ass-mar."

"If I pull logs about, I get my asthma bad. I wish I didn't, Ralph, but there it is."

The three boys went into the forest and fetched armfuls of rotten wood. Once more the smoke rose, yellow and thick.

"Let's get something to eat."

Together they went to the fruit trees, carrying their spears, saying little, cramming in haste. When they came out of the forest again the sun was setting and only embers glowed in the fire, and there was no smoke.

"I can't carry any more wood," said Eric. "I'm tired."

Ralph cleared his throat.

"We kept the fire going up there."

"Up there it was small. But this has got to be a big one."

Ralph carried a fragment to the fire and watched the smoke that drifted into the dusk.

"We've got to keep it going."

Eric flung himself down.

"I'm too tired. And what's the good?"

"Eric!" cried Ralph in a shocked voice. "Don't talk like that!"

Sam knelt by Eric.

"Well—what *is* the good?"

Ralph tried indignantly to remember. There was something good about a fire. Something overwhelmingly good.

"Ralph's told you often enough," said Piggy moodily. "How else are we going to be rescued?"

"Of course! If we don't make smoke——"

He squatted before them in the crowding dusk.

"Don't you understand? What's the good of wishing for radios and boats?"

He held out his hand and twisted the fingers into a fist.

"There's only one thing we can do to get out of this mess. Anyone can play at hunting, anyone can get us meat——"

He looked from face to face. Then, at the moment of greatest passion and conviction, that curtain flapped in his head and he forgot what he had been driving at. He knelt there, his fist clenched, gazing solemnly from one to the other. Then the curtain whisked back.

"Oh yes. So we've got to make smoke; and more smoke——"

"But we can't keep it going! Look at that!"

The fire was dying on them.

"Two to mind the fire," said Ralph, half to himself, "that's twelve hours a day."

"We can't get any more wood, Ralph——"

"—not in the dark——"

"—not at night——"

"We can light it every morning," said Piggy. "Nobody ain't going to see smoke in the dark."

Sam nodded vigorously.

"It was different when the fire was——"

"—up there."

Ralph stood up, feeling curiously defenceless with the darkness pressing in.

"Let the fire go then, for to-night."

He led the way to the first shelter, which still stood, though battered. The bed leaves lay within, dry and noisy to the touch. In the next shelter a littlun was talking in his sleep. The four biguns crept into the shelter and burrowed under the leaves. The twins lay together and Ralph and Piggy at the other end. For a while there was the continual creak and rustle of leaves as they tried for comfort.

"Piggy."

"Yeah?"

"All right?"

"S'pose so."

At length, save for an occasional rustle, the shelter was silent. An oblong of blackness relieved with brilliant spangles hung before them and there was the hollow sound of surf on the reef. Ralph settled himself for his nightly game of supposing. . . .

Supposing they could be transported home by jet, then before morning they would land at that big airfield in Wiltshire. They would go by car; no, for things to be perfect they would go by train; all the way down to Devon and take that cottage again. Then at the foot of the garden the wild ponies would come and look over the wall. . . .

Ralph turned restlessly in the leaves. Dartmoor was wild and so were the ponies. But the attraction of wildness had gone.

His mind skated to a consideration of a tamed town where savagery could not set foot. What could be safer than the bus centre with its lamps and wheels?

All at once, Ralph was dancing round a lamp standard. There was a bus crawling out of the bus station, a strange bus. . . .

"Ralph! Ralph!"

"What is it?"

"Don't make a noise like that——"

"Sorry."

From the darkness of the further end of the shelter came a dreadful moaning and they shattered the leaves in their fear. Sam and Eric, locked in an embrace, were fighting each other.

"Sam! Sam!"

"Hey—Eric!"

Presently all was quiet again.

Piggy spoke softly to Ralph.

"We got to get out of this."

"What d'you mean?"

"Get rescued."

For the first time that day, and despite the crowding blackness, Ralph sniggered.

"I mean it," whispered Piggy. "If we don't get home soon we'll be barmy."

"Round the bend."

"Bomb happy."

"Crackers."

Ralph pushed the damp tendrils of hair out of his eyes.

"You write a letter to your auntie."

Piggy considered this solemnly.

"I don't know where she is now. And I haven't got an envelope and a stamp. An' there isn't a pillar-box. Or a postman."

The success of his tiny joke overcame Ralph. His sniggers became uncontrollable, his body jumped and twitched.

Piggy rebuked him with dignity.

"I haven't said anything all that funny——"

Ralph continued to snigger though his chest hurt. His twitchings exhausted him till he lay, breathless and woe-begone, waiting for the next spasm. During one of these pauses he was ambushed by sleep.

"—Ralph! You been making a noise again. Do be quiet, Ralph—because."

Ralph heaved over among the leaves. He had reason to be thankful that his dream was broken, for the bus had been nearer and more distinct.

"Why—because?"

"Be quiet—and listen."

Ralph lay down carefully, to the accompaniment of a long sigh from the leaves. Eric moaned something and then lay still. The darkness, save for the useless oblong of stars, was blanket-thick.

"I can't hear anything."

"There's something moving outside."

Ralph's head prickled. The sound of his blood drowned all else and then subsided.

"I still can't hear anything."

"Listen. Listen for a long time."

Quite clearly and emphatically, and only a yard or so

away from the back of the shelter, a stick cracked. The blood roared again in Ralph's ears, confused images chased each other through his mind. A composite of these things was prowling round the shelters. He could feel Piggy's head against his shoulder and the convulsive grip of a hand.

"Ralph! Ralph!"

"Shut up and listen."

Desperately, Ralph prayed that the beast would prefer littluns.

A voice whispered horribly outside.

"Piggy—Piggy——"

"It's come!" gasped Piggy. "It's real!"

He clung to Ralph and reached to get his breath.

"Piggy, come outside. I want you Piggy."

Ralph's mouth was against Piggy's ear.

"Don't say anything."

"Piggy—where are you, Piggy?"

Something brushed against the back of the shelter. Piggy kept still for a moment, then he had his asthma. He arched his back and crashed among the leaves with his legs. Ralph rolled away from him.

Then there was a vicious snarling in the mouth of the shelter and the plunge and thump of living things. Someone tripped over Ralph and Piggy's corner became a complication of snarls and crashes and flying limbs. Ralph hit out; then he and what seemed like a dozen others were rolling over and over, hitting, biting, scratching. He was torn and jolted, found fingers in his mouth and bit them. A fist withdrew and came back like a piston, so that the whole shelter exploded into light. Ralph twisted sideways on top of a writhing body and felt hot breath on his cheek. He began to pound the mouth below him, using his clenched fist as a hammer; he hit with more and more passionate hysteria as the face became slippery. A knee jerked up between his legs and he fell sideways, busying himself with his pain, and the fight rolled over him. Then the shelter collapsed with smothering finality; and the anonymous shapes fought their way out and through. Dark figures drew themselves out of the wreckage and flitted away, till the screams of the littluns and Piggy's gasps were once more audible.

Ralph called out in a quavering voice.

"All you littluns, go to sleep. We've had a fight with the others. Now go to sleep."

Samneric came close and peered at Ralph.

"Are you two all right?"

"I think so——"

"—I got busted."

"So did I. How's Piggy?"

They hauled Piggy clear of the wreckage and leaned him against a tree. The night was cool and purged of immediate terror. Piggy's breathing was a little easier.

"Did you get hurt, Piggy?"

"Not much."

"That was Jack and his hunters," said Ralph bitterly. "Why can't they leave us alone?"

"We gave them something to think about," said Sam. Honesty compelled him to go on. "At least you did. I got mixed up with myself in a corner."

"I gave one of 'em what for," said Ralph, "I smashed him up all right. He won't want to come and fight us again in a hurry."

"So did I," said Eric. "When I woke up one was kicking me in the face. I got an awful bloody face, I think, Ralph. But I did him in the end."

206

"What did you do?"

"I got my knee up," said Eric with simple pride, "and I hit him with it in the pills. You should have heard him holler! He won't come back in a hurry either. So we didn't do too badly."

Ralph moved suddenly in the dark; but then he heard Eric working at his mouth.

"What's the matter?"

"Jus' a tooth loose."

Piggy drew up his legs.

"You all right, Piggy?"

"I thought they wanted the conch."

Ralph trotted down the pale beach and jumped on to the platform. The conch still glimmered by the chief's seat. He gazed for a moment or two, then went back to Piggy.

"They didn't take the conch."

"I know. They didn't come for the conch. They came for something else. Ralph—what am I going to do?"

Far off along the bowstave of beach, three figures trotted towards the Castle Rock. They kept away from the forest and down by the water. Occasionally they sang softly; occasionally they turned cartwheels down by the moving streak of phosphorescence. The chief led them, trotting steadily, exulting in his achievement. He was a chief now in truth; and he made stabbing motions with his spear. From his left hand dangled Piggy's broken glasses.

CHAPTER ELEVEN

Castle Rock

In the short chill of dawn the four boys gathered round the black smudge where the fire had been, while Ralph knelt and blew. Grey, feathery ashes scurried hither and thither at his breath but no spark shone among them. The twins watched anxiously and Piggy sat expressionless behind the luminous wall of his myopia. Ralph continued to blow till his ears were singing with the effort, but then the first breeze of dawn took the job off his hands and blinded him with ashes. He squatted back, swore, and rubbed water out of his eyes.

"No use."

Eric looked down at him through a mask of dried blood. Piggy peered in the general direction of Ralph.

"'Course it's no use, Ralph. Now we got no fire."

Ralph brought his face within a couple of feet of Piggy's.

"Can you see me?"

"A bit."

Ralph allowed the swollen flap of his cheek to close his eye again.

"They've got our fire."

Rage shrilled his voice.

"They stole it!"

208

"That's them," said Piggy. "They blinded me. See? That's Jack Merridew. You call an assembly, Ralph, we got to decide what to do."

"An assembly for only us?"

"It's all we got. Sam—let me hold on to you."

They went towards the platform.

"Blow the conch," said Piggy. "Blow as loud as you can."

The forest re-echoed; and birds lifted, crying out of the tree-tops, as on that first morning ages ago. Both ways the beach was deserted. Some littluns came from the shelters. Ralph sat down on the polished trunk and the three others stood before him. He nodded, and Samneric sat down on the right. Ralph pushed the conch into Piggy's hands. He held the shining thing carefully and blinked at Ralph.

"Go on, then."

"I just take the conch to say this. I can't see no more and I got to get my glasses back. Awful things has been done on this island. I voted for you for chief. He's the only one who ever got anything done. So now you speak, Ralph, and tell us what— Or else——"

Piggy broke off, snivelling. Ralph took back the conch as he sat down.

"Just an ordinary fire. You'd think we could do that, wouldn't you? Just a smoke signal so we can be rescued. Are we savages or what? Only now there's no signal going up. Ships may be passing. Do you remember how he went hunting and the fire went out and a ship passed by? And they all think he's best as Chief. Then there was, there was . . . that's his fault, too. If it hadn't been for him it would never have happened. Now Piggy can't see, and they came, stealing——" Ralph's voice ran up, "—at night, in darkness, and stole our fire. They stole it. We'd have given them fire if they'd asked. But they stole it and the signal's out and we can't ever be rescued. Don't you see what I mean? We'd have given them fire for themselves only they stole it. I——"

He paused lamely as the curtain flickered in his brain. Piggy held out his hands for the conch.

"What you goin' to do, Ralph? This is jus' talk without deciding. I want my glasses."

"I'm trying to think. Supposing we go, looking like we used to, washed and hair brushed—after all we aren't savages really and being rescued isn't a game——"

He opened the flap of his cheek and looked at the twins.

"We could smarten up a bit and then go——"

"We ought to take spears," said Sam. "Even Piggy."

"—because we may need them."

"You haven't got the conch!"

Piggy held up the shell.

"You can take spears if you want but I shan't. What's the good? I'll have to be led like a dog, anyhow. Yes, laugh. Go on, laugh. There's them on this island as would laugh at anything. And what happened? What's grown-ups goin' to think? Young Simon was murdered. And there was that other kid what had a mark on his face. Who's seen him since we first come here?"

"Piggy! Stop a minute!"

"I got the conch. I'm going to that Jack Merridew an' tell him, I am."

"You'll get hurt."

"What can he do more than he has? I'll tell him what's what. You let me carry the conch, Ralph. I'll show him the one thing he hasn't got."

Piggy paused for a moment and peered round at the dim

figures. The shape of the old assembly, trodden in the grass, listened to him.

"I'm going to him with this conch in my hands. I'm going to hold it out. Look, I'm goin' to say, you're stronger than I am and you haven't got asthma. You can see, I'm goin' to say, and with both eyes. But I don't ask for my glasses back, not as a favour. I don't ask you to be a sport, I'll say, not because you're strong, but because what's right's right. Give me my glasses, I'm going to say—you got to!"

Piggy ended, flushed and trembling. He pushed the conch quickly into Ralph's hands as though in a hurry to be rid of it and wiped the tears from his eyes. The green light was gentle about them and the conch lay at Ralph's feet, fragile and white. A single drop of water that had escaped Piggy's fingers now flashed on the delicate curve like a star.

At last Ralph sat up straight and drew back his hair.

"All right. I mean—you can try if you like. We'll go with you."

"He'll be painted," said Sam, timidly. "You know how he'll be——"

"—he won't think much of us——"

"—if he gets waxy we've had it——"

Ralph scowled at Sam. Dimly he remembered something that Simon had said to him once, by the rocks.

"Don't be silly," he said. And then he added quickly, "Let's go."

He held out the conch to Piggy who flushed, this time with pride.

"You must carry it."

"When we're ready I'll carry it——"

Piggy sought in his mind for words to convey his passionate willingness to carry the conch against all odds.

"—I don't mind. I'll be glad, Ralph, only I'll have to be led."

Ralph put the conch back on the shining log.

"We better eat and then get ready."

They made their way to the devastated fruit trees. Piggy was helped to his food and found some by touch. While they ate, Ralph thought of the afternoon.

"We'll be like we were. We'll wash——"

Sam gulped down a mouthful and protested.

"But we bathe every day!"

Ralph looked at the filthy objects before him and sighed.

"We ought to comb our hair. Only it's too long."

"I've got both socks left in the shelter," said Eric, "so we could pull them over our heads llke caps, sort of."

"We could find some stuff," said Piggy, "and tie your hair back."

"Like a girl!"

"No. 'Course not."

"Then we must go as we are," said Ralph, "and they won't be any better."

Eric made a detaining gesture.

"But they'll be painted! You know how it is——"

The others nodded. They understood only too well the liberation into savagery that the concealing paint brought.

"Well, we won't be painted," said Ralph, "because we aren't savages."

Samneric looked at each other.

"All the same——"

Ralph shouted.

"No paint!"

He tried to remember.

"Smoke," he said, "we want smoke."

He turned on the twins fiercely.

"I said 'smoke'! We've got to have smoke."

There was silence, except for the multitudinous murmur of the bees. At last Piggy spoke, kindly.

"'Course we have. 'Cos the smoke's a signal and we can't be rescued if we don't have smoke."

"I knew that!" shouted Ralph. He pulled his arm away from Piggy. "Are you suggesting——"

"I'm jus' saying what you always say," said Piggy hastily. "I'd thought for a moment——"

"I hadn't," said Ralph loudly. "I knew it all the time. I hadn't forgotten."

Piggy nodded propitiatingly.

"You're Chief, Ralph. You remember everything."

"I hadn't forgotten."

"'Course not."

The twins were examining Ralph curiously, as though they were seeing him for the first time.

They set off along the beach in formation. Ralph went first, limping a little, his spear carried over one shoulder. He saw things partially through the tremble of the heat haze over the flashing sands, and his own long hair and injuries. Behind him came the twins, worried now for a while but full of unquenchable vitality. They said little but trailed the butts of their wooden spears; for Piggy had found, that looking down, shielding his tired sight from the sun, he could just see these moving along the sand. He walked between the trailing butts, therefore, the conch held carefully between his two hands. The boys made a compact little group that moved over the beach, four plate-like shadows dancing and mingling beneath them. There was no sign left of the storm, and the beach was swept clean like a blade that has been scoured. The sky and the mountain were at an immense distance, shimmering in the heat; and the reef was lifted by mirage, floating in a kind of silver pool half-way up the sky.

They passed the place where the tribe had danced. The charred sticks still lay on the rocks where the rain had quenched them but the sand by the water was smooth again. They passed this in silence. No one doubted that the tribe would be found at the Castle Rock and when they came in sight of it they stopped with one accord. The densest tangle on the island, a mass of twisted stems, black and green and impenetrable, lay on their left and tall grass swayed before them. Now Ralph went forward.

Here was the crushed grass where they had all lain when he had gone to prospect. There was the neck of land, the ledge skirting the rock, up there were the red pinnacles.

Sam touched his arm.

"Smoke."

There was a tiny smudge of smoke wavering into the air on the other side of the rock.

"Some fire—I don't think."

Ralph turned.

"What are we hiding for?"

He stepped through the screen of grass on to the little open space that led to the narrow neck.

"You two follow behind. I'll go first, then Piggy a pace behind me. Keep your spears ready."

Piggy peered anxiously into the luminous veil that hung between him and the world.

214

"Is it safe? Ain't there a cliff? I can hear the sea."

"You keep right close to me."

Ralph moved forward on to the neck. He kicked a stone and it bounded into the water. Then the sea sucked down, revealing a red, weedy square forty feet beneath Ralph's left arm.

"Am I safe?" quavered Piggy. "I feel awful——"

High above them from the pinnacles came a sudden shout and then an imitation war-cry that was answered by a dozen voices from behind the rock.

"Give me the conch and stay still."

"Halt! Who goes there?"

Ralph bent back his head and glimpsed Roger's dark face at the top.

"You can see who I am!" he shouted. "Stop being silly!"

He put the conch to his lips and began to blow. Savages appeared, painted out of recognition, edging round the ledge towards the neck. They carried spears and disposed themselves to defend the entrance. Ralph went on blowing and ignored Piggy's terrors.

Roger was shouting.

"You mind out—see?"

At length Ralph took his lips away and paused to get his breath back. His first words were a gasp, but audible.

"—calling an assembly."

The savages guarding the neck muttered among them-selves but made no motion. Ralph walked forwards a couple of steps. A voice whispered urgently behind him.

"Don't leave me, Ralph."

"You kneel down," said Ralph sideways, "and wait till I come back."

He stood half-way along the neck and gazed at the savages

215

intently. Freed by the paint, they had tied their hair back and were more comfortable than he was. Ralph made a resolution to tie his own back afterwards. Indeed he felt like telling them to wait and doing it there and then; but that was impossible. The savages sniggered a bit and one gestured at Ralph with his spear. High above, Roger took his hands off the lever and leaned out to see what was going on. The boys on the neck stood in a pool of their own shadow, diminished to shaggy heads. Piggy crouched, his back shapeless as a sack.

"I'm calling an assembly."

Silence.

Roger took up a small stone and flung it between the twins, aiming to miss. They started and Sam only just kept his footing. Some source of power began to pulse in Roger's body.

Ralph spoke again, loudly.

"I'm calling an assembly."

He ran his eye over them.

"Where's Jack?"

The group of boys stirred and consulted. A painted face spoke with the voice of Robert.

"He's hunting. And he said we weren't to let you in."

"I've come to see about the fire," said Ralph, "and about Piggy's specs."

The group in front of him shifted and laughter shivered outwards from among them, light, excited laughter that went echoing among the tall rocks.

A voice spoke from behind Ralph.

"What do you want?"

The twins made a bolt past Ralph and got between him and the entry. He turned quickly. Jack, identifiable by

personality and red hair, was advancing from the forest. A
hunter crouched on either side. All three were masked in
black and green. Behind them on the grass the headless and
paunched body of a sow lay where they had dropped it.

Piggy wailed.

"Ralph! Don't leave me!"

With ludicrous care he embraced the rock, pressing himself to it above the sucking sea. The sniggering of the
savages became a loud derisive jeer.

Jack shouted above the noise.

"You go away, Ralph. You keep to your end. This is my
end and my tribe. You leave me alone."

The jeering died away.

"You pinched Piggy's specs," said Ralph, breathlessly.
"You've got to give them back."

"Got to? Who says?"

Ralph's temper blazed out.

"I say! You voted for me for Chief. Didn't you hear the
conch? You played a dirty trick—we'd have given you fire
if you'd asked for it——"

The blood was flowing in his cheeks and the bunged-up
eye throbbed.

"You could have had fire whenever you wanted. But you
didn't. You came sneaking up like a thief and stole Piggy's
glasses!"

"Say that again!"

"Thief! Thief!"

Piggy screamed.

"Ralph! Mind me!"

Jack made a rush and stabbed at Ralph's chest with his
spear. Ralph sensed the position of the weapon from the
glimpse he caught of Jack's arm and put the thrust aside

with his own butt. Then he brought the end round and caught Jack a stinger across the ear. They were chest to chest, breathing fiercely, pushing and glaring.

"Who's a thief?"

"You are!"

Jack wrenched free and swung at Ralph with his spear. By common consent they were using the spears as sabres now, no longer daring the lethal points. The blow struck Ralph's spear and slid down, to fall agonizingly on his fingers. Then they were apart once more, their positions reversed, Jack towards the Castle Rock and Ralph on the outside towards the island.

Both boys were breathing very heavily.

"Come on then——"

"Come on——"

Truculently they squared up to each other but kept just out of fighting distance.

"You come on and see what you get!"

"You come on——"

Piggy clutching the ground was trying to attract Ralph's attention. Ralph moved, bent down, kept a wary eye on Jack.

"Ralph—remember what we came for. The fire. My specs."

Ralph nodded. He relaxed his fighting muscles, stood easily and grounded the butt of his spear. Jack watched him inscrutably through his paint. Ralph glanced up at the pinnacles, then towards the group of savages.

"Listen. We've come to say this. First you've got to give back Piggy's specs. If he hasn't got them he can't see. You aren't playing the game——"

The tribe of painted savages giggled and Ralph's mind

faltered. He pushed his hair up and gazed at the green and black mask before him, trying to remember what Jack looked like.

Piggy whispered.

"And the fire."

"Oh yes. Then about the fire. I say this again. I've been saying it ever since we dropped in."

He held out his spear and pointed at the savages.

"Your only hope is keeping a signal fire going as long as there's light to see. Then maybe a ship 'll notice the smoke and come and rescue us and take us home. But without that smoke we've got to wait till some ship comes by accident. We might wait years; till we were old——"

The shivering, silvery, unreal laughter of the savages sprayed out and echoed away. A gust of rage shook Ralph. His voice cracked.

"Don't you understand, you painted fools? Sam, Eric, Piggy and me—we aren't enough. We tried to keep the fire going, but we couldn't. And then you, playing at hunting. . . ."

He pointed past them to where the trickle of smoke dispersed in the pearly air.

"Look at that! Call that a signal fire? That's a cooking fire. Now you'll eat and there'll be no smoke. Don't you understand? There may be a ship out there——"

He paused, defeated by the silence and the painted anonymity of the group guarding the entry. The chief opened a pink mouth and addressed Samneric who were between him and his tribe.

"You two. Get back."

No one answered him. The twins, puzzled, looked at each other; while Piggy, reassured by the cessation of violence, stood up carefully. Jack glanced back at Ralph and then at the twins.

"Grab them!"

No one moved. Jack shouted angrily.

"I said 'grab them'!"

The painted group moved round Samneric nervously and unhandily. Once more the silvery laughter scattered.

Samneric protested out of the heart of civilization.

"Oh, I say!"

"—honestly!"

Their spears were taken from them.

"Tie them up!"

Ralph cried out hopelessly against the black and green mask.

"Jack!"

"Go on. Tie them."

Now the painted group felt the otherness of Samneric, felt the power in their own hands. They felled the twins clumsily and excitedly. Jack was inspired. He knew that Ralph would attempt a rescue. He struck in a humming circle behind him and Ralph only just parried the blow. Beyond them the tribe and the twins were a loud and writhing heap. Piggy crouched again. Then the twins lay, astonished, and the tribe stood round them. Jack turned to Ralph and spoke between his teeth.

"See? They do what I want."

There was silence again. The twins lay, inexpertly tied up, and the tribe watched Ralph to see what he would do. He numbered them through his fringe, glimpsed the ineffectual smoke.

His temper broke. He screamed at Jack.

"You're a beast and a swine and a bloody, bloody thief!"

He charged.

Jack, knowing this was the crisis, charged too. They met with a jolt and bounced apart. Jack swung with his fist at Ralph and caught him on the ear. Ralph hit Jack in the stomach and made him grunt. Then they were facing each other again, panting and furious, but unnerved by each other's ferocity. They became aware of the noise that was the background to this fight, the steady shrill cheering of the tribe behind them.

Piggy's voice penetrated to Ralph.

"Let me speak."

He was standing in the dust of the fight, and as the tribe saw his intention the shrill cheer changed to a steady booing.

Piggy held up the conch and the booing sagged a little, then came up again to strength.

"I got the conch!"

He shouted.

"I tell you, I got the conch!"

Surprisingly, there was silence now; the tribe were curious to hear what amusing thing he might have to say.

Silence and pause; but in the silence a curious air-noise, close by Ralph's head. He gave it half his attention—and there it was again; a faint "Zup!" Someone was throwing stones: Roger was dropping them, his one hand still on the lever. Below him, Ralph was a shock of hair and Piggy a bag of fat.

"I got this to say. You're acting like a crowd of kids."

The booing rose and died again as Piggy lifted the white, magic shell.

"Which is better—to be a pack of painted niggers like you are, or to be sensible like Ralph is?"

at clamour rose among the savages. Piggy shouted

"Which is better—to have rules and agree, or to hunt and kill?"

Again the clamour and again—"Zup!"

Ralph shouted against the noise.

"Which is better, law and rescue, or hunting and breaking things up?"

Now Jack was yelling too and Ralph could no longer make himself heard. Jack had backed right against the tribe and they were a solid mass of menace that bristled with spears. The intention of a charge was forming among them; they were working up to it and the neck would be swept clear. Ralph stood facing them, a little to one side, his spear ready. By him stood Piggy still holding out the talisman, the fragile, shining beauty of the shell. The storm of sound beat at them, an incantation of hatred. High overhead, Roger, with a sense of delirious abandonment, leaned all his weight on the lever.

Ralph heard the great rock long before he saw it. He was aware of a jolt in the earth that came to him through the soles of his feet, and the breaking sound of stones at the top of the cliff. Then the monstrous red thing bounded across the neck and he flung himself flat while the tribe shrieked.

The rock struck Piggy a glancing blow from chin to knee; the conch exploded into a thousand white fragments and ceased to exist. Piggy, saying nothing, with no time for even a grunt, travelled through the air sideways from the rock, turning over as he went. The rock bounded twice and was lost in the forest. Piggy fell forty feet and landed on his back across that square, red rock in the sea. His head opened and stuff came out and turned red. Piggy's arms and legs twitched a bit, like a pig's after it has been killed. Then the sea breathed again in a long, slow sigh, the water boiled white and pink over the rock; and when it went, sucking back again, the body of Piggy was gone.

This time the silence was complete. Ralph's lips formed a word but no sound came.

Suddenly Jack bounded out from the tribe and began screaming wildly.

"See? See? That's what you'll get! I meant that! There isn't a tribe for you any more! The conch is gone——"

He ran forward, stooping.

"I'm Chief!"

Viciously, with full intention, he hurled his spear at Ralph. The point tore the skin and flesh over Ralph's ribs, then sheared off and fell in the water. Ralph stumbled, feeling not pain but panic, and the tribe, screaming now like the Chief, began to advance. Another spear, a bent one that would not fly straight, went past his face and one fell from on high where Roger was. The twins lay hidden behind the tribe and the anonymous devils' faces swarmed across the neck. Ralph turned and ran. A great noise as of sea-gulls rose behind him. He obeyed an instinct that he did not know he possessed and swerved over the open space so that the spears went wide. He saw the headless body of the sow and jumped in time. Then he was crashing through foliage and small boughs and was hidden by the forest.

The Chief stopped by the pig, turned and held up his hands.

"Back! Back to the fort!"

Presently the tribe returned noisily to the neck where Roger joined them.

The Chief spoke to him angrily.

"Why aren't you on watch?"

Roger looked at him gravely.

"I just came down——"

The hangman's horror clung round him. The Chief said no more to him but looked down at Samneric.

"You got to join the tribe."

"You lemme go——"

"——and me."

The Chief snatched one of the few spears that were left and poked Sam in the ribs.

"What d'you mean by it, eh?" said the Chief fiercely. "What d'you mean by coming with spears? What d'you mean by not joining my tribe?"

The prodding became rhythmic. Sam yelled.

"That's not the way."

Roger edged past the Chief, only just avoiding pushing him with his shoulder. The yelling ceased, and Samneric lay looking up in quiet terror. Roger advanced upon them as one wielding a nameless authority.

CHAPTER TWELVE

Cry of the Hunters

———◆———

Ralph lay in a covert, wondering about his wounds. The bruised flesh was inches in diameter over his right ribs, with a swollen and bloody scar where the spear had hit him. His hair was full of dirt and tapped like the tendrils of a creeper. All over he was scratched and bruised from his flight through the forest. By the time his breathing was normal again, he had worked out that bathing these injuries would have to wait. How could you listen for naked feet if you were splashing in water? How could you be safe by the little stream or on the open beach?

Ralph listened. He was not really far from the Castle Rock, and during the first panic he had thought he heard sounds of pursuit. But the hunters had only sneaked into the fringes of the greenery, retrieving spears perhaps, and then had rushed back to the sunny rock as if terrified of the darkness under the leaves. He had even glimpsed one of them, striped brown, black, and red, and had judged that it was Bill. But really, thought Ralph, this was not Bill. This was a savage whose image refused to blend with that ancient picture of a boy in shorts and shirt.

The afternoon died away; the circular spots of sunlight moved steadily over green fronds and brown fibre but no sound came from behind the Rock. At last Ralph wormed out of the ferns and sneaked forward to the edge of that impenetrable thicket that fronted the neck of land. He peered with elaborate caution between branches at the edge and could see Robert sitting on guard at the top of the cliff. He held a spear in his left hand and was tossing up a pebble and catching it again with the right. Behind him a column of smoke rose thickly, so that Ralph's nostrils flared and his mouth dribbled. He wiped his nose and mouth with the back of his hand and for the first time since the morning felt hungry. The tribe must be sitting round the gutted pig, watching the fat ooze and burn among the ashes. They would be intent.

Another figure, an unrecognizable one, appeared by Robert and gave him something, then turned and went back behind the rock. Robert laid his spear on the rock beside him and began to gnaw between his raised hands. So the feast was beginning and the watchman had been given his portion.

Ralph saw that for the time being he was safe. He limped away through the fruit trees, drawn by the thought of the poor food yet bitter when he remembered the feast. Feast to-day, and then to-morrow. . . .

He argued unconvincingly that they would let him alone; perhaps even make an outlaw of him. But then the fatal unreasoning knowledge came to him again. The breaking of the conch and the deaths of Piggy and Simon lay over the island like a vapour. These painted savages would go further and further. Then there was that indefinable connection between himself and Jack; who therefore would never let him alone; never.

He paused, sun-flecked, holding up a bough, prepared to

duck under it. A spasm of terror set him shaking and he cried aloud.

"No. They're not as bad as that. It was an accident."

He ducked under the bough, ran clumsily, then stopped and listened.

He came to the smashed acres of fruit and ate greedily. He saw two littluns and, not having any idea of his own appearance, wondered why they screamed and ran.

When he had eaten he went towards the beach. The sunlight was slanting now into the palms by the wrecked shelter. There was the platform and the pool. The best thing to do was to ignore this leaden feeling about the heart and rely on their common sense, their daylight sanity. Now that the tribe had eaten, the thing to do was to try again. And anyway, he couldn't stay here all night in an empty shelter by the deserted platform. His flesh crept and he shivered in the evening sun. No fire; no smoke; no rescue. He turned and limped away through the forest towards Jack's end of the island.

The slanting sticks of sunlight were lost among the branches. At length he came to a clearing in the forest where rock prevented vegetation from growing. Now it was a pool of shadows and Ralph nearly flung himself behind a tree when he saw something standing in the centre; but then he saw that the white face was bone and that the pig's skull grinned at him from the top of a stick. He walked slowly into the middle of the clearing and looked steadily at the skull that gleamed as white as ever the conch had done and seemed to jeer at him cynically. An inquisitive ant was busy in one of the eye sockets but otherwise the thing was lifeless.

Or was it?

Little prickles of sensation ran up and down his back.

He stood, the skull about on a level with his face, and held up his hair with two hands. The teeth grinned, the empty sockets seemed to hold his gaze masterfully and without effort.

What was it?

The skull regarded Ralph like one who knows all the answers and won't tell. A sick fear and rage swept him. Fiercely he hit out at the filthy thing in front of him that bobbed like a toy and came back, still grinning into his face, so that he lashed and cried out in loathing. Then he was licking his bruised knuckles and looking at the bare stick, while the skull lay in two pieces, its grin now six feet across. He wrenched the quivering stick from the crack and held it as a spear between him and the white pieces. Then he backed away, keeping his face to the skull that lay grinning at the sky.

When the green glow had gone from the horizon and night was fully accomplished, Ralph came again to the thicket in front of the Castle Rock. Peeping through, he could see that the height was still occupied, and whoever it was up there had a spear at the ready.

He knelt among the shadows and felt his isolation bitterly. They were savages it was true; but they were human, and the ambushing fears of the deep night were coming on.

Ralph moaned faintly. Tired though he was, he could not relax and fall into a well of sleep for fear of the tribe. Might it not be possible to walk boldly into the fort, say— "I've got pax," laugh lightly and sleep among the others? Pretend they were still boys, schoolboys who had said "Sir, yes, Sir"—and worn caps? Daylight might have answered yes; but darkness and the horrors of death said no. Lying there in the darkness, he knew he was an outcast.

" 'Cos I had some sense."

He rubbed his cheek along his forearm, smelling the acrid scent of salt and sweat and the staleness of dirt. Over to the left, the waves of ocean were breathing, sucking down, then boiling back over the rock.

There were sounds coming from behind the Castle Rock. Listening carefully, detaching his mind from the swing of the sea, Ralph could make out a familiar rhythm.

"Kill the beast! Cut his throat! Spill his blood!"

The tribe was dancing. Somewhere on the other side of this rocky wall there would be a dark circle, a glowing fire, and meat. They would be savouring food and the comfort of safety.

A noise nearer at hand made him quiver. Savages were clambering up the Castle Rock, right up to the top, and he could hear voices. He sneaked forward a few yards and saw the shape at the top of the rock change and enlarge. There were only two boys on the island who moved or talked like that.

Ralph put his head down on his forearms and accepted this new fact like a wound. Samneric were part of the tribe now. They were guarding the Castle Rock against him. There was no chance of rescuing them and building up an outlaw tribe at the other end of the island. Samneric were savages like the rest; Piggy was dead, and the conch smashed to powder.

At length the guard climbed down. The two that remained seemed nothing more than a dark extension of the rock. A star appeared behind them and was momentarily eclipsed by some movement.

Ralph edged forward, feeling his way over the uneven surface as though he were blind. There were miles of vague water at his right and the restless ocean lay under his left hand, as awful as the shaft of a pit. Every minute the water breathed round the death rock and flowered into a field of whiteness. Ralph crawled until he found the ledge of the entry in his grasp. The lookouts were immediately above him and he could see the end of a spear projecting over the rock.

He called very gently.

"Samneric——"

There was no reply. To carry he must speak louder; and this would rouse those striped and inimical creatures from their feasting by the fire. He set his teeth and started to climb, finding the holds by touch. The stick that had supported a skull hampered him but he would not be parted from his only weapon. He was nearly level with the twins before he spoke again.

"Samneric——"

He heard a cry and a flurry from the rock. The twins had grabbed each other and were gibbering.

"It's me. Ralph."

Terrified that they would run and give the alarm, he hauled himself up until his head and shoulders stuck over the top. Far below his armpit he saw the luminous flowering round the rock.

"It's only me. Ralph."

At length they bent forward and peered in his face.

"We thought it was——"

"—we didn't know what it was——"

"—we thought——"

Memory of their new and shameful loyalty came to them. Eric was silent but Sam tried to do his duty.

"You got to go, Ralph. You go away now——"

He wagged his spear and essayed fierceness.

"You shove off. See?"

Eric nodded agreement and jabbed his spear in the air. Ralph leaned on his arms and did not go.

"I came to see you two."

His voice was thick. His throat was hurting him now though it had received no wound.

"I came to see you two——"

Words could not express the dull pain of these things. He fell silent, while the vivid stars were spilt and danced all ways.

Sam shifted uneasily.

"Honest, Ralph, you'd better go."

Ralph looked up again.

"You two aren't painted. How can you—? If it were light——"

If it were light shame would burn them at admitting these things. But the night was dark. Eric took up; and then the twins started their antiphonal speech.

"You got to go because it's not safe——"

"—they made us. They hurt us——"

"Who? Jack?"

"Oh no——"

They bent to him and lowered their voices.

"Push off, Ralph——"

"—it's a tribe——"

"—they made us——"

"—we couldn't help it——"

When Ralph spoke again his voice was low, and seemed breathless.

"What have I done? I liked him—and I wanted us to be rescued——"

231

Again the stars spilled about the sky. Eric shook his head, earnestly.

"Listen, Ralph. Never mind what's sense. That's gone——"

"Never mind about the chief——"

"——you got to go for your own good."

"The chief and Roger——"

"——yes, Roger——"

"They hate you, Ralph. They're going to do you."

"They're going to hunt you to-morrow."

"But why?"

"I dunno. And Ralph, Jack, the Chief, says it'll be dangerous——"

"——and we've got to be careful and throw our spears like at a pig."

"We're going to spread out in a line across the island——"

"——we're going forward from this end——"

"——until we find you."

"We've got to give signals like this."

Eric raised his head and achieved a faint ululation by beating on his open mouth. Then he glanced behind him nervously.

"Like that——"

"——only louder, of course."

"But I've done nothing," whispered Ralph, urgently. "I only wanted to keep up a fire!"

He paused for a moment, thinking miserably of the morrow. A matter of overwhelming importance occurred to him.

"What are you——"

He could not bring himself to be specific at first; but then fear and loneliness goaded him.

"When they find me, what are they going to do?"

The twins were silent. Beneath him, the death rock flowered again.

"What are they—oh God! I'm hungry——"

The towering rock seemed to sway under him.

"Well—what——"

The twins answered his question indirectly.

"You got to go now, Ralph."

"For your own good."

"Keep away. As far as you can."

"Won't you come with me? Three of us—we'd stand a chance."

After a moment's silence, Sam spoke in a strangled voice.

"You don't know Roger. He's a terror."

"—And the Chief—they're both——"

"—terrors——"

"—only Roger——"

Both boys froze. Someone was climbing towards them from the tribe.

"He's coming to see if we're keeping watch. Quick, Ralph!"

As he prepared to let himself down the cliff, Ralph snatched at the last possible advantage to be wrung out of this meeting.

"I'll lie up close; in that thicket down there," he whispered, "so keep them away from it. They'll never think to look so close——"

The footsteps were still some distance away.

"Sam—I'm going to be all right, aren't I?"

The twins were silent again.

"Here!" said Sam suddenly. "Take this——"

Ralph felt a chunk of meat pushed against him and grabbed it.

"But what are you going to do when you catch me?"

Silence above. He sounded silly to himself. He lowered himself down the rock.

"What are you going to do——?"

From the top of the towering rock came the incomprehensible reply.

"Roger sharpened a stick at both ends."

Roger sharpened a stick at both ends. Ralph tried to attach a meaning to this but could not. He used all the bad words he could think of in a fit of temper that passed into yawning. How long could you go without sleep? He yearned for a bed and sheets—but the only whiteness here was the slow spilt milk, luminous round the rock forty feet below, where Piggy had fallen. Piggy was everywhere, was on this neck, was become terrible in darkness and death. If Piggy were to come back now out of the water, with his empty head—Ralph whimpered and yawned like a littlun. The stick in his hand became a crutch on which he reeled.

Then he tensed again. There were voices raised on the top of the Castle Rock. Samneric were arguing with someone. But the ferns and the grass were near. That was the place to be in, hidden, and next to the thicket that would serve for to-morrow's hide-out. Here—and his hands touched grass—was a place to be in for the night, not far from the tribe, so that if the horrors of the supernatural emerged one could at least mix with humans for the time being, even if it meant . . .

What did it mean? A stick sharpened at both ends. What was there in that? They had thrown spears and missed; all but one. Perhaps they would miss next time, too.

He squatted down in the tall grass, remembered the meat that Sam had given him, and began to tear at it ravenously.

While he was eating, he heard fresh noises—cries of pain from Samneric, cries of panic, angry voices. What did it mean? Someone besides himself was in trouble for at least one of the twins was catching it. Then the voices passed away down the rock and he ceased to think of them. He felt with his hands and found cool, delicate fronds backed against the thicket. Here then was the night's lair. At first light he would creep into the thicket, squeeze between the twisted stems, ensconce himself so deep so that only a crawler like himself could come through; and that crawler would be jabbed. There he would sit, and the search would pass him by, and the cordon waver on, ululating along the island, and he would be free.

He pulled himself between the ferns, tunnelling in. He laid the stick beside him, and huddled himself down in the blackness. One must remember to wake at first light, in order to diddle the savages—and he did not know how quickly sleep came and hurled him down a dark interior slope.

He was awake before his eyes were open, listening to a noise that was near. He opened an eye, found the mould an inch or so from his face and his fingers gripped into it, light filtering between the fronds of fern. He had just time to realize that the age-long nightmares of falling and death were past and that the morning was come, when he heard the sound again. It was an ululation over by the seashore—and now the next savage answered and the next. The cry swept by him across the narrow end of the island from sea to lagoon, like the cry of a flying bird. He took no time to consider but grabbed his sharp stick and wriggled back among the ferns. Within seconds he was worming his way into the thicket; but not before he had glimpsed the legs of a savage coming towards him. The ferns were thumped and beaten and he heard legs moving in the long grass. The savage, whoever he was, ululated twice; and the cry was repeated in both directions, then died away. Ralph crouched still, tangled in the mid-brake, and for a time he heard nothing.

At last he examined the brake itself. Certainly no one could attack him here—and moreover he had a stroke of luck. The great rock that had killed Piggy had bounded into this thicket and bounced there, right in the centre, making a smashed space a few feet in extent each way. When Ralph had wriggled into this he felt secure, and clever. He sat down carefully among the smashed stems and waited for the hunt to pass. Looking up between the leaves he caught a glimpse of something red. That must be the top of the Castle Rock, distant and unmenacing. He composed himself triumphantly, to hear the sounds of the hunt dying away.

Yet no one made a sound; and as the minutes passed, in the green shade, his feeling of triumph faded.

At last he heard a voice—Jack's voice, but hushed.

"Are you certain?"

The savage addressed said nothing. Perhaps he made a gesture.

Roger spoke.

"If you're fooling us——"

Immediately after this, there came a gasp, and a squeal of pain. Ralph crouched instinctively. One of the twins was there, outside the thicket, with Jack and Roger.

"You're sure he meant in there?"

The twin moaned faintly and then squealed again.

"He meant he'd hide in there?"

"Yes—yes—oh——!"

Silvery laughter scattered among the trees.

So they knew.

Ralph picked up his stick and prepared for battle. But what could they do? It would take them a week to break a path through the thicket; and anyone who wormed his way in would be helpless. He felt the point of his spear with his thumb and grinned without amusement. Whoever tried that would be stuck, squealing like a pig.

They were going away, back to the tower rock. He could hear feet moving and then someone sniggered. There came again that high, bird-like cry that swept along the line. So some were still watching for him; but some——?

There was a long, breathless silence. Ralph found that he had bark in his mouth from the gnawed spear. He stood and peered upwards to the Castle Rock.

As he did so, he heard Jack's voice from the top.

"Heave! Heave! Heave!"

The red rock that he could see at the top of the cliff vanished like a curtain, and he could see figures and blue sky. A moment later the earth jolted, there was a rushing sound in the air, and the top of the thicket was cuffed as with a gigantic hand. The rock bounded on, thumping and smashing towards the beach, while a shower of broken twigs and leaves fell on him. Beyond the thicket, the tribe was cheering.

Silence again.

Ralph put his fingers in his mouth and bit them. There was only one other rock up there that they might conceivably move; but that was half as big as a cottage, big as a car, a tank. He visualized its probable progress with agonizing clearness—that one would start slowly, drop from ledge to ledge, trundle across the neck like an out-size steam-roller.

"Heave! Heave! Heave!"

Ralph put down his spear, then picked it up again. He pushed his hair back irritably, took two hasty steps across the little space and then came back. He stood looking at the broken ends of branches.

Still silence.

He caught sight of the rise and fall of his diaphragm and was surprised to see how quickly he was breathing. Just left of centre, his heart-beats were visible. He put the spear down again.

"Heave! Heave! Heave!"

A shrill, prolonged cheer.

Something boomed up on the red rock, then the earth jumped and began to shake steadily, while the noise as steadily increased. Ralph was shot into the air, thrown down, dashed against branches. At his right hand, and only a few feet away, the whole thicket bent and the roots screamed as they came out of the earth together. He saw something red that turned over slowly as a mill-wheel. Then the red thing was past and the elephantine progress diminished towards the sea.

Ralph knelt on the ploughed-up soil, and waited for the earth to come back. Presently the white, broken stumps, the split sticks and the tangle of the thicket refocused. There was a kind of heavy feeling in his body where he had watched his own pulse.

Silence again.

Yet not entirely so. They were whispering out there; and suddenly the branches were shaken furiously at two places on his right. The pointed end of a stick appeared. In panic,

Ralph thrust his own stick through the crack and struck with all his might.

"Aaa-ah!"

His spear twisted a little in his hands and then he withdrew it again.

"Ooh-ooh——"

Someone was moaning outside and a babble of voices rose. A fierce argument was going on and the wounded savage kept groaning. Then when there was silence, a single voice spoke and Ralph decided that it was not Jack's.

"See? I told you—he's dangerous."

The wounded savage moaned again.

What else? What next?

Ralph fastened his hands round the chewed spear and his hair fell. Someone was muttering, only a few yards away towards the Castle Rock. He heard a savage say "No!" in a shocked voice; and then there was suppressed laughter. He squatted back on his heels and showed his teeth at the wall of branches. He raised his spear, snarled a little, and waited.

Once more the invisible group sniggered. He heard a curious trickling sound and then a louder crepitation as if someone were unwrapping great sheets of cellophane. A stick snapped and he stifled a cough. Smoke was seeping through the branches in white and yellow wisps, the patch of blue sky over head turned to the colour of a storm cloud, and then the smoke billowed round him.

Someone laughed excitedly, and a voice shouted.

"Smoke!"

He wormed his way through the thicket towards the forest, keeping as far as possible beneath the smoke. Presently he saw open space, and the green leaves of the edge of the thicket. A smallish savage was standing between him and the rest of the forest, a savage striped red and white, and carrying a spear. He was coughing and smearing the paint about his eyes with the back of his hand as he tried to see through the increasing smoke. Ralph launched himself like a cat; stabbed, snarling, with the spear, and the savage doubled up. There was a shout from beyond the thicket and then Ralph was running with the swiftness of fear through the undergrowth. He came to a pig-run, followed it for perhaps a hundred yards, and then swerved off. Behind him the ululation swept across the island once more and a single voice shouted three times. He guessed that was the signal to advance and sped away again, till his chest was like fire. Then he flung himself down under a bush and waited for a moment till his breathing steadied. He passed his tongue tentatively over his teeth and lips and heard far off the ululation of the pursuers.

There were many things he could do. He could climb a tree—but that was putting all his eggs in one basket. If he were detected, they had nothing more difficult to do than wait.

If only one had time to think!

Another double cry at the same distance gave him a clue to their plan. Any savage baulked in the forest would utter the double shout and hold up the line till he was free again. That way they might hope to keep the cordon unbroken right across the island. Ralph thought of the boar that had broken through them with such ease. If necessary, when the chase came too close, he could charge the cordon while it was still thin, burst through, and run back. But run back where? The cordon would turn and sweep again. Sooner or later he would have to sleep or eat—and then he would awaken with hands clawing at him; and the hunt would become a running down.

What was to be done, then? The tree? Burst the line like a boar? Either way the choice was terrible.

A single cry quickened his heart-beat and, leaping up, he dashed away towards the ocean side and the thick jungle till he was hung up among creepers; he stayed there for a moment with his calves quivering. If only one could have pax, a long pause, a time to think!

And there again, shrill and inevitable, was the ululation sweeping across the island. At that sound he shied like a horse among the creepers and ran once more till he was panting. He flung himself down by some ferns. The tree, or the charge? He mastered his breathing for a moment, wiped his mouth, and told himself to be calm. Samneric were somewhere in that line, and hating it. Or were they? And supposing, instead of them, he met the chief, or Roger who carried death in his hands?

Ralph pushed back his tangled hair and wiped the sweat out of his best eye. He spoke aloud.

"Think."

What was the sensible thing to do?

There was no Piggy to talk sense. There was no solemn assembly for debate nor dignity of the conch.

"Think."

Most, he was beginning to dread the curtain that might waver in his brain, blacking out the sense of danger, making a simpleton of him.

A third idea would be to hide so well that the advancing line would pass without discovering him.

He jerked his head off the ground and listened. There was another noise to attend to now—a deep grumbling noise, as though the forest itself were angry with him, a sombre noise across which the ululations were scribbled excruciatingly as on slate. He knew he had heard it before somewhere, but had no time to remember.

Break the line.

A tree.

Hide, and let them pass.

A nearer cry stood him on his feet and immediately he was away again, running fast among thorns and brambles. Suddenly he blundered into the open, found himself again in that open space—and there was the fathom-wide grin of the skull, no longer ridiculing a deep blue patch of sky but jeering up into a blanket of smoke. Then Ralph was running beneath trees, with the grumble of the forest explained. They had smoked him out and set the island on fire.

Hide was better than a tree because you had a chance of breaking the line if you were discovered.

Hide, then.

He wondered if a pig would agree, and grimaced at nothing. Find the deepest thicket, the darkest hole on the island, and creep in. Now, as he ran, he peered about him. Bars and splashes of sunlight flitted over him and sweat made glistening streaks on his dirty body. The cries were far now, and faint.

At last he found what seemed to him the right place, though the decision was desperate. Here, bushes and a wild tangle of creeper made a mat that kept out all the light of the sun. Beneath it was a space, perhaps a foot high, though it was pierced everywhere by parallel and rising stems. If you wormed into the middle of that you would be five yards from the edge, and hidden, unless the savage chose to lie down and look for you; and even then, you would be in darkness—and if the worst happened and he saw you, then you had a chance, to burst out at him, fling the whole line out of step and double back.

Cautiously, his stick trailing behind him, Ralph wormed between the rising stems. When he reached the middle of the mat he lay and listened.

The fire was a big one and the drum-roll that he had thought was left so far behind was nearer. Couldn't a fire out-run a galloping horse? He could see the sun-splashed ground over an area of perhaps fifty yards from where he lay: and as he watched, the sunlight in every patch blinked at him. This was so like the curtain that flapped in his brain that for a moment he thought the blinking was inside him. But then the patches blinked more rapidly, dulled and went out, so that he saw that a great heaviness of smoke lay between the island and the sun.

If anyone peered under the bushes and chanced to glimpse human flesh it might be Samneric who would pretend not to see and say nothing. He laid his cheek against the chocolate-coloured earth, licked his dry lips and closed his eyes. Under the thicket, the earth was vibrating very slightly; or perhaps there was a sound beneath the obvious thunder of the fire and scribbled ululations that was too low to hear.

Someone cried out. Ralph jerked his cheek off the earth and looked into the dulled light. They must be near now, he thought, and his chest began to thump. Hide, break the line, climb a tree—which was the best after all? The trouble was you only had one chance.

Now the fire was nearer; those volleying shots were great limbs, trunks even, bursting. The fools! The fools! The fire must be almost at the fruit trees—what would they eat to-morrow?

Ralph stirred restlessly in his narrow bed. One chanced nothing! What could they do? Beat him? So what? Kill him? A stick sharpened at both ends.

The cries, suddenly nearer, jerked him up. He could see a striped savage moving hastily out of a green tangle, and coming towards the mat where he hid, a savage who carried a spear. Ralph gripped his fingers into the earth. Be ready now, in case.

Ralph fumbled to hold his spear so that it was point foremost; and now he saw that the stick was sharpened at both ends.

The savage stopped fifteen yards away and uttered his cry.

Perhaps he can hear my heart over the noises of the fire. Don't scream. Get ready.

The savage moved forward so that you could only see him from the waist down. That was the butt of his spear. Now you could see him from the knee down. Don't scream.

A herd of pigs came squealing out of the greenery behind the savage and rushed away into the forest. Birds were screaming, mice shrieking, and a little hopping thing came under the mat and cowered.

Five yards away the savage stopped, standing right by the thicket, and cried out. Ralph drew his feet up and crouched. The stake was in his hands, the stake sharpened at both ends, the stake that vibrated so wildly, that grew long, short, light, heavy, light again.

The ululation spread from shore to shore. The savage knelt down by the edge of the thicket, and there were lights flickering in the forest behind him. You could see a knee disturb the mould. Now the other. Two hands. A spear.

A face.

244

The savage peered into the obscurity beneath the thicket. You could tell that he saw light on this side and on that, but not in the middle—there. In the middle was a blob of dark and the savage wrinkled up his face, trying to decipher the darkness.

The seconds lengthened. Ralph was looking straight into the savage's eyes.

Don't scream.

You'll get back.

Now he's seen you. He's making sure. A stick sharpened.

Ralph screamed, a scream of fright and anger and desperation. His legs straightened, the screams became continuous and foaming. He shot forward, burst the thicket, was in the open, screaming, snarling, bloody. He swung the stake and the savage tumbled over; but there were others coming towards him, crying out. He swerved as a spear flew past and then was silent, running. All at once the lights flickering ahead of him merged together, the roar of the forest rose to thunder and a tall bush directly in his path burst into a great fan-shaped flame. He swung to the right, running desperately fast, with the heat beating on his left side and the fire racing forward like a tide. The ululation rose behind him and spread along, a series of short sharp cries, the sighting call. A brown figure showed up at his right and fell away. They were all running, all crying out madly. He could hear them crashing in the undergrowth and on the left was the hot, bright thunder of the fire. He forgot his wounds, his hunger and thirst, and became fear; hopeless fear on flying feet, rushing through the forest towards the open beach. Spots jumped before his eyes and turned into red circles that expanded quickly till they passed out of sight. Below him, someone's legs were getting tired and the desperate ululation advanced like a jagged fringe of menace and was almost overhead.

He stumbled over a root and the cry that pursued him rose even higher. He saw a shelter burst into flames and the fire flapped at his right shoulder and there was the glitter of water. Then he was down, rolling over and over in the warm sand, crouching with arm up to ward off, trying to cry for mercy.

He staggered to his feet, tensed for more terrors, and looked up at a huge peaked cap. It was a white-topped cap, and above the green shade of the peak was a crown, an anchor, gold foliage. He saw white drill, epaulettes, a revolver, a row of gilt buttons down the front of a uniform.

A naval officer stood on the sand, looking down at Ralph in wary astonishment. On the beach behind him was a cutter, her bows hauled up and held by two ratings. In the stern-sheets another rating held a sub-machine gun.

The ululation faltered and died away.

The officer looked at Ralph doubtfully for a moment, then took his hand away from the butt of the revolver.

"Hullo."

Squirming a little, conscious of his filthy appearance, Ralph answered shyly.

"Hullo."

The officer nodded, as if a question had been answered.

"Are there any adults—any grown-ups with you?"

Dumbly, Ralph shook his head. He turned a half-pace on the sand. A semicircle of little boys, their bodies streaked with coloured clay, sharp sticks in their hands, were standing on the beach making no noise at all.

"Fun and games," said the officer.

The fire reached the coco-nut palms by the beach and swallowed them noisily. A flame, seemingly detached, swung like an acrobat and licked up the palm heads on the platform. The sky was black.

The officer grinned cheerfully at Ralph.

"We saw your smoke. What have you been doing? Having a war or something?"

Ralph nodded.

The officer inspected the little scarecrow in front of him. The kid needed a bath, a hair-cut, a nose-wipe and a good deal of ointment.

"Nobody killed, I hope? Any dead bodies?"

"Only two. And they've gone."

The officer leaned down and looked closely at Ralph.

"Two? Killed?"

Ralph nodded again. Behind him, the whole island was shuddering with flame. The officer knew, as a rule, when people were telling the truth. He whistled softly.

Other boys were appearing now, tiny tots some of them, brown, with the distended bellies of small savages. One of them came close to the officer and looked up.

"I'm, I'm——"

But there was no more to come. Percival Wemys Madison sought in his head for an incantation that had faded clean away.

The officer turned back to Ralph.

"We'll take you off. How many of you are there?"

Ralph shook his head. The officer looked past him to the group of painted boys.

"Who's boss here?"

"I am," said Ralph loudly.

A little boy who wore the remains of an extraordinary

black cap on his red hair and who carried the remains of a pair of spectacles at his waist, started forward, then changed his mind and stood still.

"We saw your smoke. And you don't know how many of you there are?"

"No, sir."

"I should have thought," said the officer as he visualized the search before him, "I should have thought that a pack of British boys—you're all British aren't you?—would have been able to put up a better show than that—I mean——"

"It was like that at first," said Ralph, "before things——"

He stopped.

"We were together then——"

The officer nodded helpfully.

"I know. Jolly good show. Like the Coral Island."

Ralph looked at him dumbly. For a moment he had a fleeting picture of the strange glamour that had once invested the beaches. But the island was scorched up like dead wood—Simon was dead—and Jack had. . . . The tears began to flow and sobs shook him. He gave himself up to them now for the first time on the island; great, shuddering spasms of grief that seemed to wrench his whole body. His voice rose under the black smoke before the burning wreckage of the island; and infected by that emotion, the other little boys began to shake and sob too. And in the middle of them, with filthy body, matted hair, and unwiped nose, Ralph wept for the end of innocence, the darkness of man's heart, and the fall through the air of the true, wise friend called Piggy.

The officer, surrounded by these noises, was moved and a little embarrassed. He turned away to give them time to pull themselves together; and waited, allowing his eyes to rest on the trim cruiser in the distance.

Fable

"**N**uncle," says the fool in *King Lear*, "thou hast pared thy wit o' both sides and left nothing i' the middle. Look—here comes one of the parings." The paring in question is Goneril and she gives him a dirty look. No one has ever been quite sure what happened to the fool later on. He disappears halfway through the play in mysterious circumstances, but we need not be surprised. He asked time and again for summary measures to be taken against him. Oh, the uncomfortable counsel he gave! "Thou did'st little good when thou mad'st thy daughters thy mothers." He tries to comfort Lear; to turn his mind from his sorrows; but ever and again the bitter truth will out. Notice that he never says "It was a piece of folly to put yourself in the power of your bloody-minded daughters". Always the truth is metaphorical. So he disappears; and though Shakespeare nowhere says so, it is plain enough to me that Lear's daughters got him in the end. For the fool was a fabulist, and fabulists are never popular. They are those people who haunt the fringes of history and appear in

First published in *The Hot Gates* (1965), this essay was originally given as a lecture in a series Golding delivered at UCLA, California, in 1962.

miscellanies of anecdotes as slaves or jesters, rash courtiers, or just plain wise men. They tell the dictator, the absolute monarch, what he ought to know but does not want to hear. Generally they are hanged, or beheaded or even bowstringed, unless they have the wit to get out of that hole with another pretty jest. It is a thankless task, to be a fabulist.

Why this is so is clear enough. The fabulist is a moralist. He cannot make a story without a human lesson tucked away in it. Arranging his signs as he does, he reaches, not profundity on many levels, but what you would expect from signs, that is overt significance. By the nature of his craft then, the fabulist is didactic, desires to inculcate a moral lesson. People do not much like moral lessons. The pill has to be sugared, has to be witty or entertaining, or engaging in some way or another. Also, the moralist has to be out of his victim's reach, when the full impact of the lesson strikes him. For the moralist has made an unforgiveable assumption; namely that he knows better than his reader; nor does a good intention save him. If the pill is not sufficiently sugared it will not be swallowed. If the moral is terrible enough he will be regarded as inhuman; and if the edge of his parable cuts deeply enough, he will be crucified.

Any of Aesop's fables will do as examples to begin with. The fox who loses his tail in a trap and then tries to persuade all the other foxes to cut their's off, because a fox looks better that way, is a situation that may be paralleled in human experience easily enough. But, you cannot make a scale model. This is why *Animal Farm*, George Orwell's splendid fable, having to choose between falsifying the human situation and falsifying the nature of animals, chooses to do the latter. Often, we forget they are animals.

Fable

They are people, and Orwell's brilliant mechanics have placed them in a situation where he can underline every moral point he cares to make. We read his funny, poignant book and consent to the lesson as much out of our own experience as out of his. There are fables from other centuries, *Gulliver's Travels*, *Pilgrim's Progress*, perhaps *Robinson Crusoe*. Children love them, since by a God-given urgency for pleasure, they duck the morals and enjoy the story. But children do not like *Animal Farm*. Why should the poor animals suffer so? Why should even animal life be without point or hope? Perhaps in the twentieth century, the sort of fables we must construct are not for children on any level.

With all its drawbacks and difficulties, it was this method of presenting the truth as I saw it in fable form which I adopted for the first of my novels which ever got published. The overall intention may be stated simply enough. Before the second world war I believed in the perfectibility of social man; that a correct structure of society would produce goodwill; and that therefore you could remove all social ills by a reorganization of society. It is possible that today I believe something of the same again; but after the war I did not because I was unable to. I had discovered what one man could do to another. I am not talking of one man killing another with a gun, or dropping a bomb on him or blowing him up or torpedoing him. I am thinking of the vileness beyond all words that went on, year after year, in the totalitarian states. It is bad enough to say that so many Jews were exterminated in this way and that, so many people liquidated, but there were things done during that period from which I still have to avert my mind lest I should be physically sick. They were not done by the headhunters of New Guinea, or by some primitive tribe in the Amazon. They were done, skilfully, coldly, by educated men, doctors, lawyers, by men with a tradition of civilization behind them, to beings of their own kind. I do not want to elaborate this. I would like to pass on; but I must say that anyone who moved through those years without understanding that man produces evil as a bee produces honey, must have been blind or wrong in the head. Let me take a parallel from a social situation. We are commonly dressed, and commonly behave, as if we had no genitalia. Taboos and prohibitions have grown up round that very necessary part of the human anatomy. But in sickness the whole structure of man must be exhibited to the doctor. When the occasion is important enough, we admit to what we have. It seems to me that in nineteenth-century and early twentieth-century society of the West, similar taboos grew up round the nature of man. He was supposed not to have in him the sad fact of his own cruelty and lust. When these capacities emerged into action they were thought aberrant. Social systems, political systems were composed, detached from the real nature of man. They were what one might call political symphonies. They would perfect most men, and at the least, reduce aberrance.

Why, then, have they never worked? How did the idealist concepts of primitive socialism turn at last into Stalinism? How could the political and philosophical idealism of Germany produce as its ultimate fruit, the rule of Adolf Hitler? My own conviction grew, that what had happened was that men were putting the cart before the horse. They were looking at the system rather than the people. It seemed to me that man's capacity for greed, his innate cruelty and selfishness was being hidden behind a kind of pair of political pants. I believed then, that man was sick—

not exceptional man, but average man. I believed that the condition of man was to be a morally diseased creation and that the best job I could do at the time was to trace the connection between his diseased nature and the international mess he gets himself into.

To many of you, this will seem trite, obvious and familiar in theological terms. Man is a fallen being. He is gripped by original sin. His nature is sinful and his state perilous. I accept the theology and admit the triteness; but what is trite is true; and a truism can become more than a truism when it is a belief passionately held. I looked round me for some convenient form in which this thesis might be worked out, and found it in the play of children. I was well situated for this, since at this time I was teaching them. Moreover, I am a son, brother, and father. I have lived for many years with small boys, and understand and know them with awful precision. I decided to take the literary convention of boys on an island, only make them real boys instead of paper cutouts with no life in them; and try to show how the shape of the society they evolved would be conditioned by their diseased, their fallen nature.

It is worth looking for a moment at the great original of boys on an island. This is *The Coral Island*, published in 1857, at the height of Victorian smugness, ignorance, and prosperity. I can do no better than quote to you Professor Carl Niemeyer's sketch of this book.

Ballantyne shipwrecks his three boys—Jack, eighteen; Ralph, the narrator, aged fifteen; and Peterkin Gay, a comic sort of boy, aged thirteen—somewhere in the South Seas on an uninhabited coral island. Jack is a natural leader, but both Ralph and Peterkin have abilities valuable for survival. Jack has the most common sense and foresight, but Peterkin turns out to be a skilful killer of pigs and Ralph, when later in the book he is separated from his friends and alone on a schooner, coolly navigates back to Coral Island by dead reckoning, a feat sufficiently impressive, if not quite equal to captain Bligh's. The boys' life on the island is idyllic; and they are themselves without malice or wickedness, tho' there are a few curious episodes in which Ballantyne seems to hint at something he himself understands as little as do his characters. . . . Ballantyne's book raises the problem of evil—which comes to the boys not from within themselves but from the outside world. Tropical nature to be sure, is kind, but the men of this non-Christian world are bad. For example the island is visited by savage cannibals, one canoeful pursuing another, who fight a cruel and bloody battle, observed by the horrified boys and then go away. A little later, the island is again visited, this time by pirates (i.e. white men who have renounced or scorned their Christian heritage) who succeed in capturing Ralph. In due time the pirates are deservedly destroyed, and in the final episode of the book the natives undergo an unmotivated conversion to Christianity, which effects a total change in their nature just in time to rescue the boys from their clutches.

Thus Ballantyne's view of man is seen to be optimistic, like his view of English boys' pluck and resourcefulness, which subdues tropical islands as triumphantly as England imposes empire and religion on lawless breeds of men.

Fable

Ballantyne's island was a nineteenth-century island inhabited by English boys; mine was to be a twentieth-century island inhabited by English boys. I condemn and detest my country's faults precisely because I am so proud of her many virtues. One of our faults is to believe that evil is somewhere else and inherent in another nation. My book was to say: you think that now the war is over and an evil thing destroyed, you are safe because you are naturally kind and decent. But I know why the thing rose in Germany. I know it could happen in any country. It could happen here.

So the boys try to construct a civilization on the island; but it breaks down in blood and terror because the boys are suffering from the terrible disease of being human.

The protagonist was Ralph, the average, rather more than average, man of goodwill and commonsense; the man who makes mistakes because he simply does not understand at first the nature of the disease from which they all suffer. The boys find an earthly paradise, a world, in fact like our world, of boundless wealth, beauty and resource. The boys were below the age of overt sex, for I did not want to complicate the issue with that relative triviality. They did not have to fight for survival, for I did not want a Marxist exegesis. If disaster came, it was not to come through the exploitation of one class by another. It was to rise, simply and solely, out of the nature of the brute. The overall picture was to be the tragic lesson that the English have had to learn over a period of one hundred years; that one lot of people is inherently like any other lot of people; and that the only enemy of man is inside him. So the picture I had in my mind of the change to be brought about was exemplified by two pictures of the little boy Ralph. The first is when he discovers he is on a real desert island and delights in the discovery.

He jumped down from the terrace. The sand was thick over his black shoes and the heat hit him. He became conscious of the weight of clothes, kicked his shoes off fiercely and ripped off each stocking with its elastic garter in a single movement. Then he leapt back on the terrace, pulled off his shirt, and stood there among the skull-like coconuts with green shadows from the palms and the forest sliding over his skin. He undid the snake-clasp of his belt, lugged off his shorts and pants, and stood there naked, looking at the dazzling beach and the water.

He was old enough, twelve years and a few months, to have lost the prominent tummy of childhood; and not yet old enough for adolescence to have made him awkward. You could see now that he might make a boxer, as far as width and heaviness of shoulders went, but there was a mildness about his mouth and eyes that proclaimed no devil. He patted the palm trunk softly; and forced at last to believe in the reality of the island, laughed delightedly again, and stood on his head. He turned neatly on to his feet, jumped down to the beach, knelt, and swept a double armful of sand into a pile against his chest. Then he sat back and looked at the water with bright, excited eyes.

This is innocence and hope; but the picture changes and the book is so designed that our last view of Ralph is very different. By the end, he has come to understand the fallen nature of man, and that what stands between him and happiness comes from inside him; a trite lesson as I have said; but one which I believed needed urgently to be driven home.

Yet if one takes the whole of the human condition as background of a fable it becomes hopelessly complex, though I worked the book out in detail.

Let us take, for example, the word "history". It seems to me that the word has two common meanings, each of them of awful importance. First there is what might be called academic, or if you like campus history. To my mind this is not only of importance, but of supreme importance. It is that objective yet devoted stare with which humanity observes its own past; and in that stare, that attempt to see how things have become what they are, where they went wrong, and where right, that our only hope lies of having some control over our own future. The exploration of the physical world is an art, with all the attendant aesthetic pleasures; but the knowledge we get from it is not immediately applicable to the problems that we have on hand. But history is a kind of selfknowledge, and it may be with care that selfknowledge will be sufficient to give us the right clue to our behaviour in the future. I say a clue; for we stand today in the same general condition as we have always stood, under sentence of death.

But there is another kind of force which we call history; and how uncontrollable that force is, even in the most detached of men, was amusingly demonstrated to me only the other day. I was being driven over the last battleground of the war between the States, a historical episode which I am able to observe with some objectivity. My driver was a southerner and scholar. His exposition to me of the situation was a model of historical balance. He explained to me how the south had embarked on a war which they could not hope

Fable

to win, in support of a pattern of society which could not hope to survive. He was, perhaps a little harder on the south than a northerner would have been; but judicially so. As the day wore on, his voice began to return to its origins. Emotion crept in—not very far, because of course he was a scholar, and scholars are detached and unemotional are they not?—At a discreet forty miles an hour we followed the wavering fortunes of battle down into Virginia. Here, he told me, Lee had performed that last incredible tactical feat in the defence of Richmond; here, Grant had sidestepped—but what was this? His voice had lost all pretence of scholarship. Insensibly the speed of the car had increased. When we came to the Appomatox, this educated, and indeed rather cynical man grunted—"Aw, shucks!" and drove past the place where Lee surrendered to Grant at seventy-five miles an hour.

This is a different force from campus history. It is history felt in the blood and bones. Sometimes it is dignified by a pretty name, but I am not sure in my own mind, that it is ever anything but pernicious. However this is a political and historical question which we need not settle here and now. My point is that however pathetic or amusing we find these lesser manifestations of prejudice, when they go beyond a certain point no one in the world can doubt that they are wholly evil. Jew and Arab in the name of religion, Jew and Nordic in the name of race, Negro and white in the name of God knows what.

And it is not only these larger more spectacular examples of frozen history which do the damage. I am a European and an optimist. But I do not believe that history is only a nominal thing. There have been many years when as I contemplate our national frontiers, I have fallen into something

258

like despair. Frontiers in Europe may be likened to wrinkles in an aged face, and all that will remove them is the death of the body. Now I know you will point out to me that Europe is already moving towards some confederation; and I would agree and add that that confederation has the full support of every man of goodwill and commonsense. But the wrinkles are so deep. And I cannot think of a confederation in history, where the members voluntarily bowed to supra-national authority without at least one of the members fighting a war to contest it. In Europe there is and has been, a terrible fund of national illwill, handed down from generation to generation. There are habits of feeling which have acquired the force of instinct. These habits of feeling may be encouraged in school or college, but they are rarely taught there. They are an unconscious legacy wished on children by their parents. A woman, like one old French lady I knew, who had gone through the business of being conquered three times, in 1870, 1914 and 1940, had acquired an attitude to the Germans which was a hate so deep that she shook when she thought of them. Indeed, as I make these words, I am aware in myself of resents, indignations and perhaps fears which have nothing to do with today, with the England and Germany of today, in a word, with reality, but are there, nevertheless. I got them from off-campus history; and unless I make a conscious effort I shall hand them on. These impulses, prejudices, even perhaps these *just* hates which are nevertheless backward-looking are what parents luxuriating in a cheap emotion can wish on their children without being properly conscious of it, and so perpetuate division through the generations. A less painful example of this is the way in which where one Englishman and one American are gathered together, that sad old story of the eighteenth century will raise its head, so that the American whose ancestors have perhaps been in the States since 1911 will be arrogating to himself all the splendours of that struggle, while the Englishman who may have spent his life in the pursuit and furtherance of liberal principles may find himself forced into the ridiculous position of defending his fellow Englishman George III. My own technique on these occasions, is to start talking about the vicious occupation of my country by the Romans and the splendid resistance to them by our own heroes, Queen Boadicea and King Arthur. Some of these examples are silly, meant to be silly, and are understood as silly by the contestants. They are less severe than the partisanship roused by games of one sort or another; nevertheless they are symptomatic. We ought not to underestimate the power or the destructiveness of these emotions. The one country to leave the British Commonwealth of Nations in recent centuries is the Union of South Africa, forced out by a universal if sometimes smug condemnation of her policy towards her own black population. But several decades ago England and Australia were shaken to the very roots of their common interests by a game of cricket. Those of you who find this incredible, either do not understand the tenuousness of the bond that holds Australia and England together, or else do not understand the fierce passions that can be roused by cricket. But the point is that many Englishmen and Australians did in fact begin to think of each other as objectionable, irrational, ill-disposed, vindictive. For a moment each nation, or at least the sillier members of each—and there are always enough silly people in any country to form a sizeable mass-movement—each nation stood squarely behind their culture heroes, the one a very fast and accurate bowler, the other a batsman who objected to being struck repeatedly on the head. If the random agglomeration of nations which is the common-wealth seems to you to have any power for good, you may consider it lucky that England and Australia are twelve thousand miles apart. Had they been separated, not by half a world, but by a relatively small ocean, Australia might have taken her bat and gone off fiercely to play cricket by herself. It was George Orwell who commented on the destructive force of international contests. Anyone who has watched a television programme of a game between two European nations must agree with him. There's savagery for you. There's bloodlust. There's ugly nationalism raising its gorgon head.

What I am trying to do is to add together those elements, some horrible, some merely funny, but all significant, which I suppose to be the forces of off-campus history. They are a failure of human sympathy, ignorance of facts, the objectiv-izing of our own inadequacies so as to make a scapegoat. At moments of optimism I have felt that education and per-haps a miracle or two would be sufficient to remove their more dangerous elements. When I feel pessimistic, then they seem to constitute a trap into which humanity has got itself with a dreary inevitability much as the dinosaur trapped itself in its own useless armour. For if humanity has a future on this planet of a hundred million years, it is unthinkable that it should spend those aeons in a ferment of national self-satisfaction and chauvinistic idiocies. I was feeling pessimistic when I tried to include a sign for this thing in a fable.

The point about off-campus history is that it is always dead. It is a cloak of national prestige which the uneducated pull round their shoulders to keep off the wind of personal self-knowledge. It is a dead thing handed on, but dead though it is, it will not lie down. It is a monstrous creature descending to us from our ancestors, producing nothing but disunity, chaos. War and disorder prolong in it the ghastly and ironic semblance of life. All the marching and counter-marching, the flags, the heroism and cruelty are galvanic twitches induced in its slaves and subjects by that hideous, parody thing. When I constructed a sign for it, therefore, it had to be something that was dead but had a kind of life. It had to be presented to my island of children by the world of grown-ups. There was only one way in which I could do this. First I must take the children at a moment when mature council and authority might have saved them as on so many occasions we might have saved our own children, might have been saved ourselves. Since a novelist ought not to preach overtly in a fable, the situation had to be highlighted by the children having some dim knowledge that wisdom, that commonsense even, is to be found in the world of grown-ups. They must yearn for it, now they have begun to find the inadequacy of their own powers. I took a moment therefore, when they had tried to hold a council meeting to discuss ways and means but had found that other questions came up—questions which they would sooner have ignored. Finally the meeting breaks down. The children who are retrogressing more rapidly have gone off into the wardance with which they fortify their own sense of power and togetherness. It is dark. The few remainder, puzzled, anxious, surrounded by half perceived threats and mysteries, faced with a problem which once looked so simple of solution, the maintenance of a fire on the mountain, but which proved to be too much for them—these few, men of goodwill, are searching for some hope, some power for good, some commonsense.

"If only they could get a message to us", cried Ralph desperately. "If only they could send us something grown-up—a sign or something."

What the grown-ups send them is indeed a sign, a sign to fit into the fable; but in the fable sense, that arbitrary sign stands for off-campus history, the thing which threatens every child everywhere, the history of blood and intolerance, of ignorance and prejudice, the thing which is dead but won't lie down.

There was no light left save that of the stars. The three bigger boys went together to the next shelter. They lay restlessly and noisily among the dry leaves, watching the patch of stars that was the opening towards the lagoon. Sometimes a little 'un cried out from the other shelters and once a big 'un spoke in the dark. Then they too fell asleep.

A sliver of moon rose over the horizon, hardly large enough to make a path of light even when it sat right down on the water; but there were other lights in the sky, that moved fast, winked or went out, though not even a faint popping came down from the battle fought at ten miles height. But a sign came down from the world of grownups, though at that time there was no child awake to read it. There was a sudden bright explosion and a corkscrew trail across the sky; then darkness again and stars. There was a speck above the island, a figure dropping swiftly beneath a parachute, a figure that hung with dangling limbs.

Fable

The changing winds of various altitudes took the figure where they would. Then, three miles up the wind steadied and bore it in a descending curve round the sky and swept it in a great slant across the reef and the lagoon towards the mountain. The figure fell and crumpled among the blue flowers of the mountainside, but now there was a gentle breeze at this height too and the parachute flopped and banged and pulled. So the figure, with feet that dragged behind it, slid up the mountain. Yard by yard, puff by puff, the breeze hauled the figure through the blue flowers, over the boulders and red stones, till it lay huddled among the shattered rocks of the mountain top. Here the breeze was fitful and allowed the strings of the parachute to tangle and festoon; and the figure sat, its helmeted head between its knees, held by a complication of lines. When the breeze blew, the lines would strain taut and some accident of this pull lifted the head and chest upright so that the figure seemed to peer across the brow of the mountain. Then, each time the wind dropped, the lines would slacken and the figure bow forward again, sinking its head between its knees. So as the stars moved across the sky, the figure sat on the mountain top and bowed and sank and bowed again.

It is worth noticing that this figure, which is dead but won't lie down, falls on the very place where the children are making their one constructive attempt to get themselves helped. It dominates the mountaintop and so prevents them keeping a fire alight there as a signal. To take an actual historical example, the fire is perhaps like the long defunct

264

Fable

but once much hoped-over League of Nations. That great effort at international sanity fell before the pressures of nationalism which were founded in ignorance, jealousy, greed—before the pressures of off-campus history which was dead but would not lie down.

Having got thus far, I must admit to a number of qualifications, not in the theory itself but in the result. Fable, as a method, depends on two things neither of which can be relied on. First the writer has to have a coherent picture of the subject; but if he takes the whole human condition as his subject, his picture is likely to get a little dim at the edges. Next a fable can only be taken as far as the parable, the parallel is exact; and these literary parallels between the fable and the underlying life do not extend to infinity. It is not just that a small scale model cannot be exact in every detail. It is because every sort of life, once referred to, brings up associations of its own within its own limits which may have no significant relationships with the matter under consideration. Thus, the fable is most successful *qua* fable, when it works within strict limits. George Orwell's *Animal Farm* confines itself to consideration and satire of a given political situation. In other words, the fable must be under strict control. Yet it is at this very point, that the imagination can get out of hand.

I had better explain that I am not referring now to normal exercises of imagination, which we are told is the selection and rearrangement of pictures already latent in the mind. There is another possible experience, which some may think admirable and others pathological. I remember, many years ago, trying to bore a hole with a drilling machine through armour plate. Armour plate is constructed to resist just such an operation—a point which had escaped me for

265

the time being. In my extreme ignorance, I put the drill in the chuck, held by half an inch of its extreme end. I seized the handle and brought the revolving drill down on the armour. It wobbled for a second; then there was a sharp explosion, the drill departed in every direction, breaking two windows and taking a piece of my uniform with it. Wiser now, I held the next drill deep in the chuck so that only the point protruded, held it mercilessly in those steel jaws and brought it down on the armour with the power behind it of many hundred horses. This operation was successful. I made a small red-hot hole in the armour, though of course I ruined the drill. If this small anecdote seems fatuous, I assure you that it is the best image I know for one sort of imaginative process. There is the same merciless concentration, the same will, the same apparently impenetrable target, the same pressure applied steadily to one small point. It is not a normal mode of life; or we should find ourselves posting mail in mailboxes which were not there. But it happens sometimes and it works. The point of the fable under imaginative consideration does not become more real than the real world, it shoves the real world on one side. The author becomes a spectator, appalled or delighted, but a spectator. At this moment, how can he be sure that he is keeping a relationship between the fable and the moralized world, when he is only conscious of one of them? I believe he cannot be sure. This experience, excellent for the novel which does not claim to be a parable, must surely lead to a distortion of the fable. Yet is it not the experience which we expect and hope the novelist to have?

It might be appropriate now to give an example of a situation in which something like this happened. For reasons it is not necessary to specify, I included a Christ-figure in my fable. This is the little boy Simon, solitary, stammering, a lover of mankind, a visionary, who reaches commonsense attitudes not by reason but by intuition. Of all the boys, he is the only one who feels the need to be alone and goes every now and then into the bushes. Since this book is one that is highly and diversely explicable, you would not believe the various interpretations that have been given of Simon's going into the bushes. But go he does, and prays, as the child Jean Vianney would go, and some other saints— though not many. He is really turning a part of the jungle into a church, not a physical one, perhaps, but a spiritual one. Here there is a scene, when civilization has already begun to break down under the combined pressures of boy-nature and the thing still ducking and bowing on the mountain-top, when the hunters bring before him, without knowing he is there, their false god, the pig's head on a stick. It was at this point of imaginative concentration that I found that the pig's head knew Simon was there. In fact the Pig's head delivered something very like a sermon to the boy; the pig's head spoke. I know because I heard it.

"You are a silly little boy," said the Lord of the Flies, "just an ignorant, silly little boy."

Simon moved his swollen tongue but said nothing.

"Don't you agree?" said the Lord of the Flies. "Aren't you just a silly little boy?" Simon answered him in the same silent voice.

"Well then," said the Lord of the Flies, "you'd better run off and play with the others. They think you're batty. You don't want Ralph to think you're batty do you? You like Ralph a lot don't you? And Piggy and Jack?"

Simon's head was tilted slightly up. His eyes could not break away and the Lord of the Flies hung in space before him.

"What are you doing out here all alone? Aren't you afraid of me?"

Simon shook.

"There isn't anyone to help you. Only me. And I'm the beast."

Simon's head laboured, brought forth audible words.

"Pig's head on a stick."

"Fancy thinking the Beast was something you could hunt and kill!" said the head. For a moment or two the forest and all the other dimly appreciated places echoed with the parody of laughter. "You knew didn't you? I'm part of you? Close, close, close! I'm the reason why it's no go? Why things are what they are?"

The laughter shivered again.

"Come now", said the Lord of the Flies. "Get back to the others and we'll forget the whole thing."

Simon's head wobbled. His eyes were half-closed as though he were imitating the obscene thing on the stick. He knew that one of his times was coming on. The Lord of the Flies was expanding like a balloon.

"This is ridiculous. You know perfectly well you'll only meet me down there—so don't try to escape!"

Simon's body was arched and stiff. The Lord of the Flies spoke in the voice of a schoolmaster.

"This has gone quite far enough. My poor, misguided child, do you think you know better than I do?"

There was a pause.

Fable

"I'm warning you. I'm going to get waxy. D'you see? You're not wanted. Understand? We are going to have fun on this island. Understand? We are going to have fun on this island! So don't try it on, my poor misguided boy, or else—"

Simon found he was looking into a vast mouth. There was blackness within, a blackness that spread.

"—Or else," said the Lord of the Flies, "we shall do you. See? Jack and Roger and Maurice and Robert and Bill and Piggy and Ralph. Do you. See?"

Simon was inside the mouth. He fell down and lost consciousness.

That then is an example of how a fable when it is extended to novel length can bid fair to get out of hand. Fortunately the Lord of the Flies' theology and mine were sufficiently alike to conceal the fact that I was writing at his dictation. I don't think the fable ever got right out of hand; but there are many places I am sure, where the fable splits at the seams and I would like to think that if this is so, the splits do not rise from ineptitude or deficiency but from a plenitude of imagination. Faults of excess seem to me more forgivable than faults of coldness, at least in the exercise of craftsmanship.

I suspect that art, like experience, is a continuum and if we try to take elements out of that continuum, they cease to be what they were, because they are no longer together. Take these words, then, as efforts to indicate trends and possibilities rather than discrete things. May it not be that at the very moments when I felt the fable to come to its own life before me it may in fact have become something more valuable, so that where I thought it was failing, it was really succeeding? I leave that consideration to the many learned and devoted persons who, in speech and the printed word, have explained to me what the story means. For I have shifted somewhat from the position I held when I wrote the book. I no longer believe that the author has a sort of *patria potestas* over his brainchildren. Once they are printed they have reached their majority and the author has no more authority over them, knows no more about them, perhaps knows less about them than the critic who comes fresh to them, and sees them not as the author hoped they would be, but as what they are.

At least the fable has caught attention, and gone out into the world. The effect on me has been diverse and not always satisfactory. It has subjected me to a steady stream of letters. I get letters from schoolmasters who want permission to turn the book into a play so that their classes can act it. I get letters from schoolmasters telling me that they *have* turned the book into a play so that their classes can act it. Now and again I get letters from mothers of boys whose schoolmasters have turned the book into a play so that their classes can act it. I get letters from psychiatrists, psychologists, clergymen—complimentary, I am glad to say; but sometimes tinged with a faint air of indignation that I should seem to know something about human nature without being officially qualified.

And at the last—students. How am I to put this gently and politely? In the first place, I am moved and fulfilled by the fact that anyone of your generation should think a book I have written is significant for you. But this is the standard form of the letters I get from most English speaking parts of the world.

Dear Mr. Golding, I and my friend so and so have read

your book *Lord of the Flies* and we think so forth and so forth. However there are some things in it which we are not able to understand. We shall be glad therefore if you will kindly answer the following forty-one questions. A prompt reply would oblige as exams start next week.

Well there it is. I cannot do your homework for you; and it is in some ways a melancholy thought that I have become a school textbook before I am properly dead and buried. To go on being a schoolmaster so that I should have time to write novels was a tactic I employed in the struggle of life. But life, clever life, has got back at me. My first novel ensured that I should be treated for the rest of my days as a schoolmaster.

W.G.

STUDY MATERIALS

Notes on the Study Materials

This section is intended to help both students and teachers with a guided reading of the text. There are chapter summaries, general discussion points, activities and study questions to help you explore this wonderful novel. The tasks focus on skills that are tested at KS3 and GCSE level but they can, and should be, expanded on by teachers, tailored to suit classes' needs and modernized where applicable. The tasks can be updated and adapted depending on the resources available in a wide range of schools, for example, diary entries can become blogs, character profiles can be structured as web-based design tasks, etc.

A glossary of teaching terms can be found on p. 324.

A separate advanced studies section follows, aimed at helping AS- and A2-level students explore some of the wider and more in-depth implications of the novel. Please note that italicized statements have been formulated to generate discussion; they are not quotations from the text itself.

CHAPTER NOTES AND QUESTIONS

Chapter One: The Sound of the Shell

Summary

The novel opens with the description of a fair-haired boy (Ralph) and a boy who is 'shorter' and 'very fat' (Piggy) moving through a jungle. Their discussion reveals that they and some other children have been in a plane crash and may be stranded on an island without any adults. They find a conch (a type of seashell) and Ralph blows it like a trumpet. Other boys, including a group of choristers led by Jack, appear on the beach. The boys vote for Ralph as their chief. Jack, Ralph and a boy called Simon set off to explore. They discover that they are indeed on an uninhabited island. While returning to the others they find a trapped piglet. Jack hesitates when he is about to kill it and it escapes. Jack claims that next time, the pig will not escape.

Discussion Points

1 Why might the boys have been on the aeroplane?
2 Can you find any examples of old-fashioned or outdated

language? What does the use of language tell us about the background of the characters?

3 Discuss the social hierarchy established in the first chapter. Who has the most power? How do you know? How does Golding use language to show this?

4 What would a world without adults be like?

5 'You're no good on a job like this' (p. 32). Discuss the concept of bullying, prejudice or class-based discrimination in Chapter One.

Activities

(Please refer to the glossary of teaching terms on p. 324 for further explanation of these tasks.)

1 Complete a research project on William Golding and aspects of his life. Students should think about, and try to make links between, his life experience and what happens in the book.

2 Refer to Ralph and Piggy's initial conversation on p. 12. Imitating Golding's style and using the characters' own language, students write the final emergency message from the plane before it crashed.

3 If you were to elect a class leader, who would it be? Students write and perform a persuasive speech on why they should be 'chief' of the class. Complete a hustings or election session and discuss the final decision.

4 Create a manifesto of rules and regulations that the class must abide by. Students use the conch rule for a group-based discussion.

5 Imagine that the teacher has not turned up for today's lesson. Students write a script based on what they think would happen.

Questions for Study

1 What relationship is created between Ralph and Piggy in Chapter One? How is it established?
2 What impression of the island is presented to the reader in Chapter One? Explore the effect of specific literary techniques and devices used by Golding.
3 How do the boys initially react to their situation? Focus on what they say and do.
4 Why do you think the boys come when Ralph blows the conch?
5 What do we learn about Jack and the choir on pp. 26–7?
6 What do the following quotations reveal about Ralph?
   > 'You could see now that he might make a boxer ... but there was a mildness about his mouth and eyes that proclaimed no devil' (p. 15).
   > 'This time Ralph expressed the intensity of his emotion by pretending to knock Simon down; and soon they were a happy, heaving pile in the under-dusk' (p. 36).
7 What do the following quotations reveal about Piggy?
   > 'They used to call me "Piggy"' (p. 16). Why are we not told Piggy's real name?
   > 'Piggy grinned reluctantly, pleased despite himself at even this much recognition' (p. 17).
   > 'Piggy ... watched Ralph's green and white body enviously' (p. 18).

8 What do the following quotations reveal about Jack?
> 'The boy who controlled them was dressed in the same way though his cap badge was golden' (p. 26).
> 'He snatched his knife out of the sheath and slammed it into a tree trunk. Next time there would be no mercy. He looked round fiercely, daring them to contradict' (p. 41).

9 Ralph dismisses Piggy from the team of explorers. Why does he do this? Use evidence from the text to support your answer.

10 Why does Jack hesitate when faced with killing the piglet? What is his excuse for this? Use evidence from the text to support your answer.

Chapter Two: Fire on the Mountain

Summary

The boys meet on the beach. Ralph declares that the conch shell will be used to determine who has the right to speak. A small boy claims that he saw a snake-like 'beastie' or monster during the night. Ralph suggests that the group build a large signal fire on top of the island's mountain to attract attention from any passing ships. The boys rush off to build the fire, realizing that they can use the lenses from Piggy's glasses to light it, but the fire gets out of control. The small boy, who told the other boys about the 'beastie', goes missing; they pretend that nothing has happened.

Discussion Points

1 Find examples in the text of the boys behaving co-operatively. If you were in their situation, what would you do? Would you and your friends co-operate, or would you argue? Give reasons for your answers.

2 What are the characteristics of a good 'leader'? Who would you vote for as your leader if you were on the island? Give reasons for your choice.

3 'We've got to have rules and obey them. After all, we're not savages' (p. 55). To what extent are the boys a

'community'? Are rules necessary for a 'community'?
Give reasons for your answer.

4 What is the beast? Refer to Golding's language, use of
   techniques and style to support your response.

5 What do you think happened to the little 'un? Why do the
   boys react as they do? Would you react in a similar way?

Activities

(Please refer to the glossary of teaching terms on p. 324 for
further explanation of these tasks.)

1 Message in a bottle task: students imagine they are one
   of the boys trapped on the island. They write a note to
   be put in a bottle and cast into the sea. It should explain
   their situation and ask for help.

2 Diary task: students write a diary entry as Piggy, Ralph or
   Jack. Explain how they feel about what has happened so
   far and what they think of the others on the island.

3 Soundscape task: make a list of all the sounds that might
   be heard on the island. Make an aural soundscape by re-
   creating these sounds and noises.

4 Tableau task: create a freeze-frame of the key events of
   the chapter. Thought tap certain characters and ask them
   how they feel.

5 Ralph says, 'This is our island. It's a good island' (p. 45).
   Create a travel brochure which either informs people
   about the island or persuades them to visit.

6 Desert island task: imagine you are going to be stranded
   on an island. What five items would you take with you?
   What five pieces of music would you take with you?

Chapter Notes and Questions

Questions for Study

1. 'Treasure Island—' 'Swallows and Amazons—' 'Coral Island—'
   What is the significance of the literary texts referred to on p. 45?

2. Explain how Ralph's 'leadership' begins to break down in Chapter Two. Use evidence from the text to support your answer.

3. How is Jack's character developed in Chapter Two? How does Golding use language to show negative aspects of Jack's character?

4. How does Piggy's status within the group change during this chapter? How is this shown in the speech and behaviour of Piggy and the other boys?

5. Why does Piggy feel betrayed by Ralph? Is he justified?

6. 'He still says he saw the beastie. It came and went away again an' came back and wanted to eat him—' (p. 47). How does the idea of the 'beastie' affect the boys' state of mind?

7. Find three examples of moments of doubt in the chapter when the boys fear they may not be rescued and the island may not be 'good' after all. What do the boys decide to do about this?

8. Examine the description of the fire on p. 57. How does Golding make the fire seem alive? How effective is the animal imagery?

9. 'I got the conch! Just you listen!' (p. 58) What does the conch symbolize?

10. 'My father's in the navy. He said there aren't any unknown islands left. He says the Queen has a big room full of maps

and all the islands in the world are drawn there. So the Queen's got a picture of this island' (pp. 48–9). How are the concepts of *empire* and *imperialism* presented? Refer to the Britain and Imperialism section on p. 1.

Chapter Three: Huts on the Beach

Summary

Chapter Three begins with Jack practising his skills as a hunter like an animal alone in the wild. When he returns to the beach, he finds Ralph and Simon struggling to build shelters; the rest of the boys are not helping as they had promised. It becomes increasingly clear that Jack and Ralph have different priorities on the island. The two boys have a tense exchange about the fact that the shelters have not been built and that Jack and the hunters have still not killed a pig. Simon reminds the boys of their fear of the 'beastie' on the island. When Ralph and Jack leave to go and continue the hunt, Simon is left to contemplate the situation on the island on his own.

Discussion Points

1 Consider the significance of Jack hunting wearing few clothes. What do clothes represent on the island and what are the implications of no longer wearing them?

2 'They walked along, two continents of experience and feeling, unable to communicate' (p. 70). Discuss the power struggle between Jack and Ralph. Who has the most power? Why? How do you know?

3 Is obsession part of everyday life? Is obsession part of the human condition?

4 The island is made to seem menacing and alive, 'As if it wasn't a good island' (p. 66). Discuss. Is Golding's language effective in creating atmosphere?

5 *Golding uses Simon as a plot device to plant seeds of doubt and fear in the boys*. Discuss.

Activities

(Please refer to the glossary of teaching terms on p. 324 for further explanation of these tasks.)

1 Produce a Venn diagram of the characteristics of Ralph and Jack to highlight the similarities and differences between the two boys.

2 Hotseat the characters Simon, Piggy, Ralph and Jack. Students ask questions about these characters' thoughts and feelings.

3 Balloon debate task: students write persuasive speeches as characters from the novel; invite the class to decide who deserves to stay in the imaginary hot air balloon.

4 Gallery drama task: students sculpt each other to show changes in a character, for example, Jack. One student acts as a sculptor whilst the other is ready to be physically moulded into shape. In pairs, 'A's create a pose which portrays Jack as he first appeared on the island. 'B's strike a pose showing what he has become at the beginning of Chapter Three.

5 Pupils draw, describe or act out their own interpretation of the beastie. Encourage students to notice the

284

differences between their ideas and the implications this has for the novel.

Questions for Study

1 What do the following quotations reveal about Jack? Consider if, and how, his character has evolved since Chapter One.

> 'Then dog-like, uncomfortably on all fours yet unheeding his discomfort, he stole forward five yards and stopped' (p. 61).

> 'A sharpened stick about five feet long trailed from his right hand; and except for a pair of tattered shorts held up by his knife-belt he was naked' (p. 61).

> 'The forest and he were very still' (p. 62).

> 'Jack stood there, streaming with sweat, streaked with brown earth, stained by all the vicissitudes of a day's hunting' (p. 63).

2 How has Jack's sense of morality changed since the beginning of the novel? How does Golding demonstrate this change in morality?

3 How and why does Golding build up a sense of tension on p. 62 when Jack is hunting? Predict what event(s) this description could foreshadow later on in the novel.

4 How does Golding create a sense of conflict between Jack and Ralph through his use of language on pp. 64–5? Why do they argue and how do they resolve this conflict?

5 In what ways are the thoughts and feelings of Jack and Ralph similar in this chapter? What is the significance of their differing obsessions? What are the priorities of the other children?

6 What might Jack and Ralph's different priorities on the island represent in terms of human nature?

7 The symbol or motif of 'eyes' or 'glasses' is recurrent throughout the novel. Look at the following quotations and analyse what Golding's description of these different characters' eyes could reveal about them:
   > Ralph: 'eyes that proclaimed no devil' (Chapter One, p. 15).
   > Jack: 'They were bright blue, eyes that in this frustration seemed bolting and nearly mad' (p. 62).
   > Jack: 'The madness came into his eyes again' (p. 65).
   > Simon: 'his eyes so bright they had deceived Ralph into thinking him delightfully gay and wicked' (p. 70).

8 What impression of Simon is created in the following quotations?
   > 'Simon spoke from inside the shelter' (p. 63).
   > 'Simon's contrite face appeared in the hole' (p. 64).
   > 'Simon poked his head out carefully' (p. 64).
   > 'Simon found for them the fruit they could not reach, pulled off the choicest from up in the foliage, passed them back down to the endless, outstretched hands' (p. 71).

9 'As if ... the beastie, the beastie or the snake-thing, was real. Remember?' (p. 66). How does Simon highlight the darker side of the island and what could this fore-shadow?

10 'He's queer. He's funny' (p. 69). At the end of the chapter, how does Golding create a sense that Simon is different from the other boys?

Chapter Four: Painted Faces and Long Hair

Summary

Roger throws stones near a 'littlun' but does not hurt the boy because he remembers the rules of the adult world. Ralph and Piggy are stunned when a ship passes the island and they realize that the hunters have let the fire and smoke signal die out. Meanwhile, Jack has camouflaged his face and succeeds in killing a pig. Ralph and Piggy argue with the returning hunters about the fire and then watch enviously as the boys re-enact the pig's capture in a celebratory, tribal dance.

Discussion Points

1 'Roger led the way straight through the castles, kicking them over, burying the flowers, scattering the chosen stones' (p. 76). Discuss what role Roger might have later on in the narrative.

2 'Belly flop! Belly flop!' (p. 82). Why does Golding remind the reader that they are children?

3 Consider how Ralph and Jack attempt to assert their authority. In what different ways do Ralph and Jack show leadership qualities? What does this suggest about the future of their friendship?

4 'For hunting. Like in the war. You know—dazzle paint. Like things trying to look like something else' (p. 79). Discuss Jack's use of concealing paint. How can the idea of a mask be symbolic to the novel? What are the boys trying to hide? What or who are the boys trying to look like? Why?

5 Discuss what separates humans from animals.

6 Debate the concept of nature versus nurture.

Activities

(Please refer to the glossary of teaching terms on p. 324 for further explanation of these tasks.)

1 Students design and create a mask; think about how the mask could compel the wearer to act differently in any given situation.

2 Devise a choral drama performance based on the song and dance at the end of the chapter. Think carefully about the positioning of Ralph and Piggy.

3 Watch examples of animal behaviour in the wild and explore the similarities or differences in the boys' behaviour.

4 Create an island menu – decide what food and drink is available.

5 Revisit the Venn diagram from Chapter Three. Have the similarities and differences between Ralph and Jack changed? Could students add any more personality traits to the diagram? Add key quotations to this Venn diagram for revision purposes.

Extension Activity

Research and create presentations on the context and background of Golding's writing. Could the novel have a political or social agenda? (Explore the essays in the advanced studies section and refer to the Post-War British Society essay on p. 4.)

Questions for Study

1 How does Golding use language and literary techniques to create atmosphere? Explore specific techniques such as anthropomorphism and pathetic fallacy.
   > 'the heat ... became a blow that they ducked'.
   > 'Strange things happened at midday. The glittering sea rose up ...'
   > 'Sometimes land loomed where there was no land and flicked out like a bubble as the children watched.'
   > 'no boy could reach even the reef ... where the snapping sharks waited ...' (all p. 73).

2 How does Golding's omniscient narrative make the reader feel about the littluns' experience on the island?

3 'Roger's arm was conditioned by a civilization that knew nothing of him and was in ruins' (p. 78). Roger's violent behaviour highlights a menacing undertone in the book. How does this line create a sense of tension and even horror?

4 What do these quotations from p. 80 reveal about the effect of the mask on both Jack and the other characters?
   > 'his sinewy body held up a mask that drew their eyes and appalled them'.

> 'He began to dance and his laughter became a blood-thirsty snarling.'
> 'the mask was a thing on its own, behind which Jack hid, liberated from shame and self-consciousness'.
> 'The mask compelled them.'

5 How does Piggy try to maintain a connection with civiliz-ation in this chapter? Are his ideas shared by Ralph and the others?

6 What do the following quotations reveal about Ralph?
> 'Ralph continued to watch the ship, ravenously' (p. 83).
> 'He did desperate violence to his naked body ... so that blood was sliding over him' (p. 84).
> 'Ralph dribbled. He meant to refuse meat but ... accepted a piece of half-raw meat and gnawed it like a wolf' (p. 92).

7 'Piggy was a bore; his fat, his ass-mar and his matter-of-fact ideas were dull: but there was always a little pleasure to be got out of pulling his leg' (p. 81). How is Piggy shown to be a victim? How does Ralph, Jack and Simon's treatment of Piggy make us feel about them? How does Golding present the narrator's view of Piggy?

8 What does the repetition of the 'unfriendly side' of the island symbolize (pp. 85 and 93)? What could it indicate about the boys and their 'unfriendly side'?

9 What is the significance of the motif of blood in this chapter?

10 What is the significance of the tribal dance? What could it show about the boys' state of mind and evolving characters?

Chapter Five: Beast from Water

Summary

As he walks along the beach, Ralph thinks about the qualities a chief needs and how he can fulfil the role. He holds an assembly to try to get everyone to take their responsibilities seriously; he insists they keep the fire going in the hope of being rescued. The 'littluns' voice their fears about 'the beast' and it becomes apparent that they are very frightened, especially Percival. Jack decides that he and his hunters will search for the beast. He quarrels with Piggy before breaking up the assembly. Most of the boys follow him, except for Ralph, Piggy and Simon who are left alone on the beach.

Discussion Points

1 '... maybe there is a beast' (p. 110). Are the worst fears real or imagined? How does Golding's use of uncertain language, such as the word 'maybe', emphasize rather than reduce this fear?

2 'What I mean is ... maybe it's only us' (p. 111). Is fear a part of being human? What is Golding telling us about the nature of evil in this quotation? Is 'the beast' necessarily an external force or does 'the beast' exist within the boys themselves?

3 *A social hierarchy is natural and necessary*. Discuss using evidence from the text to support your response.
4 'The fire is the most important thing on the island' (p. 100). Do you agree?
5 'You voted me for chief. Now you do what I say' (p. 101). What is the best way to get people to do what you want or need them to do? Is Ralph successful in persuading the boys? Discuss with reference to the language Ralph uses in his speech to the boys.

Activities

(Please refer to the glossary of teaching terms on p. 324 for further explanation of these tasks.)

1 Draw a seating plan of the assembly area described on p. 96. Compare this to the seating arrangements in a parliamentary system. Discuss the similarities and differences.
2 Diamond nine task: arrange a diamond nine of all the characters mentioned so far. Put the one with most power at the top, leading down to least powerful at the bottom.
3 Students imagine they are Ralph. Write a diary entry to explain how you feel when Piggy tells you that Jack hates you.
4 Students draw a picture of their interpretation of the 'beast from water' and label it with quotations from the text.
5 Using the title of the chapter for inspiration, create a storyboard for a film entitled *Beast from Water*. Create a

trailer for the film adhering to codes and conventions for trailers, such as voiceovers.

Questions for Study

1 Pre-reading question: Ralph calls a meeting which 'must not be fun, but business' (p. 95). What do you think he will say? How will the others react?

2 'Only, decided Ralph as he faced the chief's seat, I can't think. Not like Piggy' (p. 97). How does Golding use punctuation and language to show Ralph's feelings towards Piggy? Are these feelings reflected in his actions?

3 'They had never had an assembly as late before' (p. 97). What techniques are used to show that there is a change in atmosphere here? Why is the change significant?

4 How does Golding create an atmosphere of fear through his description of nature in Chapter Five? Use evidence from the text to support your ideas.

5 '. . . looking beyond them at nothing, remembering the beastie, the snake, the fire, the talk of fear' (p. 102). What does the use of the word 'beastie' rather than 'beast' suggest about Ralph's character and attitude towards the beast?

6 '. . . talk of a thing, a dark thing, a beast, some sort of animal' (p. 103). What are the other characters' attitudes towards 'the beast'? Analyse the language used by different characters when discussing the beast and discuss what this tells us about the character.

7 '"Pig." "We eat pig." "Piggy!"' (p. 104) What might Golding's play on the word 'pig' and the

name 'Piggy' anticipate or foreshadow? Find evidence to support your response.

8 Find evidence in the text that suggests democracy in the camp is starting to fail. Why might this be?

9 'What are we? Humans? Or animals? Or savages?' (p. 113). Explore the significance of Piggy's outburst.

10 'If only they could send us something grown-up ... a sign or something' (p. 117). How is the adult world viewed at the end of this chapter?

Chapter Six: Beast from Air

Summary

During the night a dead aircrew member drops down by parachute into the trees. None of the boys see this. Sam and Eric, who are supposed to be watching the fire, fall asleep. When they wake up they believe they have seen 'the beast' and run back to the camp. The boys go on a hunt for the beast and discover a part of the island where they have not been before. They are initially scared but then want to build a fort and play in what they call 'Castle Rock'. Ralph reminds them that they have to go back and build the fire.

Discussion Points

1 'But a sign came down from the world of grown-ups, though at the time there was no child awake to read it' (p. 118). What is the significance of the 'beast from air' and what does he represent?

2 '... though not even a faint popping came down from the battle fought at ten miles' height' (p. 118). Are the boys in a real or imaginary world?

3 Is it always best to face your fears?

4 The boys are torn between creating a fort and keeping the fire alight. Doing what you want or doing what is right: which is more important?

5 *The boys become increasingly wild and savage as they are isolated from the adult world.* Discuss the similarities and differences between civilization and savagery.

Activities

(Please refer to the glossary of teaching terms on p. 324 for further explanation of these tasks.)

1 Creative writing task: use a variety of visual or auditory stimuli and ask students to imagine staying outside in a place with no artificial light (for example in a jungle or on a beach). Students then write a creative piece using sensory description to create atmosphere and describe how they feel and what they are thinking.

2 Students imagine they are film directors. How would you direct the scene with Sam and Eric and the fire? Consider costumes, setting, character movement, character voice (pitch and tone), lighting and sound.

3 Draw, and annotate with quotations, a picture of the 'beast from air'.

4 Describe the island and the boys from the perspective of the 'beast from air'.

5 Revisit the diamond nine activity from Chapter Five: how has the power shifted between characters?

Chapter Notes and Questions

Questions for Study

1 'There was no light left save that of the stars' (p. 118). What atmosphere does this opening sentence create? Consider Golding's use of alliteration and assonance in your response.

2 'The figure fell and crumpled ... and the parachute flopped and banged and pulled' (p. 119). Consider the connotations of each word used to describe 'the beast'. What mood does Golding create here?

3 'They became motionless, gripped in each other's arms, four unwinking eyes aimed and two mouths open.' How does Golding use the twins as a device to build tension on pp. 119–22? Can their interaction be seen as humorous too?

4 How do the boys' reactions to the idea of the 'beast from air' and the 'beast from water' differ? What do their decisions highlight about their state of mind?

5 'Soon the darkness was full of claws, full of the awful unknown and menace' (p. 123). Why is the world outside the shelter seen as 'impossibly dangerous'?

6 Explore the interaction between Jack and Ralph on pp. 125–8. What are Jack's and Ralph's motivations for going on the hunt?

7 Investigate the significance of, and the reaction to, Simon's claim that he does not 'believe in the beast' on p. 130.

8 > 'Jack was excited. "What a place for a fort!"' (p. 131).
   > Ralph: 'This is a rotten place' (p. 132).
   How and why do Jack's and Ralph's reactions to the unexplored part of the island differ?

9 Are Jack and Ralph becoming polarized characters or is the line between them becoming increasingly blurred? Consider the importance of their obsessions.
   > 'Shove a palm trunk under that and if an enemy came—look!' (p. 132).
   > 'We want smoke. And you go wasting your time. You roll rocks' (p. 133).
10 Who is in charge at the end of the chapter?
   > 'I'm chief. We've got to make certain' (p. 134).
   > 'Jack led the way down the rock and across the bridge' (p. 134).

Chapter Seven: Shadows and Tall Trees

Summary

Ralph is starting to give up on the idea of ever being able to escape from the island. Simon reassures Ralph that he will get home. That afternoon, the hunters find pig droppings and Jack suggests they hunt the pig. The boys track a large boar and chase it. The boar escapes, but the boys are thrilled with the chase and re-enact the scene with Robert as the pig. Jack challenges Ralph to continue the hunt for the beast and he eventually agrees. Ralph, Roger and Jack start to climb the mountain. Jack claims to have seen the beast, which Ralph and Roger then confirm. The three boys flee from the mountain-top in terror.

Discussion Points

1 What does Simon mean when he tries to reassure Ralph by saying, 'You'll get back to where you came from' (p. 137)?

2 'The desire to squeeze and hurt was over-mastering' (p. 142). Are the boys particularly cruel savages or is this an innate quality – a primitive instinct that all humans have?

3 Discuss the concept of mob mentality. Have you ever behaved differently in a group or a crowd compared to how you might behave if you were on your own?

4 'I'll go if you like. I don't mind, honestly' (p. 145). *Simon is the bravest character*. Discuss.

5 *Jack and Ralph hate each other*. Discuss.

Activities

(Please refer to the glossary of teaching terms on p. 324 for further explanation of these tasks.)

1 Place four boxes in front of a student (the selected student should not be able to see what is in each box). Each box should contain an everyday object (preferably with a strange texture). Pupils must describe how they feel about the boxes before they put their hands in. This is an opportunity for pupils to empathize with the boys and experience the 'fear of the unknown'.

2 Write a letter home from Simon. Think carefully about what he would say has happened. How would he describe the other boys?

3 *Ding Dong, What's the Score?* Students chart the power struggle between Jack and Ralph throughout the chapter, awarding a point to a character each time he does something to raise his status. Create a tally chart for discussion at the end and decide who has the most power.

4 Draw a cartoon version of Jack and Ralph's conversation about, and perception of, the beast on pp. 150–3. Include speech and thought bubbles that highlight the difference between their actions and their internal fears.

5 Students hotseat the characters of Ralph, Simon, Jack and Piggy in a series of trials that test their survival skills. Members of the audience then ask what they would do

in different scenarios on the island. Characters' responses must be based on textual detail/evidence. Ultimately, students decide who would make the best leader and why.

Questions for Study

1 'If you could shut your ears to the slow suck down of the sea ... there was a chance that you might put the beast out of mind and dream for a while' (p. 135). How does the narrative perspective invite the reader to empathize with the boys and imagine how they are now feeling?

2 'He would like to ... cut this filthy hair right back to half an inch ... have a bath, a proper wallow with soap' (p. 135). How does Ralph's physical condition relate to the state of the island's society? Refer to Golding's use of animal imagery in your answer.

3 Golding describes Ralph noticing that the boys' faces had been 'marked in the less accessible angles with a kind of shadow' (p. 136). With close reference to Golding's use of language, what do you suggest has happened to the boys?

4 Whilst Jack 'was in charge of the hunt', Ralph daydreams about home, 'Mummy had still been with them and Daddy had come home every day' (pp. 138–9). What is the significance of Ralph's flashback here?

5 What is treated with greater respect by the boys – Ralph wounding the pig or Jack being wounded by it (pp. 140–1)? Which do you think deserves more respect?

6 'The circle moved in and round. Robert squealed in mock terror, then in real pain ... Robert was screaming and struggling with the strength of frenzy ... *Kill the pig! Cut*

his throat! Kill the pig! Bash him in!'" What has changed between the re-enactment of the hunt at the end of Chapter Four and the one in this chapter (pp. 141–2)? What effect does the chant and accompanying tribal dance have on the boys now?

7 What does Jack suggest the boys use instead of a pig in their future re-enactments (p. 143)? What is the significance of the boys' reaction to the suggestion?

8 '"Coming?" ... The word was too good, too bitter, too successfully daunting to be repeated' (p. 148). How does Jack persuade Ralph to come with him up the mountain? Why is he so successful? Make close reference to Golding's technique.

9 'Why do you hate me?' (p. 146). Why does Ralph's open expression of emotion or sentiment create such tension? How does Ralph feel about the 'stain that was Jack' (p. 149) and what is implied by this metaphor?

10 What descriptive detail is the reader given about what the boys have seen on the top of the mountain (pp. 152–3)? Why do you think we are given so little information?

Chapter Eight: Gift for the Darkness

Summary

Jack calls an assembly using the conch. He tells the others about 'the beast' and claims that Ralph is a coward and should no longer be the leader. The other boys refuse to vote Ralph out of power and Jack leaves the group in tears. Piggy suggests to Ralph that they build a new fire on the beach whilst many of the older boys leave to join Jack's group. Jack declares himself the chief of the new tribe and they kill a sow, leaving the head as an offering to the beast. Jack's group steal fire from Ralph's group and invite them to their feast. Meanwhile, Simon has slipped away from the group and finds the pig's head, which speaks to Simon as the 'Lord of the Flies', terrifying Simon into a faint.

Discussion Points

1 'He's like Piggy. He says things like Piggy. He isn't a proper chief' (p. 157). In what ways is Ralph like Piggy?

2 Would you join Jack's hunter gang or stay with Ralph and look after the fire?

3 'The island was getting worse and worse' (p. 172). Discuss.

4 If the 'beast' isn't 'something you could hunt and kill' (p. 177), what is it?

5 What are the two uses of the fire on the island and which one does each tribe prioritize (pp. 174–5)? Debate the idea that fire is a symbol of both civilization and savagery.

Activities

(Please refer to the glossary of teaching terms on p. 324 for further explanation of these tasks.)

1 Complete a research project on political leaders during the Second World War. Contrast Jack and Ralph with historically famous political leaders.

2 Draw a poster/leaflet advertising the benefits of being in Jack's or Ralph's gang.

3 Write a diary entry as Simon. Explore his thoughts and feelings after communicating with the Lord of the Flies on pp. 177–8.

4 Dramatize the interaction between Simon and the Lord of the Flies in pairs: consider how to vary pitch and volume to emphasize important words. Write and perform an extended monologue as the Lord of the Flies – offer suggestions for your purpose or role, explain your view of the boys and the island. Write and perform an extended monologue as Simon in response to the Lord of the Flies. Be imaginative and creative.

5 Complete diagrams or an essay exploring a psychoanalytical approach to understanding the text: Jack as the id, Ralph as the ego and Piggy as the superego. Use Freud's theory to examine the characters' reactions to

the Lord of the Flies (refer to Critical Interpretations: A Psychoanalytic Approach in the advanced studies section on pp. 336–7).

Questions for Study

1 Has the boys' view of the beast changed since their encounter with it on the mountain-top (p. 154)? Where do the boys suggest the beast comes from (p. 156)? What could this symbolize? What do they suggest the beast is doing?

2 Why does Jack say he has called the meeting (p. 156)? Do you think this is his real motivation?

3 'He isn't a proper chief ... He's a coward himself ... He's not a hunter' (p. 157). How does Jack try to take over as chief from Ralph?

4 'I'm not going to play any longer. Not with you' (p. 158). How does Jack react when he fails to usurp power at the assembly? Why does he react in this way? Does Golding's description create sympathy for Jack?

5 Which character suggests climbing the mountain (p. 159)? Why might this be a surprise?

6 'For the first time on the island, Piggy himself removed his one glass, knelt down and focused the sun on tinder. Soon there was a ceiling of smoke and a bush of yellow flame' (p. 161). Why is fire so important to the boys? What does it symbolize? Is it significant that Piggy lights the fire here?

7 Explore the significance of Simon's solitary journey in the jungle beginning on p. 164. Can Simon be seen as

a Christ-like figure? Consider Golding's use of religious imagery.

8 'I'm going to be chief' (p. 165). How is this different to how Ralph became chief? Does this foreshadow any similarities or differences between the two tribes?

9 '... what makes things break up like they do?' (p. 173). To what extent does Ralph depend on Piggy? Has Piggy's role changed in this chapter?

10 'You knew, didn't you? I'm part of you?' What does Simon's interaction with the Lord of the Flies (pp. 177–8) mean? Is it a hallucination or a dream? Is he communing with nature? Is the Lord of the Flies the voice of the island? Why does Simon faint at the end of this interaction? What do you think the function of the Lord of the Flies is? Consider the overarching religious theme in this passage.

Chapter Nine: A View to a Death

Summary

Simon awakens from his 'fit', climbs the mountain and encounters the dead parachutist. He realizes that this is what the boys have mistaken for the beast. He frees the parachutist from the rocks and goes to tell the boys what he has seen. Meanwhile Ralph and Piggy go to Jack's feast in the hope that they will be able to regain control. The majority of the boys decide to join Jack's tribe; they dance and chant in frenzied excitement after joining in the feast. Simon emerges from the forest; the boys assume he is the beast and they kill him in a moment of hysteria.

Discussion Points

1 Explore the idea of the individual versus the mob. Consider possible links between historical or recent social events that can be related to the mob mentality of the boys.
2 *Tribalism leads to violence*. Discuss.
3 Is a faith system necessary in a society? Investigate the themes of belief and spirituality on the island.
4 Debate whether the boys' society on the island would work best as a dictatorship or a democracy.
5 *Simon's death is the result of primitive instinct*. Debate.

Study Materials

Activities

(Please refer to the glossary of teaching terms on p. 324 for further explanation of these tasks.)

1 Conscience alley/corridor drama task: create a conscience corridor where opposing lines of students chant *'Kill the beast! Cut his throat! Spill his blood!'* Students act in role as various characters and walk through the corridor of chanting students. Students should think about, and feed back on, the physical and emotional responses they have.

2 Draw a silhouette (or use a gingerbread man outline) and write in it as many things as possible that you are not allowed to do in society. Write a similar list of things around the outside that you are expected to do. Use this silhouette as a stimulus to explore how the contrast between what you can and cannot do in society is presented in the novel.

3 Create the rule book for Jack and Ralph's 'tribes'.

4 Dramatize the slaughter of Simon in groups; include the chant and a tribal dance. Think carefully about the positioning of Ralph and Piggy.

5 Students create a poster about 'tribalism' and its connotations that can be presented to their peers.

Questions for Study

1 'Colours drained from water and trees ... and the white and brown clouds brooded' p. 179. How does Golding use language and writing techniques to create

atmosphere? Pay particular attention to the use of pathetic fallacy.

2 'The flies had found the figure too' (p. 181). Is nature presented as a menacing force in the novel?

3 'The beast was harmless and horrible; and the news must reach the others as soon as possible' (p. 181). How does Simon behave when he discovers the 'beast from air'?

4 Read pp. 182–3, starting 'Ralph dived into the pool' and ending 'Ralph squirted water again'. How has the relationship between Ralph and Piggy changed?

5 'Jack, painted and garlanded, sat there like an idol' (p. 183). '"I gave you food," said Jack, "and my hunters will protect you from the beast. Who will join my tribe?"' (p. 185). How does Golding use dialogue to show Jack's leadership qualities? How does Jack gain dominance over Ralph in this chapter?

6 'And the conch doesn't count at this end of the island' (p. 186). How and why does the conch lose its power in this chapter?

7 'Between the flashes of lightning the air was dark and terrible …' (p. 187). Why, at this point in the novel, does Golding use the language and imagery of light and dark? What mood and atmosphere does this language create?

8 'There was the throb and stamp of a single organism' (p. 187). How and why is the unity of the boys reinforced?

9 What does the nature of Simon's death show about the boys? What do you think the possible outcomes and repercussions of Simon's death might be?

10 'The line of his cheek silvered and the turn of his shoulder became sculptured marble' (p. 190). What does

the final image of Simon reveal about his role on the island?

11 Look closely at Golding's choice of language when the boys eat the meat, on p. 184. What atmosphere is created by Golding's description?

12 Identify examples of Golding's personification of the island. What effect do these descriptions have on the reader?

Chapter Ten: The Shell and the Glasses

Summary

The morning after the death of Simon, Piggy and Ralph are ashamed of their actions. Piggy believes Simon's death was an accident whereas Ralph insists it was murder. Everyone but Sam and Eric and a few littluns have joined Jack's tribe. At Castle Rock, Jack is a brutal leader and the boys are punished for no apparent reason. Jack states that they must continue to guard against 'the beast' for it can never be truly dead. Jack sends a group of boys to attack Ralph's camp; they beat Ralph and the others badly and steal Piggy's glasses.

Discussion Points

1 *Paranoia is an inherent part of human nature.* Discuss.
2 *Power and respect need to be earned and not simply assumed through assertion.* Discuss and consider the theme of power and status in the novel.
3 *We understand and shape our own identity by exploring differences in others.* Discuss the use of binary opposites in this chapter.
4 How are the themes of hope and despair presented simultaneously in this chapter? How and why are these ideas juxtaposed?

5 *The island has clear links to Hitler's totalitarian state.*
   True or false?

Activities

(Please refer to the glossary of teaching terms on p. 324 for further explanation of these tasks.)

1 Enact a courtroom trial: using the characters' own defence of their role in Simon's death, create a prosecution and a defence to decide who is guilty of Simon's murder. Assign each student a different role and evaluate the outcome at the end of proceedings.
2 Use the diamond nine activity to place characters in order of who is most responsible for Simon's death. Be prepared to justify your choice.
3 Use the diamond nine activity to discuss which symbols or motifs are the most important in the novel so far, for example: the conch, glasses, fire, smoke, shelter, food, spears, water, clothes and blood.
4 Prepare and present news coverage of Simon's death. Students work in groups and prepare a news-room report which switches/links to an on-location report. Ensure students cover the 5 Ws (who, what, when, why and where) and include eyewitness accounts from the characters.
5 Complete research presentations on totalitarian states. Can students create links between these states and the society on the island?

Chapter Notes and Questions

Questions for Study

1 '"Didn't you see what we—what they did?" There was loathing, and at the same time a kind of feverish excitement in his voice' (p. 193). How does Ralph react in the aftermath of Simon's death?

2 Read from the bottom of p. 192 to p. 195. What avoidance tactics do the other boys employ to deny they were involved in Simon's death? Pay particular attention to the use and effect of the personal pronouns 'we' and 'they' in this chapter.

3 'He's going to beat Wilfred.' 'What for?' ... 'I don't know. He didn't say' (p. 196).
What evidence can you find to suggest that the island has become a dictatorship?

4 'He came—disguised. He may come again even though we gave him the head of our kill to eat' (pp. 197–8). How and why does Jack manipulate the boys into believing the beast is still alive?

5 '... feeling curiously defenceless with the darkness pressing in' (p. 202). What does the darkness represent?

6 'His mind skated to a consideration of a tamed town where savagery could not set foot.' Looking at pp. 202–3, what images do the boys draw on to stay hopeful about their own salvation?

7 'This was the first time he had admitted the double function of the fire. Certainly one was to send up a beckoning column of smoke; but the other was to be a hearth now and a comfort until they slept' (p. 199). What is the impact on Ralph and Piggy of losing the fire?

8 'Then the shelter collapsed with smothering finality; and the anonymous shapes fought their way out and through' (p. 206). The boys end up fighting amongst themselves. How does Golding suggest that the island has affected them?

9 'They didn't come for the conch. They came for something else. Ralph—what am I going to do?' (p. 207). What is the significance of Piggy's glasses being stolen? What is the significance of the chapter's title?

10 'He was a chief now in truth; and he made stabbing motions with his spear. From his left hand dangled Piggy's broken glasses' (p. 207). Who is the leader of the boys at the end of this chapter? How do you know?

11 Golding uses fractured dialogue to convey Ralph and Piggy's feelings about Simon's death. How do the fractured dialogue, adjectives and adverbs used to describe their speech and movements evoke their mental state?

12 Jack is now referred to by the boys, and by Golding, as 'The Chief'. What effect does this have on the reader and the moral nature of the novel? (Refer to Golding's 'Fable' essay for further information.)

Chapter Eleven: Castle Rock

Summary

Sam, Eric, Ralph and Piggy go to the other end of the island to see Jack and demand Piggy's glasses. Roger sees the boys and defends the entrance at Castle Rock. Jack returns from hunting and argues with Ralph, while Piggy begs for Ralph's protection. The argument becomes violent as Jack and Ralph fight. Sam and Eric are tied up and the boys clash again, while Piggy protests. The tribe listen for a moment, but Roger releases a rock which hits Piggy and kills him, breaking the conch. Ralph gets injured in the chaos that results, but runs away from the tribe as Roger asserts authority.

Discussion Points

1 Do you think that the narrator passes judgement on characters and events? How does this affect the reader's judgement?
2 Which driving force motivates the boys: brute force or logic and reason?
3 'Which is better, law and rescue, or hunting and breaking things up?' (p. 222). Which political power models are in conflict according to Piggy?

4 'One of our faults is to believe that evil is somewhere else and inherent in another nation' (See 'Fable' essay, p. 255). Do the boys try to displace the evil within themselves? If so, how?

5 'Which is better—to be a pack of painted niggers like you are, or to be sensible like Ralph is?' (p. 221). What is the impact of this racist term on modern readers?

Activities

(Please refer to the glossary of teaching terms on p. 324 for further explanation of these tasks.)

1 Complete another election session. Students write persuasive speeches as one of the boys and perform to the class. Compare the tone and language choices in each character's speech and then compare the results to the election completed after Chapter One.

2 Revisit the diamond nine activity and organize the characters into positions of power in a final version of the social hierarchy.

3 Students design a mask that they would wear if they were elected leader of a group or tribe.

4 Write diary entries, blogs or monologues as a member of Ralph's tribe as they walk towards Castle Rock 'in formation' (p. 213). Imagine their thoughts and feelings in detail.

5 Mime task: re-enact Piggy's death scene in groups. End the scene with a tableau or freeze-frame and complete thought tracks for each character. Enable each character to offer a perspective on the scene.

Chapter Notes and Questions

Questions for Study

1 'You let me carry the conch, Ralph. I'll show him the one thing he hasn't got' (p. 210). What does the conch symbolize?

2 'Then they were apart once more, their positions reversed' (p. 218). To what extent are Jack and Ralph 'reversed' binary opposites of each other? Consider how this relates to the wider idea of opposition in the novel.

3 'They understood only too well the liberation into savagery that the concealing paint brought' (p. 212). Who wears an imaginary and/or literal mask? How does the use of paint show the difference between Ralph's and Jack's tribes? In what ways can the mask be seen as a symbolic barrier between civilization and savagery?

4 'They set off along the beach in formation' (p. 213). Analyse the use of war imagery in this passage. Why has Golding chosen this specific description in the penultimate chapter?

5 'Don't leave me, Ralph' (p. 215). Does Piggy's language inspire sympathy from the reader?

6 'Jack made a rush and stabbed at Ralph's chest with his spear' (p. 217). Explore the significance of the violent language used to describe Jack's initial attack on Ralph. How does it relate to the hunting imagery in the novel?

7 How is the viciousness of the hunters shown through the description of Piggy's death, the attack on Ralph and the slaughter of yet another sow?

8 To what extent is nature presented as a menacing force in the novel? '. . . when it went, sucking back again, the body of Piggy was gone' (p. 223); 'Simon's dead body

moved out towards the open sea' (Chapter Nine, p. 190). What could the sea be a metaphor for?

9 How does Golding use language to skilfully demonstrate the shifting identity of the boys? For example, how important is it that Jack is now simply known by the term 'Chief'?

10 'Roger advanced upon them as one wielding a nameless authority' (p. 224). How is Roger presented in this chapter? What effect does Golding intend to have on the reader?

Chapter Twelve: Cry of the Hunters

Summary

Ralph is wounded and in hiding, fearful for his life. He debates whether he should stay on his own or try to join Jack's tribe. He discovers and destroys the pig skull (the Lord of the Flies), thinking it is alive. He approaches Sam and Eric who warn him that he is in danger. He spends the night hiding while the tribe chant and feast. Sam and Eric are forced to betray Ralph and reveal his hiding place. The hunters drive him out into the open by setting fire to the undergrowth. They chase him across the island. He flees to the beach and collapses at the feet of a naval officer, whose ship has spotted the smoke and has come to investigate. The boys realize they are rescued and begin to weep for themselves and their lost friends.

Discussion Points

1 '. . . the only enemy of man is inside him' ('Fable' essay, p. 255). How can this statement be applied to *Lord of the Flies*?

2 'Man is a fallen being. He is gripped by original sin' ('Fable' essay, p. 253). How can this statement be applied to *Lord of the Flies*?

3 Consider the absence of women and the issue of sex and gender in the novel. What is the significance of not having any females on the island apart from the sows? Is this a reason for the collapse of the boys' society?

4 How does Golding present the relationship between the adult world of experience and the childhood world of innocence in the novel?

5 The naval officer is emblematic of the British Empire. How do you think Golding wished to make the reader feel about the rescue?

Activities

(Please refer to the glossary of teaching terms on p. 324 for further explanation of these tasks.)

1 Create cards with binary opposite themes, for example: *Good/Evil*, *Natural/Man-made*, *Savagery/Civilization*, *Adulthood/Childhood*, *Innocence/Experience*, *Power/ Weakness*, *Conflict/Harmony* and *Light/Dark*. Students decide which theme is dominant in the text. Which characters or settings are associated with each theme? Students find key quotations from the text to support their views. Create a series of debates/discussions/ presentations based on the importance of these themes.

2 Create a list from the text of descriptions of the island. Students then analyse each of the quotations and assign them a black or white card. Students discuss and decide which colour is more dominant and explain what this suggests about the island. (The interpretation of these colours is to be decided by the students.)

Chapter Notes and Questions

3 Display a range of colours and/or shapes; invite students to discuss and match each character to a colour and/or shape. They must explain the choices they have made.

4 Drama task: what is going on while Ralph is in the thicket? One student could perform a monologue as Ralph whilst he is in the thicket. Other students could act out what the other characters are doing and include the 'ululation' described on p. 245.

5 Create a tension graph or an alternative visual representation of how the narrative progresses in *Lord of the Flies*. Analyse significant moments of climactic tension.

6 Investigate the significance of chapter titles. Explore connections and try to spot patterns between key events, chapter headings and tension in the novel.

Questions for Study

1 'Then there was that indefinable connection between himself and Jack; who therefore would never let him alone; never' (p. 226). How does Golding present the relationship between Ralph and Jack at this point in the novel?

2 'No fire; no smoke; no rescue' (p. 227). To what extent are Ralph and Jack consumed by their respective obsessions?

3 'A sick fear and rage swept him' (p. 228). Why does Ralph react so violently towards the Lord of the Flies?

4 'They're going to hunt you to-morrow' (p. 232). How does Golding build tension in this chapter?

5 'Ralph felt a chunk of meat pushed against him and grabbed it' (p. 233). Is Ralph a sympathetic character?

6 'There was no Piggy to talk sense. There was no solemn assembly for debate nor dignity of the conch' (p. 241). How does Ralph's admission suggest the boys have declined into savagery?

7 Why does Golding continually refer to light and dark imagery in the last chapter?

8 '... a huge peaked cap ... a white-topped cap, and above the green shade of the peak was a crown, an anchor, gold foliage' (p. 246). What is significant about the appearance of a naval officer and the 'trim cruiser' at the end of the book? What do they represent?

9 'I should have thought that a pack of British boys—you're all British aren't you?—would have been able to put up a better show than that' (p. 248). How does Golding present the boys as undermining Britishness or the image of Britain? Consider links to the decline of empire and imperialism. (Refer to the Britain and Imperialism essay in the introductory materials , p. 1.)

10 '... infected by that emotion, the other little boys began to shake and sob too' (p. 248). Why does Golding present fear as an 'infection' in the novel?

11 'Ralph wept for the end of innocence, the darkness of man's heart, and the fall through the air of the true, wise friend called Piggy' (p. 248). What does Ralph's emotional outburst reveal about the boys' spiritual journey on the island? What have they learned, if anything?

Suggested Post-Reading Activities

1 Write the next chapter of the book – consider how the boys might change when they return to the mainland. Consider the different perspectives of the characters – would they be remorseful? Would they try to forget the events on the island or would they honour the memory of Simon and Piggy, by holding a memorial service, for example? Consider what might be left of civilization on the mainland. Might events in the children's world be paralleled by events in the adult world?

2 Write a newspaper article which gives details about the events on the island. You could compare and contrast the tone used in a tabloid and a broadsheet article – what details would these types of newspapers concentrate on and why?

3 Divide the class into groups and assign each either a theme or a character – they must present ideas to the class to help them understand the novel in greater detail.

4 Students draw and label their own map of the island.

balloon debate: The class imagines a range of characters in a hot-air balloon. The imaginary balloon is losing height rapidly and will soon crash because it is overweight; therefore you have to get rid of some of the passengers! Students have to come up with persuasive arguments as to why their character should be allowed to stay in the balloon. After all the arguments have been heard, a decision is made about who will be forced to leave the balloon.

conscience corridor/alley: The majority of the class form two lines facing each other. Individual students adopt the role of a character (perhaps experiencing internal conflict about a difficult decision) and walk between the lines. The students in these lines offer their advice verbally – they can invent this advice independently or repeat key quotations from the text. It can be organised so that those on one side give opposing advice to those on the other. When the individual student reaches the end of the alley, they should make a decision as that character and suggest what they would do next in their situation.

diamond nine: Key words, statements or pictures are placed on nine cards which are diamond shaped. Students then place them in order of importance: their opinion of what is the most important on the top, followed by a row of two less important below, then a row of three, then another row of two and finally the least important at the bottom, creating a diamond shape. This activity can be used to analyse a variety of aspects of the text.

gallery drama: Students make still images with their bodies to represent a scene. This can be done in pairs where one student acts as the sculptor and one as a metaphorical 'lump of clay' ready to be moulded into shape. When directed, the other members of the group move around the tableaux inspecting the sculptures and considering their motivations for creating certain positions. This activity is particularly good for exploring themes.

hotseating: A student takes on the role of a character. They are given a central seat in the classroom and are then questioned by the group about his or her background, behaviour and motivation. Students move from the 'hot seat' quickly to allow another student to take on their role.

soundscape: The class creates a chorus of sound using their voices. The class paints a *soundscape* of a particular theme or mood, for example the beach. This can begin with one group's noises and then other groups are invited to join in to make a melee of sound. The designated leader can control the shape of the piece by raising their hand to increase the volume or bringing it to the floor for silence.

tableaux: Students make a still image or freeze frame (independently, in pairs or in groups) that represents analysis of characters or themes. Other students analyse the positioning of these students and discuss key ideas and representation.

thought tap: A group makes a still image (freeze frame or tableau) and individuals are invited to speak their thoughts or feelings aloud. This can be done by tapping each person on the shoulder. Alternatively, other members of the class can be invited to voice one character's thoughts aloud for them.

Venn diagram: A mathematical diagram that uses overlapping circles to explore the relationship between different characters or themes. This can be used to help students compare and contrast terms or concepts. Similarities between ideas are indicated by the area where the circles overlap.

ADVANCED STUDIES SECTION

Introduction

This section introduces some key concepts, ideas and suggestions for wider reading that could be explored alongside Golding's *Lord of the Flies*. The section is designed for students wishing to develop a broader understanding and critical appreciation of the novel.

These are brief introductions to the topics and provide no more than a basis for beginning further independent research. Students will be provided both with questions for discussion and suggested reading on each topic, to help them formulate their own ideas.

Golding's Life and Influences

Golding was born in 1911, a period still characterized by a harsh division between social classes. However, there was also an emerging socialist movement in which politicians and writers were critical of social inequality. Golding would have been aware of this during his childhood in Marlborough, Wiltshire, since his father, Alec, was a teacher with openly socialist views. Golding's mother, Mildred, campaigned for women's right to vote.

After leaving Marlborough Grammar School, Golding attended the University of Oxford where he studied Natural Sciences for two years before transferring to English Literature.

Golding married Ann Brookfield, an analytical chemist, in 1939 and they had two children, David and Judith.

In the autumn of 1935, Golding was employed as a teacher of English and music at a school in Streatham which followed the teachings of Rudolf Steiner. Steiner schools did not conform to the traditional patterns of teaching and learning, and instead emphasized the role of the imagination.

In December 1940, Golding left his second teaching post at a boy's grammar school, Bishop Wordsworth's School, Salisbury, to join the navy where he served until the end of the Second World War in 1945. His service during the war gave him direct experience of the human capacity for brutality. Golding himself said that these horrors lay behind his descriptions of the behaviour of the boys on the island.

After the war, Golding returned to Bishop Wordsworth's School where he remained until 1961. Writing always remained his primary passion and focus; however, teaching gave him further invaluable insights into human behaviour.

In *Lord of the Flies* the narrative suggests that evil is inherent within all of us. We cannot be certain about Golding's religious beliefs, but some critics have seen the novel as an allegory depicting Man's fall from grace. However, it could also be read as a critique of the growing cruelty and destruction that mankind is capable of inflicting, which Golding witnessed first-hand during wartime.

Questions for Discussion

1 To what extent is the novel autobiographical?
2 *Golding's life experience is evident in the characters, setting and plot of the novel*. Discuss.

3 *Is Golding himself the omniscient narrator, ever-present in the text?* Discuss the implications of your answer in terms of the structure of the novel.

Wider Reading

Other works by Golding include:

The Inheritors (novel) 1955
The Brass Butterfly (play) 1955
The Spire (novel) 1964
The Scorpion God (three short novels) 1971
Rites of Passage (novel) 1980
Close Quarters (novel) 1987
Fire Down Below (novel) 1989
The Hot Gates (a collection of essays) 1965
A Moving Target (a collection of essays) 1982

(All the above are published by Faber and Faber.)

Critical Works on Golding

Mark Kinkead-Weekes and Ian Gregor, *William Golding: A Critical Study of the Novels*, 3rd edn (London: Faber, 2002)
Virginia Tiger, *William Golding: The Unmoved Target* (London: Marion Boyars, 2003)
John Carey, *William Golding: The Man Who Wrote Lord of the Flies* (London: Faber, 2009)

In order to explore the literary context in which Golding was writing, it may be useful for students to consider his contemporaries:

Early 1900s – social reform:

H. G. Wells
George Bernard Shaw

Fiction and drama – 1940s/1950s

J. B. Priestley
Graham Greene
J. R. R. Tolkien
Iris Murdoch
Kingsley Amis
Lawrence Durrell
Anthony Burgess
Margaret Drabble
Tom Stoppard
John Osborne
Samuel Beckett

Poetry

Dylan Thomas
T. S. Eliot
W. H. Auden
Philip Larkin
John Betjeman

Castaway Novels

The 'castaway' genre produced such famous novels as *Treasure Island* (1883; serialized 1881–2) by Robert Louis Stevenson and *Swallows and Amazons* (1930) by Arthur Ransome. One of the aims of a castaway novel was to create the scene for a classic 'boys' own' adventure. Young men, especially public schoolboys, were expected to become soldiers and civil servants who would travel to the farthest reaches of the British Empire. The portrayal of adventure, heroism and success in this type of novel was exemplified in the many stories by G. A. Henty. Golding himself owned two of Henty's stories. Such stories encouraged boys to take up similar roles. Tales of young men – always European, often British – overcoming the threats inherent in the unexplored and apparently uncivilized parts of the world gave the impression that Western men could conquer nature itself. Indigenous inhabitants were often cast merely as a natural phenomenon.

The removal of influential adults from the narrative is a device often used in children's literature. It allows the young protagonists the freedom to evolve as characters and leaders without adults to influence, help or pass judgement on their actions. It was a convenient way of making youngsters demonstrate their independence and courage but could also allow the writer to show human nature unconstrained by the supposedly civilizing bonds of society.

In 1731 the German critic Johann Gottfried Schnabel invented the term *Robinsonades* to describe the growing number of castaway novels inspired by Defoe's *Robinson*

Crusoe (1719). Golding was an enthusiast of the Robinsonade genre and wrote about it in the essay 'Islands' (see *The Hot Gates*, pp. 106–10). The role uninhabited islands could play in removing civilization's constraints held a particular fascination for him; he immersed himself in stories such as *Treasure Island* (1883) and *The Swiss Family Robinson* (1812) where people, separated from 'civilization', are changed by their experiences. In *Lord of the Flies*, Golding references this tradition, when he has the boys say in Chapter Two, 'It's like in a book . . . Treasure Island . . . Coral Island' (p. 45).

The Robinsonade which most directly inspired Golding was R. M. Ballantyne's children's novel, *The Coral Island*, published in 1857 when the British Empire and its attendant beliefs and attitudes were at their zenith. The protagonists are white boys who perform a series of daring feats which demonstrate their moral, intellectual and physical superiority to the 'natives' whom they encounter. Later critics, including the adult Golding, understood the novel as a colonialist text which portrays the arrival of white boys on a remote island as a civilizing influence on the savage, barbarous cannibals who live there.

Golding could not accept the notion of the innate moral superiority of Westerners, especially after his experiences in the Second World War; he wrote *Lord of the Flies* partly as a response to the Victorian text and its assumptions. The boys stranded on Golding's island share some of the Coral Islanders' names. Jack and Ralph, for example, occur prominently in both novels; the third boy in *The Coral Island*, whose name is Peterkin, is referenced by Golding in his character of Simon, as in Simon Peter the Apostle. Part of the effectiveness of reusing these names is in the contrasts and similarities between the characters' personalities and behaviour in the two novels.

The Coral Island is mentioned again at the end of *Lord of the Flies* by the naval officer who rescues the boys. He remarks, 'I know. Jolly good show. Like The Coral Island.' (p. 248) The reader is only too aware of the dreadful irony of these words and of the naivety of the officer's assumptions about the boys' conduct on the island. Any reader familiar with *The Coral Island* will also be conscious of the gulf between Ballantyne's and Golding's views of human nature. Golding's overt references to Ballantyne's novel indicate that he clearly intends the reader to make these comparisons.

There are no aborigines on Golding's island, no natives to subjugate or dispossess. Most of the boys believe in the presence of a 'beast' which could be thought to represent a native brutishness to be overcome. But Golding consistently suggests that the beast is something innate in the boys. Simon, the visionary, understands this, and it is on his return from a heroic exploration of the jungle and mountain, a courageous quest which ironically mirrors the heroism of the 'boys' own' explorers, that he himself is mistaken for the beast, and killed by the other boys. Jack, a true demagogue, understands the potential of the 'beast''s *otherness* as a rationale for violence and the acquisition of power, and declares that it can never be killed. Brilliantly manipulating his audience, he remarks, 'You can't tell what he [the beast] might do.' (p. 198)

A colonialist reading of *The Coral Island* locates evil in the native savages; the boys are paragons of virtue and civilization. Ballantyne's view of man is blandly optimistic; his view of English boys' pluck and resourcefulness suggests that they can subdue tropical islands as triumphantly as

England imposes Empire and Christianity on lawless breeds of men. Where there is white civilization, he believes there will inevitably be justice, goodness and mercy. At the end of *Lord of the Flies*, Golding makes the boys' rescuer say, 'I should have thought that a pack of British boys . . . would have been able to put up a better show than that' (p. 248). In the final paragraph, the rescuer gazes, with implicit satisfaction, on the 'trim cruiser', no doubt fully equipped with advanced weaponry, in the distance.

Questions for Discussion

1 Discuss the effects of the removal of adults as a narrative device with reference to *Lord of the Flies*.
2 How would the castaway novel encourage young boys to be independent?
3 How does *Lord of the Flies* subvert the castaway genre? Discuss with close reference to the text.
4 Compare and contrast the views of castaway societies presented in Ballantyne's *The Coral Island* and Golding's *Lord of the Flies*.

Critical Interpretations

When interpreting *Lord of the Flies*, it is possible to read the events of the story through a literal or a figurative point of view, or a combination of the two. One interesting approach is to view *Lord of the Flies* as a straightforward commentary on childhood. Golding has set his young protagonists on an island, surrounded by an impassable ocean. What happens to the boys can be viewed as a type of social experiment whereby their innocence and status as children are abruptly replaced by the harsh necessities of a more adult world. When the boys first find themselves on the island, they see authority and power as having been removed, and they take pleasure in this. As the novel progresses, they gradually reassert governance through differing power models, good and bad.

A Symbolic Approach

Alternatively, *Lord of the Flies* can be read more figuratively. The island may simply be a device that Golding uses to make a wider and far more troubling comment on society. The boys' descent into primitive hunting, savage fighting and inter-tribal conflict could be seen as portraying the emergence of their collective unconscious desires as they revert to type. They lose their individual characters and act as a group. This process has a drastically disinhibiting effect, even on such 'good' characters as Ralph and Piggy, and it seems likely that Golding here is directly referencing the terrifying aspects of mob rule, and specifically the behaviour of Hitler's followers in Nazi Germany. The island provides catalysing processes – hunting, the spreading of fire, the presence of the jungle – for the emergence of the boys' instinctual behaviours: they prove to be murderous and predatory. This in itself is a frightening prospect for the boys: their deepest desires are revealed, exposing them to a self-knowledge they have no help with. They do not recognize these feelings as being in themselves, and they create the mysterious 'beast' as a metaphorical vessel to carry them. Simon's attempt to explain this is met with derision, which perhaps masks fear. Moreover, the reaction of the naval officer and rescuer at the end of the novel offers no recognition or acceptance of the trauma the children have lived through, even though by then he observes that they have been 'having a war' (as he is) and have killed people. Golding offers the boys' behaviour as a demonstration of what society can be without the veneer of the rules and expectations that govern us, as in foreign wars or domestic riots. It is possible that the absence of females on the island is meant to indicate that the 'society' on the island is unsustainable; or that the boys are to be seen as a militarized section of society, which might offer protection to females and children, at the price of domination.

A Psychoanalytic Approach

It may also be that the boys' characters represent different parts of the *personality*. Golding himself recorded his own distrust of the ideas of Freud, but nevertheless it is interesting for the reader to draw upon a psychoanalytic framework, and to look to Freud and his conception of the 'psyche' – the individual personality. Freud believed the psyche is made up of three parts: the *id* which is concerned with our basic needs and desires; the *superego* which is centred on moral imperatives and (especially) prohibitions; and the *ego* which is concerned with negotiating a reality, striking a balance between the id and the superego. On the island, Jack reverts to basic, id-like desires, quickly taking on the role of hunter and provider. However, the fact that he never gains complete power over the boys suggests that bowing to our basic desires can be dangerous and unsatisfying. Piggy could therefore represent the concerns of the superego as he worries about fairness, order and rules. The reader therefore needs to question why the boys destroy Piggy and similarly destroy all the rules on the island. Ralph is the intermediary between Jack and Piggy. As the metaphorical ego, he tries to maintain cohesion in the group by being friends with both boys and trying to find a compromise between them.

Questions for Discussion

1 What do you think is the significance of the island being solely inhabited by boys?
2 What other symbols are there in the novel? Research Carl Jung's concept of the *Shadow* and explain how it applies.
3 Explore in detail how Jack can be seen as the id, Piggy as the superego and Ralph as the ego. In what ways can the boys be seen to act out these roles on the island?
4 Consider the role of the sea, literally and figuratively, in the novel. Compare with other works by Golding in which the sea figures prominently.

Colonialism and War

During the early twentieth century, many of those people administering European empires still believed in their civilizing mission over far-reaching parts of the globe. European literature and historical studies of the colonial period tended to assume the superiority of Western civilization and Westerners as well. Little heed was paid to the cultures and viewpoints of the colonized peoples. Such ideas were increasingly challenged during the era following the Second World War, both in movements seeking freedom from Western rule and in the emerging academic field of post-colonial studies.

Post-colonial thinking has developed as a historical and moral critique of the process of Western colonization which has taken place since the early sixteenth century. The post-colonial perspective deals with those areas where racialized populations were subjected to brutal exploitation such as slavery and forced labour, but it also includes 'settler societies', such as Australia, Canada and the USA, where exclusionary and even genocidal policies were pursued against indigenous or 'first' peoples. It also covers immigrant and so-called 'hybrid' cultures that grew up in the large cities in the rich countries of Western Europe.

Post-colonial thought functions as a corrective to the colonialist view that Western countries had a civilizing mission to govern, educate and develop other peoples and cultures supposedly for those peoples' and cultures' own benefit. Writers such as Joseph Conrad (*Heart of Darkness*, 1899) and Edward Said (*Orientalism*, 1978) portrayed the corrupting effects of power on the colonizers and dominant cultures through their practice of constructing racialized *others* who were supposedly childlike and inferior.

From the very opening of *Lord of the Flies*, themes of colonialism are clearly visible: a group of English schoolboys arrive on an island and try to construct a social system, confident in their 'English superiority'. Throughout, Golding undermines and corrodes the sense of 'Englishness' in the novel; the island certainly does not become a civilized paradise after the boys' arrival. Instead, Golding invites us to explore an apparently universal human capacity not just to do evil but to organize evil-doing politically.

The naval officer, who arrives at the end of the novel, believes – just like the boys at the start of the novel – in the natural superiority of the dominant power, in this case, the British. Having experienced the events of the novel, we are left in little doubt that the naval officer is as wrong as the boys; Golding has completely undermined the officer's role as an authoritative speaker. However, in our brief glimpse of the boys through his eyes, we are allowed to see them to scale – Jack, for example, that terrifying figure of capricious and brutal authority, becomes once again a 'little boy'.

Golding's text thus presents us with colonialist presumptions, before compelling us to see the limitations of these platitudes, something not offered in R. M. Ballantyne's *The Coral Island*.

Questions for Discussion

1 To what extent does Golding undermine a colonialist concept of Britishness?
2 Is *Lord of the Flies* a colonial or a post-colonial text?
3 How are the effects of the two twentieth-century World Wars explored in the text of the novel?

Postmodernism

Golding's *Lord of the Flies* is arguably a novel that revels in destruction, presenting a world in which society's boundaries collapse and become inverted. These ideas are central to the concept of postmodernism, which is characterized by the *crisis of representation*. This crisis is the result of a rejection of the assumed certainty and stability of scientific or objective efforts to represent and explain reality. As such, postmodernism is an interrogation of the very foundations of reality, and hence of society and the individual's place within it.

Collapse of Boundaries and Disintegration of the Self

In *Lord of the Flies*, Golding highlights the futility of the boys' efforts to maintain society's rules and routines in another setting. The boundaries between good and evil, animal and human, and self and other become blurred and ultimately disintegrate within the novel. Postmodernism postulates that many, if not all, apparent realities are only social constructs and are therefore subject to change. The individual is at risk of losing a definite subject position. In the novel, the characters Sam and Eric cease to be separate entities and ultimately dissolve into one another, becoming 'Samneric'. Through this, Golding is perhaps suggesting that the conditions under which identity is traditionally understood are unstable, dependent to a great extent on social assumptions or repetitive interactions between individuals within a group. Yet what constitutes the individual has a tendency to become fragmented when conditions change. This can be seen in the confrontation between Ralph and Jack in Chapter Eleven when the two characters become indistinguishable, and then 'apart once more, their positions reversed' (p. 218).

Advanced Studies Section

History and Grand Narratives

For postmodernist thinkers, history is a system or narrative, and should be challenged. Postmodernism claims that there is no absolute truth; the way people perceive the world is subjective. History, for Michel Foucault, is only interpretations of interpretations; in other words the history we are given is fictional, and we should be suspicious of it. Golding himself provides an alternative 'island paradise' narrative, subverting the work of predecessors such as R. M. Ballantyne (*The Coral Island*) with his dystopian vision. His narrative itself becomes almost mythical as the story comes to a close. The change of viewpoint at the end, whereby the boys are suddenly seen as little and vulnerable, makes the reader realize that earlier presumptions were not secure; the initial certainties have the potential to fragment and reverse. The reader may even come to question whether the boys have been truly rescued by the arrival of the naval officer, leaving Golding's narrative open to endless interpretation and modern adaptation.

Questions for Discussion

1 At what points do the boundaries between good/evil, man/animal, self/other collapse in the novel?
2 Postmodernism can be seen as an interrogation of the individual's place in society. How does Golding produce this interrogation?
3 In the final chapter, how does Golding make the reader question the events of the entire narrative?
4 Undertake a postmodern analysis of cinematic adaptations of the text. What perspectives are depicted

341

or favoured by the directors? With close reference to critical reviews, explore the impact of these texts on contemporary and modern audiences.

Other Points to Consider

There is insufficient scope in this section to explore all of the themes and concepts present in the text. Advanced readers should always be open-minded and strive to offer new interpretations of the characters, events, themes and ideas. They should develop probing questions that explore the relationship between the author's intention and the readers' interpretations. They should be keen to tackle the explicit and inferred or implicit meaning of themes and ideas. For example, advanced readers might explore the wider issues of gender the novel is concerned with: why are there no females on the island apart from sows? Why are the sows sacrificed? What does the lack of female presence imply about the boys' ability to function as a society? Is the fact that there are no human females on the island the reason the boys' society ultimately breaks down? What is the relationship between this 'society' and militarized warfare? How would the plot have developed if there had been females on the island? Is Golding presenting a dystopian vision of society without women?

A close reading of *Lord of the Flies* should generate more questions than it answers; advanced readers should be prepared to undertake independent reading on related genres and critical theories which may inform their interpretation of the text.

Further Suggested Reading

About William Golding

John Carey, *William Golding: The Man Who Wrote Lord of the Flies* (2009)

William Golding, *The Paper Men* (1983)

www.william-golding.co.uk

Castaway novels and stories

William Shakespeare, *The Tempest* (first performed 1611)

Daniel Defoe, *Robinson Crusoe* (1719)

Johann David Wyss, *The Swiss Family Robinson* (1812)

R. M. Ballantyne, *The Coral Island* (1857)

Robert Louis Stevenson, *Treasure Island* (1883)

Novels of childhood

Rudyard Kipling, *Stalky and Co.* (1899)

Ian McEwan, *The Cement Garden* (1978)

Utopian/dystopian works

Voltaire, *Candide* (1759)

Samuel Butler, *Erewhon* (1872)

William Morris, *News from Nowhere* (1890)

Aldous Huxley, *Brave New World* (1932)

George Orwell, *1984* (1934)

Study Materials

Hunting as colonialism

R. M. Ballantyne, *The Gorilla Hunters* (1861)
Angela Carter, 'Master' in *Fireworks* (1974)

'Boys' Own' stories

G. A. Henty, *By Sheer Pluck: A Tale of the Ashanti War* (1884)
G. A. Henty, *With Clive in India* (1884)
H. Rider Haggard, *King Solomon's Mines* (1885)
H. Rider Haggard, *She* (1887)
John Buchan, *The Thirty-Nine Steps* (1915)

Post-colonial texts

Joseph Conrad, *Heart of Darkness* (1899)
Chinua Achebe, *Things Fall Apart* (1958)
Edward Said, *Orientalism* (1978)

Psychoanalytic interpretations

Works of Sigmund Freud
Works of Carl Jung

Postmodernist fiction

Chuck Palahniuk, *Fight Club* (1996)
Thomas Pynchon, *The Crying of Lot 49* (1966)
Works of Jorge Luis Borges
Works of Philip K. Dick

GLOSSARY

Chapter 1: The Sound of the Shell

p. 17	efflorescence	reflective / shimmering quality
p. 18	specious	false / hollow
p. 20	effulgence	brightness
p. 21	decorous	well behaved / proper / correct
p. 22	fulcrum	pivot / hinge
p. 23	strident	loud / shrill
p. 25	tow	pale-coloured fibres of flax, hemp or jute
p. 26	hambone frill	a decorative frill around the collar
p. 28	precentor	a person who leads singing or organizes services in a church
p. 32	pallor	paleness / whiteness
p. 35	pliant	flexible / bendy
p. 35	immured	imprisoned / enclosed
p. 37	cirque	a semicircular hollow in a mountain with steep walls formed by erosion

Chapter 2: Fire on the Mountain

p. 51	quota	allowance / ration
p. 53	officious	bossy / intrusive
p. 54	coign	an external corner of a wall
p. 57	festooned	decorated / draped
p. 58	pall	a dark covering

Chapter 3: Huts on the Beach

p. 62	gaudy	garish / colourful / lurid
p. 62	inscrutable	mysterious / enigmatic
p. 63	castanet	hand-held wooden or plastic percussion / rhythm instrument
p. 63	vicissitudes	difficulties
p. 64	contrite	sorry / regretful / ashamed / repentant
p. 65	antagonism	resentment / dislike / bitterness
p. 67	opaque	cloudy / misty
p. 68	declivities	downward inclinations / slopes
p. 69	tacit	unspoken / wordless
p. 71	clamorously	loudly / noisily / demanding attention
p. 72	furtive	secretive / cautious

| p. 72 | susurration | murmuring / whispering |
| p. 72 | sepals | outer leaves enclosing the petals of a flower |

Chapter 4: Painted Faces and Long Hair

p. 73	perpendicular	vertical / upright
p. 73	opalescence	shimmering milky colours
p. 75	belligerence	hostility / antagonism
p. 76	chastisement	reprimand / punishment
p. 77	detritus	debris / waste / leftovers
p. 77	myriad	many / innumerable
p. 77	runnels	channels / furrows
p. 77	bole	trunk / stalk
p. 77	crooning	singing / murmuring
p. 78	taboo	unmentionable / forbidden
p. 79	mere	lake
p. 82	irked	annoyed / upset
p. 82	balm	comfort / relief
p. 90	malevolently	wickedly / unkindly
p. 90	parody	imitation / mockery
p. 92	ha'porth	half a penny's worth, hence a very small amount

Chapter 5: Beast from Water

p. 96	lamentably	unfortunately
p. 97	apex	top / peak
p. 98	reverence	respect / devotion
p. 98	solemnity	seriousness
p. 107	derisive	mocking / sarcastic
p. 108	effigy	image / statue
p. 108	lamentation	weeping / crying
p. 109	sough	soft murmuring / sighing
p. 111	decorum	dignity / correct behaviour
p. 112	indignant	outraged / angry
p. 113	tempestuously	emotionally / stormily
p. 117	incantation	chant / prayer / spell

Chapter 6: Beast from Air

p. 123	paling	diminishing / fading
p. 123	tremulously	unsteadily / shakily
p. 128	incredulity	disbelief / amazement
p. 128	diffidently	hesitantly / shyly
p. 131	polyp	inactive stage of sea invertebrate which attaches to rock
p. 131	leviathan	sea monster
p. 131	guano	accumulated animal droppings

Glossary

p. 133	sombrely	seriously / sadly
p. 134	mutinously	disobediently / rebelliously

Chapter 7: Shadows and Tall Trees

p. 135	dun	bleak and depressing
p. 135	coverts	woods / thickets
p. 137	obtuseness	stupidity / slowness
p. 142	ruefully	regretfully / humbly
p. 144	luxuriance	profusion / abundance
p. 144	traverses	passes through / crosses

Chapter 8: Gift for the Darkness

p. 155	serenading	singing to / entertaining
p. 165	fervour	passion / dedication
p. 168	paunched	ripped open the belly of / disembowelled
p. 171	iridescent	lustrous / shimmering

Chapter 9: A View to a Death

p. 181	corpulent	fat / plump
p. 182	primly	prudishly / formally
p. 183	garlanded	decorated / decked

p. 184	bourdon	a bass noise
p. 185	sauntered	walked casually / strolled
p. 189	clefts	cracks / splits
p. 189	phosphorescence	the emission of light without heat, in this case generated by sea creatures

Chapter 10: The Shell and the Glasses

p. 192	befouled	dirtied / polluted
p. 195	convulsively	moving uncontrollably
p. 197	torrid	hot / stifling
p. 197	assimilating	understanding
p. 198	interrogative	questioning / probing
p. 198	theological	religious
p. 200	dredged	searched / scoured
p. 202	spangles	stars
p. 204	tendrils	stems / vines
p. 204	rebuked	reprimanded / reproached
p. 204	woebegone	sorrowful / sad

Chapter 11: Castle Rock

| p. 208 | myopia | short-sightedness |
| p. 213 | multitudinous | countless / infinite |

Glossary

Chapter 12: Cry of the Hunter

p. 225	fronds	leaves / ferns
p. 227	leaden	heavy / ponderous
p. 228	pax	'the kiss of peace' – used to express a call for a truce in children's games
p. 229	acrid	pungent / harsh / choking
p. 232	ululation	a hooting cry
p. 239	crepitation	a crackling sound
p. 240	baulked	recoiled / hesitated / drew back from
p. 246	epaulettes	ornamental shoulder badges worn on military uniforms
p. 246	cutter	a type of small boat
p. 246	ratings	ordinary seamen
p. 246	stern-sheets	the rear part of a boat

ABOUT LOXFORD SCHOOL OF SCIENCE AND TECHNOLOGY

Loxford School of Science and Technology provides young people with the highest-quality education, accessible to students of all abilities. We emphasise traditional standards of uniform, good manners, discipline and respect whilst providing a very relevant and modern education which will enable our students to succeed in the workplace and society in the twenty-first century. The students of Loxford School enjoy state-of-the-art facilities for all subject areas which provide an atmosphere of life-long learning. A new building for the primary-school phase is underway and this will provide an all-through educational experience for learners between the ages of three and eighteen. As an 'all-through' school, we will seek further improvement in learners' academic achievements and raise their aspirations, confidence and self-esteem. Our school ethos supports the importance of reading for pleasure and at 3.10 p.m. every Thursday, all 2,000 members of the school community settle down to enjoy 'whole school reading'. We all hope you will enjoy exploring the story, themes and ideas in *Lord of the Flies* and believe that it is a version that will be studied for years to come at Loxford and beyond.

The outstanding English Department is a group of dedicated teachers with a variety of expertise and experience, who consistently achieve excellent examination results. Working collaboratively is what we do best; this exciting opportunity to develop an educational edition of *Lord of the Flies* has been an honour and it has been a privilege to be part of English cultural history. If ever a group of teachers were so humbled, it is us. Not only do we get to work with each other on a daily basis but we have been able to translate our teamwork and inspirational spirit into print by working on a timeless classic. We have provided a variety of creative tasks which will enable students to explore the complexities of language, structure and form as well as characters, themes, motifs and symbols in more detail. And, most importantly, we hope you enjoy using this edition of the novel.

Elâ Tűrker-Glodowska has led the *Lord of the Flies* educational edition project since its inception and has been responsible for co-ordinating and inspiring the creativity of the vibrant and dynamic Loxford English Department. They are: Jenny Baldwin, Philip Bayley, Katie Burningham, Francesca Hand, Lucy Hyams, Dani Kelly, Nicola Kober, Janette Price, Michael Rowley, Ciara Ryan, Yasmin Sadek, Frances Steel, Russ Tannahill, Kate Thackray, Elâ Tűrker-Glodowska and Olivia Walker.

With special thanks to Louise Kanolik for her unfaltering positivity and dedication to the project, our headteacher Anita Johnson for her continued support and belief, and Richard Steel and Pawel Glodowski for their patient proofreading and invaluable wisdom.

ff

William Golding's
Lord of the Flies

adapted for the stage by
Nigel Williams

Playwright and novelist Nigel William's stage adaptation of Golding's modern classic was first professionally produced by the Royal Shakespeare Company at Stratford-upon-Avon in July 1995. The special acting edition, particularly suitable for schools and amateur groups, contains the full playtext as well as notes on staging, a full properties list and lighting and sound cues.

'Remarkably true to the novel in spirit . . . the theatre lends itself particularly well to the ritualistic aspects of the story – chanting, dancing, marching, forming a circle round the victim, stamping out the fire . . . you end up feeling you have seen a fable of infinite implications enacted in a little room.'
SUNDAY TELEGRAPH